# Forgiven
## Tabor Heights, Year 1, Book 6

Michelle L. Levigne

*www.MtZionRidgePress.com*

Mt Zion Ridge Press
295 Gum Springs Rd, NW
Georgetown, TN 37366

https://www.mtzionridgepress.com



Published in the United States of America
Publication Date: November 15, 2024

Editor-In-Chief: Michelle Levigne
Executive Editor: Tamera Lynn Kraft

Cover Art Copyright by Mt Zion Ridge Press © 2024

*Welcome to Tabor Heights:*
*A friendly little town on Ohio's North Coast, where sweet*
*romance is always in the air.*

*Here you'll be able to explore the lives of the members of the*
*congregation of Tabor Christian Church in the space of two years.*
*The stories overlap, and there's no one right place to start.*

*Just like any small town, you come in, you meet someone, you*
*hear their story and get to know them, and they introduce you to*
*their friends, tell you something about them, and you learn those*
*stories. As you get to know these new friends, they introduce you*
*to other people, and tell you about other interesting stories in*
*town.*

*It's the same way with Tabor Heights. Start with the story that*
*interests you the most, and then branch out.*

*Settle back and enjoy your visit.*
*Welcome!*


## Year One

**THE SECOND TIME AROUND**
**DETOURS**
**COMMON GROUNDS**
**WHITE ROSES**
**THE FAMILY WAY**
**FORGIVEN**
**FIRESONG**
**BEHIND THE SCENES**
**THE MISSION**
**ACCIDENTAL HEARTS**
**A QUIET PLACE**

# Chapter One

*Friday, March 22*
*Quarry Hall, Akron, Ohio*

"How do you feel about going away for a while for a project?" Joan said, meeting Nikki on the massive natural stone patio of Quarry Hall when she came back from her morning walk around the estate.

"What kind of project?" Nikki grinned at her half-sister and knelt on the top step. Her companion dog, Gray Brother, obediently raised one paw after another to let her check for any mud he might have picked up, to clean his feet before they went indoors. "Where?"

For just a moment, their matching hazel eyes locked gazes and Nikki shivered slightly from the sensation that struck at the oddest times: that when she looked at Joan, twelve years her senior, she looked in a blurred mirror. The same wide cheekbones, shoulder-length dark hair with a touch of red in bright sunlight, hazel eyes... and the same ghost pain in those eyes. Today they had even dressed similarly, though Nikki was sure it was pure coincidence. For those who worked behind-the-scenes at Quarry Hall and the Arc Foundation, faded jeans, hiking boots and plain t-shirts were the uniform of the day.

Joan shrugged, offering a crooked smile, and tucked her tangled, dark hair behind an ear. "Tabor." She turned to go indoors with her Akita, Ulysses, a silent, watchful shadow.

"How long?" Nikki followed her through the french doors, through the Great Hall, to the stairway up to the living quarters for Joan's father and stepmother.

"We won't know until you're already hip-deep in it," was all Joan said.

Nikki bit back a smart remark about being hip-deep in alligators. Her first solo mission for the Arc Foundation, last summer, was supposed to just be a courier run. An easy assignment became complicated when she stopped in a small mountain town to pick up Brooklyn, was falsely accused of kidnapping, then was kidnapped herself and held prisoner with Brooklyn and the local sheriff. She had never been so grateful to have a big sister, when she learned how Joan had dropped everything to drive cross-country, ready to tear the little mountain town apart with her bare hands to find her.

"Nikki, good, Joan found you." Elizabeth Carter greeted the sisters with a smile when they stepped into the office. She finished setting down the tea tray and gestured with a nod toward the massive desk where Harrison Carter, Joan's father, leaned back in his black leather chair, talking on the phone, his voice a pleasant rumble.

Though she had only been part of the Arc Foundation for less than two years, Nikki felt as close to the people here as if she had grown up with them. She was glad to see that Joan's father, whom she called Uncle Harrison, was having a good day today. No wheelchair, or a robe for extra warmth over his crisp white Oxford shirt and chocolate brown trousers. His white hair didn't look quite so thin and lifeless, and his big, elegant hands didn't look quite so skeletal and crooked with pain.

Elizabeth wore her usual outfit of a simple silvery-gray calf-length skirt, matching sweater, and loafers. Today her blouse was a pearly blue that added its tint to her gray eyes and hid the silver streaks among her golden hair, caught up in its usual casual chignon. Nikki had found it hard at first, when she came to Quarry Hall, to accept that Joan and her stepmother got along so well. Wasn't Elizabeth supposed to despise the daughter of "the other woman," a visual reminder of her husband's momentary infidelity? Soon, Nikki was grateful for that relationship, because Elizabeth's acceptance and love extended to her, as Joan's sister.

Joan, Elizabeth and Nikki stayed quiet, filling their cups and helping themselves to the generous plate of cookies Brooklyn had sent up from the kitchen, while Carter finished his phone call. Ulysses and Gray settled on either side of the door, reminding Nikki of the stone lions guarding the pavement in some ancient temple.

"One more detail cleared away." Carter hung up the phone. "Thank you, dear," he said, chuckling, when Elizabeth handed him a cup already prepared for him, with three chocolate-iced oatmeal-raisin cookies sitting on the saucer. "Well, Nikki, are you bored yet?"

"How can I be bored with Vincent beating up on me all the time?" Nikki laughed with the other three. She was proud to be able to say that even if she couldn't flip the foundation's security chief on his back yet, or bomb him with water balloons during Quarry Hall's version of war games, she could sometimes hold her own during self-defense lessons.

"Anne had an interesting talk with Lisa Montgomery the other day. Do you know her?"

"Dad was her advisor, but we really didn't spend much time together."

"Have your parents kept you up-to-date on the progress with the Mission at Tabor Christian?"

"They were just finishing the first phase of renovations at the old Eloise Elementary school when I ran away," she said, nodding. "They're talking about expanding the food cupboard and meal delivery program and opening up a couple of rooms for shelters for homeless people in the winter. There's a local band, Firesong, that's having a concert next week, I think, to raise money."

"Exactly. That's how Lisa comes into it. She's designing the cover art for their coming CD, and she suggested to Anne that the Mission would be a good outreach opportunity. We're considering partnering with Tabor Christian," Elizabeth said. "We want to send a representative to evaluate the situation, see where there are needs, and determine if it is even possible to partner with the church without taking over or stirring resentment."

"And you want me to do that?"

Nikki didn't know what made her heart race more. Going back to Tabor Heights, among the people who knew the wretched mess she had made of her life, or the responsibility the Arc Foundation was willing to put on her shoulders.

"You don't have to," Joan said, resting a hand on Nikki's wrist. "I know how hard it is to face all those people."

"So that makes me more of a coward, doesn't it, if I stay here, within spitting distance, and pretend..." Nikki sighed and put down her cup so she could rub her temples. Her head ached. "It's the right thing to do. For my sake, maybe even more than the Mission. But I don't know if I can."

"We won't make you," Carter said. "Jennifer is the next choice, but we'd like to give her a few more months to recover from surgery, make sure the damage isn't deeper than the doctors say."

"I think I need to take a walk. Think it over." Nikki got up, grateful her knees weren't wobbly. Gray was on his feet, waiting in the hall, before she could open her mouth to command him.

Nikki's thoughts leaped back and forth between the two opposing reactions to the proposal as she hurried through the house and outside. First, there was the pressure of doing a good job for the foundation, helping the Mission, doing something worthwhile for the church where she had grown up. Then there was the discomfort of facing all those people she had grown up with, who had watched her turn her back on all her values and break her foster parents' hearts. Nikki knew she was forgiven, by the Holwoods, by the people in her church family who really mattered, and by God, but that didn't make it any easier.

She ended up in one of the lower, sheltered gardens of the massive old estate, where the willow trees were still misty bright green with fresh growth. Nikki thought she would have ended up there in the willow garden, even if she had come out here in the middle of the night, in a raging storm, with her eyes closed. Her heart led her here.

"Hey, sweetheart," she whispered, and went to her knees in front of the brass marker set in the polished chunk of stone. Nikki brushed a few cherry blossom petals off the plaque, blown over from a garden several levels up in the terraces, and her fingers traced the raised letters spelling out *Mercy Grace Kathryn.* "Mommy's here."

At times of stress, she could still feel the ache in her womb and the bruises and cuts that came from the car wreck when Ringo, Brock's former boss, had rammed a roadblock and rolled his car. He had kidnapped her to use her as a human shield when he fled the authorities. She had been seven months pregnant. The doctors said her daughter would have survived being born prematurely, but the injuries from the accident eventually led to her death. What made the loss so ironic was that Brock had ordered her to abort when she first told him she was pregnant, but Ringo wanted her baby to provide another layer of camouflage for his drug running operations.

"So, do you think I should do it?" Nikki adjusted her position so she sat with her legs drawn up to her chest, arms wrapped tight around her legs, and her chin resting on her knees. "Time to face the music?"

Gray settled down next to her, his muzzle resting on her foot.

There were so many reasons to go back to Tabor Heights, to face her past and her shame, look people in the eye when they sneered at her, and go on with her life. She would be able to prove she had gotten past her adolescent, selfish stupidity, by bringing something beneficial to the town. How long could she justify staying in the safe, warm, nurturing nest of Quarry Hall and the Arc Foundation?

How long could she keep visiting her daughter's grave and vow to make up for her bad choices before she actually fulfilled that promise?

Just a few feet away, another bronze marker lay half-buried in grass that needed cutting. Nikki stared at it as the quiet of the morning seeped into her mind and body. Finally, she scooted around and went on her knees to the other marker, to brush the blades of grass aside. There were no dates, nothing but the word *Faith* on the marker. There were no ashes in a sealed marble box under the marker, like under Mercy Grace's.

Joan had miscarried before she even knew she was pregnant. She had been with Nikki when Mercy Grace died, and held her and wept with her, and confessed the secret she had carried so long. Nikki knew Joan had done it to help her heal. There was nothing to bury, but Joan had placed the marker for her child as a reminder of all she had gone through, and all the changes she had made in her life since then.

Confessing years of secrecy to that baby's father had probably been the hardest thing Joan could ever have done. Nikki considered her half-sister the bravest person she had ever met.

If Joan could face her sins and failures and move on, Nikki decided she could and should do the same.

"Please, God... it's going to be so hard. Bring good out of this, please?"

She sat between the two markers, letting the peace soak in again, until Gray nudged her and whined, and looked toward the house, hidden by the trees and raw stone walls and the sloping terraces of Quarry Hall's grounds. Nikki nodded and slowly got to her feet.

"I'll be back. I promise," she whispered.


*Sunday, March 24*
*Valleyford, PA*


"You're risking your life," Paul Hunter said, pitching his voice low.

As one person, Brock Pierson and Paul glanced at the next picnic table in the park, where Paul's five-year-old daughter, Sammy, played with her Larrymobile and the beanbag figures of Bob, Larry, Larryboy and Junior Asparagus. The little girl giggled and pushed the two cucumber toys together, side-by-side, her white-blond head bobbing up and down with the force of her chatter to her toys. Brock decided Sammy hadn't heard a thing he had said to her father since the two men sat down to talk half an hour ago. He was relieved.

"It's the right thing to do," Brock said, shrugging. He reached for his travel mug of coffee and tipped it back, grimacing when he found it empty. He had done that three times already. It just showed how distracted he had been since he had made up his mind.

"The Feds offered you witness protection and a new identity because you're valuable to them. You did a good job."

"They're hoping I'll remember more details some time in the future, to testify against anyone else they manage to bring in."

"True." Paul slapped his hand down on his Bible as the freshening breeze stirred the pages. "She must be worth it."

"More than worth it." Brock sighed, feeling about ten degrees of tension uncoil in his gut and shoulders. Paul had been there as a counselor since his first days of incarceration, before the trial to put away Ringo Esteverde had even been put on the docket. He had helped Brock finish the last steps of the path he had chosen the day Nikki fled him, when he ordered her to abort and then hit her hard enough to fling her across the hotel room bed, to hit the wall.

Remembering those horrific days, when he had been secretly working for the DEA and feared for Nikki's life more than his own, Brock stroked the Bible he had carried with him from that hotel. He had caught Nikki reading it, crying over the pages, and tore it out of her hands, ripping it down the spine into three pieces. When she fled the hotel, he had found the pieces in the wastebasket, pieced the Bible together, and started reading it.

When Ringo had found Nikki and kidnapped her, Brock realized he had read that Bible because he wanted to find a way to end up in Heaven, just so he could see Nikki again and apologize.

And tell her that he loved her.

"I've paid for my crimes," Brock finally said, raising his head to meet Paul's gaze. He had the same piercing blue eyes as his daughter, the same white-blond tangle of hair. If Sammy exuded innocence and joy, her father radiated strength and integrity and a demand for honesty and honor. "I helped put Ringo away. I served time in prison. By some miracle, I wasn't charged with statutory rape." He shuddered, remembering how the authorities had actually put that charge on the list. Nikki's sister, Joan, testified that Nikki's birthday was three months sooner than the official records said. Brock had escaped that rape charge by two days. "It's time I make things right with Nikki."

"She hasn't written to you. I'll bet she doesn't even know you've been released."

"I haven't written to her, either." He sighed and rested his face in his hands. "Paul, she's the only truly good, beautiful thing in my life. We made a baby together! I have to try to fix things."

"If you're hoping to win her back..." Paul shook his head and reached across the table to grip Brock's shoulder and shake it. "I'll be praying for you, brother."

"You're not talking me out of it?" He could almost have laughed as he straightened up.

"I think you're an idiot, going around with your own identity, sitting where Ringo's men can still find you. A smart man would opt for the Feds' new identity and fresh start."

"When are you going to get that fresh start, yourself?" Brock asked. He glanced at Sammy, who chortled as she jammed Junior Asparagus and Bob the Tomato into the Larrymobile and shoved it up and down the tabletop. "She's getting old enough to hear the whispers. When will she be old enough to be hurt by what the people in this town say about her mother and grandfather?"

"I'm praying on it." Paul nodded slowly, his smile dimming a little. "Maybe when you find your new place—after you clear things up with your Nikki—you'll find me a decent job."

"I owe you a whole lot more than that." He held out his hand and the two men shook.

"Take some advice?" He waited until Brock nodded. "Make your apologies, accept whatever Nikki gives you, either forgiveness or telling you to stay out of her life permanently, and let yourself move on. You have to consider that what you feel is more guilt than love."

"I know." Brock's mouth twisted in a pained smile, and he nearly admitted he had considered that possibility quite often in the weeks since he had decided he needed to see Nikki and try to win her heart again. He didn't want to believe that the aching, empty, torn-in-half feeling that haunted him was just guilt over seducing an innocent, pure girl into abandoning her family, using her as camouflage in his drug-running business — and then not having the guts to admit to her when he decided to work with the Feds. Brock had changed his life because of Nikki, but he hadn't had the courage or opportunity to tell her that yet.

He would find her, apologize, and move on. It was the only smart thing to do.

But he loved her, and he had known very few people who had ever said love was even in the same universe as "smart."

The place to start was to visit her parents and apologize to them for the pain he had caused. If Dr. Holwood and his wife were as generous and understanding, and as strong of Christians as Brock remembered, then maybe he could ask for their advice on how to approach Nikki. Or if he should approach her at all.

*Tuesday, March 26*
*Quarry Hall*

Nikki had so much on her mind, preparing for the move back to Tabor Heights, she didn't react at first when Kurt Green walked into Quarry Hall that morning to meet with the Carters. She had front door duty and knew a representative from the Allen Michaels Evangelistic Association was due that day. Vincent had called from the gatehouse to say he had sent the visitor up to the main house. She stepped into the kitchen to put the tea tray into the dumb waiter, to send upstairs, and went out the side door to hurry to the parking lot, to meet Kurt and lead him to the house. She even knew his name but didn't make the connection until she had led him through the front door and they were heading down the front hallway to the main stairs.

His name and face registered in her memories just as they started up the stairs. She stumbled on the second step, turning to look at him again. What was more disconcerting was the puzzled expression Kurt wore on his handsome, golden face, the comprehension waiting to dawn. She guessed he recognized her, but wasn't sure from where, and she laughed.

"Kurt Green." She grappled at the carved mahogany banister to keep from falling. "Katie's cousin, right?"

"Right. How do you..." Kurt's mouth dropped open. "Nikki... James. From Tabor. From Tabor Christian. What are you doing here?"

"Besides doing a lousy job as a tour guide?" She grinned and turned back around on the stairs, gesturing up to the second floor. "I work for the foundation now. Like, duh." It relieved her more than she wanted to admit, when he laughed with her. "So Allen Michaels is having a crusade in Ohio this year?"

"This summer, Cuyahoga County Fairgrounds. I'm the first part of the team. Investigating resources, making arrangements, that sort of thing."

"And Quarry Hall is a part of it. I think it's so cool, Uncle Harrison being a friend of Rev. Michaels."

"Uncle?" Kurt slowed as they neared the door to Carter's office.

"Long story. The short version is, I have a half-sister, his daughter, and it's just easier to call him Uncle."

"Oh. Okay."

Then they were at the office. She stepped back into the hall, and gestured for him to go in. "We can talk when you're finished here, okay?"

"You better believe it." Kurt winked at her, then stepped into the office, holding out his hand to Elizabeth, who crossed the room to greet him.

"Maybe it's a test," Joan said, when Nikki found her ten minutes later in the gym, going through her flexibility routine. "If you can survive running into one old friend, you'll do fine when you go home. Kind of like a warm-up."

# Chapter Two

"For one thing, Kurt wasn't exactly an old friend. He's six or seven years older than me and Katie." Nikki sighed and leaned back against the wall, letting herself slide down to sit on the wood floor. Gray immediately settled down next to her and put his head on her ankles. "For another, Kurt left Tabor years before Brock showed up."

"Nikki." Joan straightened up from her twisting maneuver that always made Nikki feel like her spine would snap. "You don't have to do this. If you're not ready, then give the job to someone else."

"I'm a coward."

"You haven't forgiven yourself yet." She muffled a bark of laughter when Nikki flinched at her words. "Listen to the expert in guilt trips. If I had told you about our mother, if I had told you we were sisters when I first landed in Tabor, you might have had a totally different attitude about guys. You might not have even been in the right place to meet Brock when he first came to town. You might never have let him take you out on that first date. Everything would be different. For both of us. Faith never would have been conceived. Sophie might not be in her wheelchair. We both would have done a thousand things differently."

"You might not be a Christian now," Nikki whispered.

"You don't know that. My point is, I could let guilt eat me up every day, but I had to learn to let go. I had to stop saying 'If only,' every time I turned around. If I didn't, I'd be useless—to the foundation, to Dad, to you, to God. I waited four years before I got the guts to tell Matt about our baby. I hurt him and damaged our friendship... Sometimes I wonder where we'd be if I had told him right away."

"Do you think the two of you would be married by now?" She lost her breath for a moment when Joan closed her eyes and blushed. "You're in love with him, aren't you?"

Her sister claimed it was just stress sex, reacting to a life-and-death situation, when she and Matt Cameron had slept together four years ago. Nikki had always believed Matt had been in love with her. After all, he had hounded her for weeks to marry him.

"Doesn't matter."

"Yes, it does! Matt is perfect for you."

"Doesn't matter." Joan dropped to one knee in front of Nikki and grasped her younger sister by her shoulders. "The past and what might have been don't matter. What matters is what we do *now*. And you'll be crippling yourself if you don't forgive yourself. Understand?"

"Yeah," Nikki whispered. "I think so."

~~~~~

"You know, I remember coming here on a field trip when I was in junior high." Kurt Green looked through the french doors, out over the rain-soaked lawn and the sprawling theme gardens behind the Great Hall, now that the tour Nikki and Joan had given him of Quarry Hall had finished. "It's kind of hard to wrap my mind around..." He turned back to face them. "Sisters. I mean, yeah, seeing the two of you together, it's obvious."

"So obvious, nobody saw it for the four years I was living in Tabor, maneuvering to run into Nikki as often as I could." Joan settled down on a hassock with Ulysses next to her.

"There is none so blind as she who will not see," Nikki offered. She stepped over next to him and glanced out at the wet afternoon. Even when the day had gone gray and drippy, Quarry Hall was beautiful. A pang twisted her insides for a moment. "I'm going to miss this place." She bit her lip when a memory flashed into her mind's eye, of the same type of weather, looking out the back door of her foster parents' home on the back yard. The pang turned into an ache to be standing there in the kitchen, helping Doria bake cookies, talking about high school concerns and homework.

"Thirty miles away," Joan offered with a smirk.

"What are you talking about?" Kurt looked back and forth between them, clearly puzzled.

Joan explained about Nikki's coming assignment, to assess the Mission to see if the Arc Foundation would partner with Tabor Christian in the community outreach center. Talk switched to where the idea had come from, then to Lisa Montgomery designing the cover art for Firesong's coming CD, and the upcoming fundraising concert for the Mission.

Kurt was taking an apartment in Tabor Heights, close to the church, and would be within walking distance of the Mission. He and Nikki made tentative arrangements to try to meet up for lunch once or twice while they were both staying in town, and more solid arrangements to meet up at the Firesong concert the next week.

"You've got something nice to look forward to," Joan remarked, as she and Nikki watched Kurt drive away an hour later. She snorted when Nikki gave her a confused look. "The concert. A friendly face in town."

"Lots of friendly faces," Nikki said. "There's Katie and Dani and some other girls in our class at church. They'll be nice. They certainly won't be a bunch of nasty old Pharisees. Then there's Max and some of the older girls.
~~~~~

It won't be so bad."

"And Xander and Hannah, if you're feeling lost. And gee, we're not that far away. You could come home for lunch every day if you wanted." Joan laughed when Nikki glared at her.

The next moment, she laughed with her older sister, despite feeling like a kid going off to first grade. The knowledge that she could indeed run home to Quarry Hall if she felt unwanted and outnumbered did give her some sense of security.

And increased her determination not to let anything drive her away from Tabor Heights before her job was done.

*Monday, March 31*
*Tabor Heights, Ohio*

Coming up Sackley Road from the Hyburg I-71 exit into Tabor, Nikki stopped to buy flowers at the roadside stand by the fairgrounds' entrance. It had been there since before she came to the Holwoods as a foster child, and Nikki supposed it would always be there. She liked that sense of stability, something to rely on. Some things didn't change and never would. That was good.

Some things had to change, though, and for that, she gave thanks with all her heart and soul and every breath she took.

Gray sniffed suspiciously at the hodgepodge of carnations and gladiolas and blue-tinted daisies, wrapped up in crinkly white tissue paper. The dog woofed softly and sat up in the front seat of the dark blue Jeep as Nikki pulled out into the lazy, pre-lunch traffic.

She rolled down the window and leaned her elbow out, grinning at the tickle of the cool breeze on her winter-pale skin. She glanced at herself in the side mirror and wondered if anyone would recognize her.

"All grown up, you think, Gray?" she murmured, and raked a hand through her shoulder-length hair. She had always worn it long and in braids until she ran away with Brock and had all the money she wanted to experiment with hair and makeup and clothes. Some people in Tabor were so set in their patterns, just the change in hair might make her unrecognizable. Nikki considered that she might be a little thinner, with a few lines around her mouth and eyes from pain and guilt, but otherwise she hadn't changed much. In her faded jeans, blue gingham shirt, and hiking boots, she could have been coming home for lunch from high school.

Nikki shook her head as she drove past Tabor High School on her right. On her left, the sprawling horseshoe of single-story buildings for Tabor Children's Home—where she would have spent her childhood if the Holwoods hadn't taken her. Then all around her, scattered throughout the town as if it held Tabor on the map, the ivy-clad sandstone buildings of Butler-Williams University.

She was home. With butterflies battling in her stomach, Nikki admitted that Tabor Heights would always be home, no matter where she went or how long she was gone. She had work to do for the Arc Foundation, which had given her a new life and purpose. All the tears in the world wouldn't bring her child back from the dead — what was the use of tormenting herself with memories?

Other memories came to her as she turned left on Main with its hodgepodge of quaint, old houses that had been turned into shops and apartments, then took another left on Stephen. She had grown up here, treating the entire Butler-Williams University campus as her back yard. Her foster father was head of the Humanities Department; her foster mother, a part-time tutor for the music department. Nikki had always been on campus when she wasn't doing something with the other foster children or the youth at Tabor Christian Church.

"Didn't keep me out of trouble, did it, Gray?" she murmured, slowing to travel the one-way street lined with clumps of oaks and elms that cast all the sprawling Century homes into perpetual shade. "I should have seen the warning when Rich turned his back on everything we believed in. When he broke his promises to me, he was betraying God. I was so upset over my broken heart, it never occurred to me that I would do the same thing half a year later." She turned left on Church, with the Holwoods' house in sight. "Guess we really were a pair after all, huh?" The big Akita snorted and nuzzled her hand on the steering wheel. "We're here. You behave yourself and don't eat anybody, hear me?"

She parked against the curb and sat a few moments after turning off the engine, just looking. Nothing had changed. Not the pristine white paint and forest green shutters on the three-story tall Century house. Not the sprinkling of buttery dandelions on the mossy lawn. Not the crooked, uneven slate sidewalks that had provided such dangerous, exciting paths for hordes of roller-skating children.

There were cars parked in the street and in driveways, and bikes abandoned by front and side doors. Lunchtime in Tabor Heights still meant coming home from school and work whenever possible. A green sedan with temporary tags sat in the driveway of the Holwood house. Probably another parent who finally got her life together enough — job and home and car — to take back her child. Nikki knew with all the praying the Holwoods did for the children in their care, their lives were bound to continue improving when they returned to their parents. She was the only failure her foster parents ever had, as far as Nikki knew, and even she had ended up all right.

"Ready, Gray?" She opened the door, slid out onto the crumbling curb splashed with asphalt from the last paving job, and held the door open until the big dog climbed across the driver's seat to follow her. She left everything in the back seat. Coming home, it was best to leave her arms empty for hugs. Nikki tucked her ring of keys in her left pocket and reached into her right pocket to pull out a single key hanging from a ring with a white ceramic dove attached.

It was the key to the Holwoods' house. Doria had brought it with her when she went to be with Nikki in the hospital, recovering from the accident that killed Mercy Grace. She had given it to her foster daughter almost before Nikki could begin apologizing like the Prodigal Son, and told her she would always be able to come home.

Nikki squeezed the key once for reassurance and slid it back into her pocket. She didn't need the key during the day. The door to the Holwoods' house was always open. University students needing advice could come and walk in and call to announce their presence. Co-workers at the university or from church were welcome any time. What was the use of locking the door during the day, when foster children were in and out at all hours? The only time the door was ever locked was when everyone was away from home, and that was only a concession to the criminal element that reached to touch even quiet, gentle Tabor.

The heavy, forest green door groaned softly as the latch clicked and Nikki pushed it open. She smiled, remembering all the times she had watched and then helped Dr. Holwood oil the hinges, and still the door refused to be quiet. That door and the lack of trees to climb outside her attic bedroom window had forced her to stick to curfews when she fell into her rebellious phase.

"Mum?" she called, pausing in the shadowy hardwood foyer with the stairs in front of her, the living room on her right and the door into the dining room on her left. Nikki tapped the spotty bronze dove-shaped doorknocker twice. "Daddy? I'm home."

"Nikki?" Doria Holwood hurried around the corner of the dining room from the kitchen, wiping her hands on her apron. Her coffee-colored face lit and she spread her arms wide. "Sweetheart, you're early."

"Didn't want to miss lunch." She hugged her foster mother hard to fight the twinge in her gut. Did Doria seem smaller than the last time she had been home?

No. Nikki blamed the thick soles of her boots. She had been able to look her foster mother in the eye since she was fourteen, and nothing had changed there, either.

"More like that monster of yours didn't want to miss lunch," Dr. Rance Holwood rumbled, stepping through the doorway from the kitchen, as his wife led Nikki through the dining room. "Welcome home, baby." He wrapped his massive arms around her, nearly lifting her off her feet. A dead ringer for James Earl Jones, he made his slim, elegant wife look elfin by comparison. He grasped Nikki by her shoulders and held her off at arm's length, looking her up and down. "You look good. Those folks at Arc aren't running you ragged, are they? Are you taking good care of our girl, Gray?"

Gray woofed, then sneezed, and settled down next to the kitchen doorway with a "that's that" expression on his gray and black-streaked face. The other three laughed.

"I'm interrupting something," Nikki said, after glancing around the dining room. The table was set for three for lunch. Her foster parents weren't expecting her until mid-afternoon, and they never ate in the dining room except for special occasions. Guests were in that category. Doria's pale green print dress and the fact that Dr. Holwood hadn't taken off his jacket were further clues. "Somebody's folks here to pick them up? And where are the kids, anyway?"

"A field trip all day," Doria said, and glanced at the doorway into the kitchen.

"It works out well," Dr. Holwood added. He glanced down at his jacket and prepared to take it off.

"Let me get my gear up to my room and get Gray settled outside, and you can get on with things." She took a step back toward the front door.

"Nikki?" The soft baritone voice coming from the kitchen stopped her dead in her tracks.

Myriad images flashed through her mind. Emotions and sensations from dozens of highs and lows in her life flooded her memory, knocking her off balance in heart and body. Nikki reached out a hand for the pale oak chair at the head of the dining room table.

That voice had laughed with her and teased, argued and shouted and cursed. The man had held her in his arms and seduced her into setting aside what she thought she believed, and when she returned to those principles, he had slapped her hard enough to fling her across their hotel room.

"I hoped to see you while I was here, but I didn't think it would be so soon." Brock Pierson stepped into the doorway between kitchen and dining room.

His hair was shorter. Nikki was used to it curling down the back of his neck. She used to like stroking the silky blackness to soothe away his headaches. He had shaved his beard and moustache, and his square face looked thinner than she had thought it would.

For a moment, she wondered what it would be like to kiss him without all that hair to tickle her. Fury twisted through her, along with a nauseous sense of guilt. If she had never let Brock kiss her, none of the last four years would have happened.

His wide shoulders didn't look quite so stooped with pressures and anger as they had the last few times she saw him. He didn't wear any of the stylish sport coats he had liked when he worked for Ringo. Nikki supposed his fancy wardrobe, expensive sports car, jewelry, everything he valued had all been lost when Ringo went to prison. She felt a flicker of satisfaction, even as she remembered that Brock had voluntarily forfeited all that wealth when he contacted the DEA to work for them against Ringo and his organization. He actually looked good in new jeans, blue work shirt, sans tie—but she refused to consider that after the first moment.

Brock was out of her life. She had repented and given her life back to God. She was making up for her stupidity and rebellion. Brock was no part of her new life. He had almost gotten her killed. Knowing that he had been working with the DEA, providing them information on Ringo's drug operation for eight months before Mercy Grace had died didn't change anything between them. Brock had ordered her to abort their daughter, had hit her for the first time when she refused, and hadn't come after her when she left him, to work her way home to Tabor. She still wasn't sure what hurt her the most. Knowing he had become one of the "good guys" could never make up for how he had hurt and lied to and used her.

"What are you doing here?" she asked, her voice thin but even. She was proud she hadn't shouted or burst into tears. Proud she hadn't asked what he was doing out of prison so soon. He still had to serve prison time, despite all the bargains he had made with the authorities. Nikki had been glad he had to go to prison, and she wasn't ashamed of her vindictive feelings.

"Trying to set things right, mostly." Brock glanced at the Holwoods, who watched Nikki. "Starting at the top and working my way down the ladder. I was planning to go to Quarry Hall next, but I called and they said you would be working here for a while."

"That's right. I have work to do." Nikki wanted to flee back to her Jeep, maybe all the way back to Akron and Quarry Hall. She dug her boots more securely into the dark green Berber carpet of the dining room and sent up a silent prayer for help.

Why wasn't Gray reacting to any of this? He was her bodyguard, her four-legged conscience and jerk-detector. The big dog just lay there and watched Brock, his ears pricked forward and his massive gray head resting on his paws.

"Nikki—"

"You have no business being here." She pressed her hand against her left cheek, as if she could still feel that shattering blow from his hand.

"Sweetheart." Doria reached out a hand to rest on Nikki's shoulder.

"Brock's here to make things right."

"He can't." She almost shrugged off her mother's calming touch, and that shocked her worse than seeing Brock again.

"He's a Christian now," Dr. Holwood said.

"I don't care! That doesn't fix anything." Nikki wrapped her arms hard around herself, flashing back to that terrifying ride in the trunk of Ringo's car, when he had used her as a shield against the police on his trail. She relived the twisting, empty ache inside when she woke in the hospital and learned her baby fought for her life in an incubator. Nikki thought she had made her peace with that pain and guilt and anger. What good was peace that went away when the man she used to love stood there and expected her to go on as if nothing had ever happened?

"Look, Nikki, I want to do what's right." Brock took two steps toward her, hesitated, and when she didn't retreat, he took another step and held out a hand to her. "I want to make things up to you. I think it's what God wants me to do." He tried to smile. "Did you... did you bury our baby? I'd like to see the place."

Let him come to Quarry Hall? Walk through the gardens that had become her sanctuary and show him the shadowy, green place where she had buried the ashes of their daughter? Did he know what he was asking? How much more did he want to hurt her?

# Chapter Three

Then an image filled her mind: Brock falling backward in the kitchen of the rented townhouse, thrown by the force of Ringo's gunshot; bleeding in an explosive burst that made Nikki think he died instantly. He had tried to free her from Ringo and his enraged boss had shot him.

Brock had cried when the prosecutor announced in court that Mercy Grace had lived a little more than a week in the hospital pediatric ICU and died of the injuries that brought about her premature birth. Nikki had never thought she would ever see Brock cry.

She pushed away the moment of softness toward him. Brock was responsible for so much pain and waste in her life.

*Just as responsible as you are,* that guiding voice in her heart whispered. *If you can finally forgive yourself, why can't you forgive him? He still loves you.*

*No he doesn't. He never loved me. He was only using me,* she fought back. Brock had romanced her away from her home and beliefs to use her as a shield, a front, a distraction for those who got suspicious about the questions he asked and the connections he made.

"I don't think—I can't," she finally said, when the silence grew thick and tense.

"Honey, why don't you get your things up to your room and wash up?" Doria murmured and gently turned Nikki toward the door.

Dr. Holwood beckoned and guided Brock before him, back into the kitchen.

"What is he doing here, Mum?" Nikki whispered as she stumbled down the front steps and down the slate sidewalk to the curb.

"Exactly what he says. I have to admit, I was shocked when he showed up at the door an hour or so ago with your father."

"He went to Daddy, first?" She stopped short, just a few feet from the curb. "That must have taken a lot of nerve."

"Oh, quite the opposite, I think." Doria held out her hand and Nikki gave her the keys. "I think he really is telling the truth. God had to knock him to rock bottom before he would listen, and now he's setting everything right. When he showed up at the door, he was sweating and so white, I thought he would pass out right there on the doorstep." She chuckled as she unlocked the Jeep. "He's a far cry from the young man who romanced you right out from under our noses."

"He lied to us before. How can I be sure he's telling the truth now?"

"Nikki... If we judged everyone based on their past performances, we'd never trust anyone, never get anything accomplished in this world. We'd all be living in solitary, dark little holes with lots of chains and bars on the doors and emptiness in our hearts." She gently stroked an errant strand of hair out of Nikki's eyes. "Why should your father and I believe you when you say you've changed?"

"Because I'm —" She swallowed hard. "Brock says he's a Christian now, huh? What if that's just another scam? Mum, he was using me to cover up his trail. People saw a guy with his innocent little girlfriend and thought he was on the level, not front-man and numbers-cruncher for a drug ring!"

"He almost died, protecting you."

"Yeah. So did I." She reached into the Jeep and pulled her backpack and computer case from the floor in the front.

~~~~~

Brock was still there when Nikki finished unpacking and settling into her old room in the attic, and came back downstairs. She wasn't surprised. She had heard voices talking softly in the dining room and hadn't heard any doors open or close, or car engines start up, or tires crunch on the gravel drive. Gray let out a soft whine of warning as he followed her down the stairs. He didn't growl, and that disappointed her. Then again, he stayed at her side when they reached the first floor and didn't respond to the hand Brock held out to him in an attempt to make friends. No more than Nikki responded to the wobbly smile he gave her.

"Could I see her grave?" he asked, getting up slowly, like a creaky old grandfather, from the bench against the wall parallel to the stairs. It was a good guess that he had been waiting for her to come downstairs.

Nikki was just too tired to argue. This wasn't like all the times she swallowed misgivings to make Brock happy. She wasn't scalding her conscience to do stupid things. She would never again throw aside what she knew was right to make someone else happy. No matter how much she thought she loved him.

This was keeping the peace, so he would leave as quickly and quietly as possible. Still, she couldn't help resisting a little bit.

"Why? She's not really there."

"I know that. It's just... I was getting all geared up to learn how to be a daddy... and now I'll never know."

"If I had aborted her like you ordered me, there wouldn't even be a marker."

"Nikki!" He stomped away a few steps, whirled and spread his arms as if he would lunge at her. Or hug her. Nikki held her ground, stunned to realize she hoped he would hit her so she could fight back. Vincent and Joan had taught her to hold her ground and defend herself — but never to
~~~~~

provoke arguments, never trick someone into attacking her. What was wrong with her?

Arguing and deliberately baiting someone wasn't approved behavior for a representative of the Arc Foundation. Nikki knew Joan and the Carters would be disappointed, at the very least.

Worse, Jesus would be disappointed. She worked for the Arc Foundation to do good in the world, to heal wounds — and here she was picking at her own wounds, and Brock's, deliberately making them worse. What was wrong with her? Was it just fatigue? Or hadn't she healed as much as she thought?

Maybe Joan was right, and she hadn't forgiven herself yet, so that made it impossible for her to forgive Brock?

"Look." He raked the fingers of one hand through his hair. "I understand why you hate me. I hate myself. But you loved me once. I loved you. Doesn't that mean anything?"

"That wasn't love. Not real love. We went at it all wrong," she whispered, and sank down onto the second step. "Everything we did was wrong, Brock. Look where it's brought us."

"I'm a Christian, now. I probably wouldn't have stayed around long enough to listen, if you had given me the brush-off like you were supposed to. Does that make up for any of it?" He tried to smile.

"My baby died!" Nikki gripped the banister post to keep from jumping up and running away.

"My baby, too. It hurts."

"You will never know how much it hurts!" She stood, almost falling off balance. Gray moved over in front of her, effectively keeping her from throwing herself at Brock, fists flying.

Was she really planning on pounding him? Gray seemed to think so; her furry conscience.

"Nikki—"

"I'll probably never be able to have more kids."

The scene in the townhouse kitchen flashed before her eyes. Ringo with his gun. Brock, bare-chested and sleepy, falling to the tiles with a geyser of blood like a weird flower blooming from his chest. Everything was black and white and red; the decor of the kitchen, the night outside, Brock's blood.

"I'm sorry," he whispered. "I'd give anything to turn back the clock. I'd marry you, Nikki. I'd be the best daddy our little girl could ever want. I'd take care of you. I swear."

"Don't." Suddenly she was just too tired to fight, to think, to feel. "You can follow me back to Quarry Hall, I'll show you where the grave is and you can — we can all get on with our lives."

"Sure. Anything you want."

~~~~~

Gray got in her way, when Nikki stepped into the willow garden, keeping her from going directly to Mercy Grace's marker. She reached down to grasp his collar to turn him aside, but something in the big dog's eyes made her shiver and pause. She saw Brock move past her and turned to watch him.

His legs wobbled a little. His shoulders hunched, just enough to be noticeable. He clenched his fists.

"Oh, please," she whispered.

What bothered her more? The sympathy she felt for his pain? Or her anger? What right did he have to hurt for their murdered child? He had ordered her to abort when Mercy Grace was little more than a handful, not even visible inside her mother's body. He had slapped her and tore up the Gideon Bible she had found in the nightstand and devoured, begging God for guidance and strength.

"I'm sorry, baby," Brock whispered, and bent over, reaching out as if to touch the bronze marker and the new carpet of cherry blossom petals strewn across it.

A tear fell off the tip of his nose, sparkling in the afternoon sunlight as it tumbled down to the marker.

*Lord, please help me forgive him. I can't accept Your forgiveness to me, for all the stupid, selfish things I did, until I can forgive him.*

Nikki choked on mixed laughter and tears as her prayer echoed through her mind and heart. How many times had Joan and Vincent and the Carters counseled her on being forgiving and accepting forgiveness? So many times, she had lost count.

She thought she had forgiven Brock, until she saw him again.

"How did you get out of prison so soon?" she asked. Her voice creaked a little, startling her.

"Good behavior." He shrugged and knuckled his eyes before turning completely to face her. Gray strands in his hair gleamed in a single stray sunbeam for a moment. "I testified against Ringo. Gave the authorities a lot of people in the organization, a lot of contacts. And I just wasn't high up enough to be worth the trouble."

"They let you out because they were afraid someone would kill you inside," she guessed, listening to the shiver that ran up her spine. Nikki blamed the suspense novels she had read.

"That, too."

"Shouldn't you be in Witness Protection or something?"

"Probably. But Ringo got himself killed two months ago—territory fight inside the prison—and things are so shredded, with people fighting over what's left of his territory, I'm more of a benefactor to the winners than an enemy. If it wasn't for me, they wouldn't be on top now."
~~~~~

"That's sick."

"That's the world I was living in." He took a deep breath, let it out, jammed his hands in his pockets. "Nikki, I swear, I tried to protect you from that. Keep you sweet and innocent."

"Ignorant, you mean. And I guess I'm grateful," she added, her voice cracking.

"I really did love you."

"Brock —" Nikki shook her head. She had to get out of here. She had to head back to Tabor and get to work, focus on her reasons for being home, not dwell on the past. Learning from the past was one thing. Regretting it and trying to change it was something else altogether. "You know how to get here now. I have to get going. I have work to do..." She stared at him for a few racing heartbeats, wondering why in the world she was telling him all this. "I'll — I'll probably see you again before you leave town, huh?"

"Invitation?" He tried to smile.

"No. More like giving in to the inevitable."

"I don't want to hurt you anymore, Nikki."

"Thanks," she whispered.

For a few more seconds she watched him, seeing the moisture in his eyes, the aching that pressed on his shoulders. She imagined him clenching and unclenching his fists in his jacket pockets. Brock kept so much inside, she knew. It was his habit. She had always admired his self-control. It had been more shock at the sudden violence than pain when he hit her, and that shock had prompted her to run away.

Nikki nodded, unable to say good-bye for some reason, and turned to take the long way around the estate to get to the parking lot. The last thing she wanted was to run into anyone and have to explain what she was doing back, when she had driven to Tabor Heights only three hours ago. Worse was having to explain what Brock was doing there. Gray pressed against her leg as she walked. She welcomed his warmth even as he nearly knocked her off balance with every step.

~~~~~

Brock watched Nikki and her dog leave. When they had vanished through the trees, he turned back to the little bronze marker. This time he dropped to his knees. He pushed aside the carpet of petals and tall grass and traced the raised letters with his index finger.

"Your mommy knew what she was talking about when she named you, huh?" he whispered. "Mercy is when we don't get what we deserve. Grace is when we get what we don't deserve. I hurt your mommy really bad, and I hurt you. But I love you, Mercy Grace. Even though I never saw you. God taught me that." He caught his breath, knuckled away another tear. "I still love your mommy. I love her so much more, now."
~~~~~

He was supposed to go on to a job waiting for him in Kentucky, part of the reformation program he was involved in. Suddenly, that felt like the absolutely wrong thing to do. He thought for a moment, then headed for his rental car and the notebook holding all his important phone numbers. Open Doors, the prison ministry he had joined before he was assigned his bunk in prison, had boarding houses and contacts here in northeast Ohio. Paul had told him to contact Mandy Gordon if he needed any help or needed to talk to someone. Maybe it wasn't a coincidence that she happened to live in Tabor Heights?

After all his close calls and the miracles that had allowed him to turn his life around, Brock was willing to believe in divine intervention, and didn't hesitate to pray for some right now.

~~~~~

"Mom Holwood, there's a huge dog in our back yard!" a little girl shrieked, accompanied by the kitchen door groaning open.

"You didn't hurt him, did you?" Doria asked calmly and gave Nikki a wide-eyed look of mock innocence.

"He's bigger than me!" the child said, punctuated with a stomp that would have been more effective if she had been wearing boots instead of little pink sneakers.

She stopped short, all blonde curls and pink baseball jacket and jeans. Her head barely topped the scarred oak kitchen table. She stared at Nikki, who continued working on the salad for their dinner.

"Brandy, this is Nikki. You've heard Dad Holwood and me talk about her." Doria gestured at the row of three glasses of milk and three napkins with a brownie on each one sitting on the table. "Are you going to eat your snack or are you going to stand there, catching flies with your mouth hanging open?"

The little girl blinked, then a grin wiped away the stare that Nikki had been sure was about to transform into hysterics at being faced by a stranger. She scurried up onto the closest chair and surveyed the treats, then reached for the napkin with the largest brownie, and scooped up the cup with the most milk in it.

The Holwoods had told her about the three foster children currently staying with them, when Nikki called to tell them about her assignment. Brandy, at eight, was the youngest and had been with the Holwoods almost six months now. Her mother had run out on her Navy hospital corpsman father. When he shipped out more than a year ago, he left her with his parents. Both were frail, with health issues, and couldn't cope with a rambunctious, strong-willed child with a voice that could bend steel—according to Dr. Holwood. They were members of Tabor Christian and had asked the Holwoods to take Brandy. That way they could see her on a regular basis and be part of her life, and not worry what would
~~~~~

happen to the girl if either one or both of them became incapacitated.

Brandy spent time with her grandparents several times a week and stayed over most weekends. She had been visiting her grandparents the last few times Nikki had come home for a visit or at holidays, or when the Holwoods went to Quarry Hall for holidays and parties.

The other two foster children, Davie and Danny, were cousins, ten years old, born three months apart, and looked enough alike they were mistaken for twins. That seemed to be their greatest source of pride. They were blue-eyed and dark-haired, chubby and given to exaggeration and silliness at the most socially awkward times. Davie's mother had died at birth, so her sister took the boy to raise with her son. Neither father was locatable, and when Danny's mother was arrested for soliciting for the fifth time, the system took the boys away. The cousins had been with the Holwoods for two months now. According to their caseworker, it looked like their mother was going to lose all parental rights if she continued to backslide in her rehabilitation program.

"Is that your dog?" Brandy asked, after chugging nearly half the glass of milk without stopping to breathe. She plunked the glass down onto the table and wiped her milk moustache with her sleeve.

"His name is Gray Brother, and he's more like my partner." Nikki dumped the last of the celery into the salad and took the cutting board to the sink to rinse it.

"Huh?"

"Gray is Nikki's bodyguard. She does a lot of traveling for her job, and Gray keeps her safe," Doria said. She shook her head, even as she smiled at her daughter.

"There's a big dog in the back yard!" a boy yelped as the kitchen door banged open and two boys barreled through together.

"Mom Holwood! Come look!" the second one called. "He followed us home. Can we keep him?"

Nikki stepped back, blinking as the comments shifted from one boy to the other without any change in voice. Her foster mother had been right. It was hard to tell where one boy ended and the other began. She could only tell who spoke by watching their lips move.

"No, you cannot keep him and no, Gray didn't follow you home. He's been here all afternoon," Doria said, and calmly continued pulling the butter and the pickles from the refrigerator.

The cousins stopped short, staring at Nikki, who leaned back against the counter, crossed her arms and waited for whatever their response would be. According to her foster parents, the boys would either take to her immediately, or spend the duration of her visit darting into other rooms or watching her from under their shaggy mops of tangled black hair.

"Who are you?" one boy asked, his voice almost a whisper.

"This is Nikki, dope," Brandy said. She sighed and shook her head, in perfect imitation of Doria. "Don't you remember Mom and Dad Holwood telling us she was coming home?"

"You have the attic room, don't you?" the other boy asked. He barely waited for Nikki to nod before blurting, "Can I have it when you leave again?"

"That attic room is Nikki's forever and ever," Doria said. "And that particular topic of conversation is closed. Now sit down and eat your snack before it's time to start setting the table."

Both boys hurried to slam themselves into their chairs and gobble their brownies. Nikki and Doria exchanged grins. The rule in the Holwood house was that snacks were permitted until someone started setting the table, then no treats until two hours after dinner had ended.

Nikki let the children get used to her presence and stayed in the background during the dinner preparations. She liked listening to them chatter about their day with their foster mother. It made her feel like nothing had really changed, and she was still the big sister in this ever-changing household. She liked knowing the children accepted her presence enough to go on with their usual routine. Nikki wasn't sure what she would have done if the children sat like little mute lumps and just watched her. Leave? Where would she go? She hadn't kept in contact with any of her friends from church or school. Maybe that was another reason for coming home; to mend more broken bridges and repair lines of communication.

# Chapter Four

Dr. Holwood came home with a briefcase full of papers to read and grade, as usual. He left it at the foot of the stairs, as usual. Just in time, because all three children abandoned their various chores and ran to greet him. Nikki paused in putting the corn in the microwave and listened to the squeals and laughter, the thumps, and Dr. Holwood's fake protests of helplessness.

"Feel like you're really home now, honey?" Doria murmured.

"As long as there are kids in this house, it'll always be home." She swallowed a thick lump trying to lodge high in her throat. "How come God lets us be so stupid?"

"So we learn and grow. And so we can help other people when they're suffering from their own stupidity. How can we help when we can't sympathize?"

Dr. Holwood shuffled into the kitchen, with Brandy in his arms and a boy half-riding each leg. He staggered over to his chair at the table, which was pulled out and waiting, and sank down into it. The boys tumbled to the ground, laughing.

"Whew! I'm getting too old for this," he grumbled, and set Brandy down on her own feet with a thud. The little girl giggled and scampered back to her job of filling water glasses with ice. He settled back in his chair, watching his wife and daughter finishing their preparations. "Now this is what I like to see. My whole family all in one place."

Gray, who had taken up his chosen spot on the rug next to the back door, raised his head and gave a soft woof as if agreeing with him.

~~~~~

Brock slowed and studied the big old house as he drove past. All was quiet out front, and after a glance at the dashboard clock, he guessed everyone was in the kitchen in the back of the house, settling down to dinner. Nodding, his mouth stretching into a small, tight smile, he continued down the street. He glanced at a piece of paper sitting on the seat next to him, comparing the house numbers, until he came to a three-story olive-green house across the street and three houses down from the Holwoods. A metal fire escape painted to match the house peered out from behind the skinny poplars lining the side yard between it and the next house. Brock parked in front and got out to head to the door. Before he could take more than three steps, a short woman with ebony and gray
~~~~~

curls waddled out to meet him, her violet and emerald caftan snapping briskly against her pudgy legs.

"Well, Mr. Pierson, you didn't dawdle, did you?"

"No, ma'am, Mrs. Gordon. I'm really anxious to settle down. You have no idea how much I appreciate this."

"Oh, I can guess." She looked him up and down, and Brock waited while she made her inspection.

Mandy Gordon was a "character," according to his contact at Open Doors, who had arranged permission from all the authorities for Brock to change his plans and settle here in Tabor Heights. Brock supposed she had to be a character to be willing to help newly released convicts get a footing back in the real world.

"Ready to see your place? It's all cleaned up and stocked. You don't have to buy any groceries for a week. I got a schedule all made up for when people can use the laundry room. I expect you to keep your rooms clean." She led him up the slate walkway to the wide wooden porch and the front door. "General rules: No loud music between eleven at night and seven in the morning. No alcohol or smoking in my house. If you gotta, you do it somewhere else and don't bring the residue back here. Got that?" She glanced over her round shoulder at him.

"Yes, ma'am. I don't do either."

"That's good. Less work to do on straightening you out. Now, one big rule is, you gotta go to church if you stay at my place."

"I already have one picked out." Brock followed her into the house. His contact at Open Doors had emailed him the floor plans and the house rules. The bottom floor was the common area for the six men who rented two-room suites in the house. Three men to a floor, with a shared bathroom. Each suite had a mini kitchen, but there was also a shared kitchen on the ground floor as well as laundry facilities and a den to study in, for those who were attending school.

"Good for you. Which one?" She pointed at the stairs that faced the front door and they headed up. Brock had rooms on the top floor, also accessible by the fire escape.

"Tabor Christian."

"Good church. I go there myself." She chuckled. "Any particular reason?"

"I know somebody who goes there."

"Uh huh." She hauled herself up to the third-floor landing and fumbled a jangling ring of keys from her sagging pocket. "Your girl, I'll just bet."

"Ma'am?" Brock nearly took a step backward and almost went tumbling down the stairs.

"Joey told me why he thinks you changed your plans to stay here. He says you got a girl here in Tabor."

"I *had* a girl here in Tabor." He took a deep breath, fighting the ache that dug into his chest every time he thought about Nikki and Mercy Grace. If he wasn't guilty of murder for what he had done to her and their daughter, then what could it be called?

"And you want to get her back. Well, love isn't the worst reason for straightening out your life. Won't be any good unless you get straight with God, first." She paused with the door open three inches and the key still in the lock. "Did Joey warn you I'm a Bible-thumper?"

"Yes, ma'am." Brock grinned now. "I told him I'll take all the thumping I can get."

"You'll do. Let's see about finding you a job tomorrow, and then we can work on getting your girl back."


*Tuesday, April 1*


First thing the next morning, after the children had shuffled off to school, Nikki went to the Mission. She had considered just showing up yesterday, even before going home and settling in. That wouldn't be fair, she knew. The staff expected her today. Other places, it might have been all right to show up early and short-circuit attempts to clean up things or hide damaging or dangerous evidence and even people. But Nikki knew the people at the Mission. It had been started by her home church. Pastor Wally had been a grandfather figure since before she could talk.

She wore her business clothes for this first visit: black blazer, black slacks, sensible black loafers, and a purse and briefcase instead of her usual backpack. She put a leash on Gray. He didn't complain but gave her that sorrowful puppy look of reproach that made her want to laugh and cry.

"As soon as everybody knows you, I swear you'll lose the leash," Nikki promised as she led him out to the Jeep, to drive to the Mission.

She could have walked from her parents' house, but image was everything, as Brooklyn regularly lectured the girls at Quarry Hall. Nikki had walked to the site of the Mission when it was an elementary school, but now she was here on official Arc Foundation business.

The Mission's building was typical forties school construction: one long central hallway with a peaked roof; individual exits for each classroom that opened onto the lawn on one side, the parking lot on the other; a boxy addition holding the gymnasium and cafeteria stuck on the back side; and a small extension out the front for the office area and lobby. Nikki parked on the street where the flagstone path from the front door met the sidewalk and got out slowly. She felt like she had been called to the principal's office, and that was ridiculous.

Despite her resolution to follow through and accept this assignment, she had still felt some doubts as she went through all the paperwork and the details of the Mission's financial and legal status that Sophie had dug up with her almost magical Internet acumen. Not that Nikki minded being given work in her hometown. She wanted to come home and do something worthwhile for the town, but she had just been taken from courier status to full-fledged representative for Arc. Shouldn't she have more experience under her belt before she took such a personal assignment?

*"You'll see things the rest of us would miss, just because we don't know the territory,"* Elizabeth had said, when Nikki confided in her about her questions and misgivings. *"We all trust you, Nikki. Trust yourself."*

"Trust myself," Nikki whispered as she and Gray marched up the walk to the front door.

They stepped through the door into the lobby. The former principal's office with its floor-to-ceiling plate glass window sat on the other side of the lobby. From her desk, gnarled, wrinkled Miss Steary had been able to see down the hall in both directions and knew everything going on. A slender, strawberry-blonde woman in a simple, sleeveless blue dress sat at Miss Steary's desk. She only gave Gray one faintly surprised look before she stood and went to the open office door.

"Nikki James?" she asked, summoning up a smile that felt totally genuine to Nikki.

"How'd you guess?" Nikki liked her right away. She searched her memories of Tabor to try to match that pretty, unpainted, gray-eyed face with a name. She came up blank.

"Xander warned us about your bodyguard, when he heard that the Arc Foundation was considering partnering with us. Hi, boy. You're a beauty, aren't you?" She didn't hold out a hand in a misguided attempt at friendship or drop to her knees or do anything to ingratiate herself with Gray. She only stood still and let him finish nosing around her knees and ankles. Nikki was impressed.

"Standard issue equipment. You are?"

"Oh—sorry. Claire Donnelly." She held out her hand.

"Right!" Nikki liked the feel of her hand; solid, smooth, dry; a working hand. "You put together the fundraiser with Firesong for this weekend. I've been warned about your brother, to protect my toes from his wheelchair, and protect my brain from his warped sense of humor."

"You do know a lot about us." Claire led her into the office and gestured for her to have a seat on the same wooden benches that had lined the office when Nikki was seven.

"Connections. People who are excited about the Mission..." She paused, a little disoriented to see a long rack of shelves where the school's trophy case had been.

"I'll go get Pastor Wally." She vanished down the short hallway that used to lead to the teachers' lounge and Principal Thornwood's office. Before Nikki could even consider putting down her briefcase, Claire returned, followed by a massive shape.

Pastor Wally had been white-haired since Nikki could remember. His bristly walrus moustache had gone from iron-gray to brilliant white in the four years since she had been gone, and the flesh sagged a little more on his solid neck. The chocolate brown slacks and white shirt with sleeves rolled up to his elbows and open at the neck were his usual costume. Nikki just grinned to see the big man lumber down the short hall into the office.

"Well, Miss James, it's a real pleasure to work with you." Pastor Wally frowned a little. He took off his thick, copper-rimmed glasses, rubbed his eyes and leaned closer. "Do I know you?" Mischief sparkled in his eyes.

"Pastor Wally!"

"Give me a hug, little girl." He opened his arms wide, then stopped, his mouth dropping open at the sight of Gray watching him. "Who let that bear in here?"

"That's my bodyguard. Gray, this is Pastor Wally. He's a friend." Nikki held out her hand in the signal that brought Gray up next to her. "Claire, Pastor Wally, hold out your hands in fists." She waited until they complied. "Gray Brother. Friend. Friend." She gripped Gray's collar and guided his head, back and forth between their fists, letting him sniff their skin multiple times.

"That's all it takes?" Claire settled down on the front of her desk, a thoughtful frown on her face.

"The dogs trained by the Arc Foundation are... superior. Intelligent, yes, but some people have said they swear there's a person looking out through their eyes." Nikki knelt next to Gray and wrapped an arm around his neck while she rubbed the bib of thick fur on his chest, signaling her approval and love. "Gray knows you're safe, that you're a friend, and if I'm separated from him and he sees you, he'll come to you if you call."

"Interesting." Pastor Wally shook his head. "What sort of people have you gotten yourself involved with?"

"Good people." She took a deep breath. "Do you remember Joan Archer?"

"She was there when I visited you in the hospital. A friend of the Camerons, I think."

"She's my sister. Half-sister. She was here when I was dumped in the river as a baby, and she came back to find me when she grew up. Joan's father started the Arc Foundation. We do a lot of good work in the world, and that's why I'm here now."

"I told your folks to leave you in God's hands." He nodded sagely, then ruined the effect by winking. "I knew you'd turn up again."

"Bad penny, huh?"

"Lucky penny. Give me that hug, little girl." Pastor Wally didn't wait for her, but wrapped his arms tight around her. His chuckle sounded ragged. When he released her, he had to wipe his eyes. "Well, let's make ourselves comfortable before we get to work."

He linked his arm through hers and led her to his office. They settled down, he behind his battered desk overflowing with paperwork, and she in the equally battered, scratchy brown easy chair she remembered from his office at church when he was in charge of all the Sunday schools.

He cocked a bushy white eyebrow at her. "Xander says the Arc Foundation does a lot more than fund missions and orphanages and give scholarships to future pastors."

"Reclamation work. They saved my life, literally, and helped me get back on my feet and got me back on track with God." She patted her leg and Gray came from his post in the doorway to settle down next to her feet. "It is okay he's in here?"

"From what I've heard about the bodyguards Arc sends out, do I dare say no?" He grinned. Everyone knew Pastor Wally loved all "critters," as he called them.

"Gray is part of the process. He can read people's souls, seems like. He's my walking lie detector, danger spotter, and a dozen other jobs, whatever I need. If his reaction to people or situations is different from mine, I only get in trouble if I ignore him."

"Do I dare hope he likes us?"

"Oh, yeah."

"So." He thumped his hands flat on his desk, in the only small open space available. "Where do we get started, Miss James from the Arc Foundation?"

"How about a tour? I still see this place as Eloise Elementary."

"Lots of things have changed since you went away."

"Including me."

"That too." He tipped his head to one side and studied her for a moment. "Your folks didn't say what you'd been doing, said it was nobody's business unless you decided to talk about it. If you need a sounding board, I hope you can still come to me."

"If I had come to you when Brock was twisting my head and heart around..." Nikki shrugged. "What's past is past."

"That it is. But you know, you shouldn't go kicking yourself. It wasn't entirely your fault. You had a broken heart, and Brock happened to look like the right kind of medicine, just sent from heaven." Pastor Wally frowned, paused a moment, then shook his head. "Wrong tack to follow.

Now, how about I tell you what we're doing here, and then we take the tour, so you can match rooms up with activities and such?"

"Sounds good."

An hour later, Nikki followed Pastor Wally out of the office to start the tour. He waved to Claire, who was hard at work on the computer, and answering the phone.

"Don't know what we'd do without Claire and her brother," Pastor Wally murmured as they took a right and headed down the hall. "Tommy's in a wheelchair, did they tell you? Nice guy, education and counseling degree, the kids love him, they'll talk to him when you'd swear their lips are sewn shut. But what he's really good at is making people laugh. He's got this knack for just twisting your head around and leaving you breathless, and he just sits there with that innocent little grin on his face. If someone who's built like the Incredible Hulk from the waist up can look innocent."

Nikki chuckled at the mental image and let him ramble as they walked. He pointed out the various rooms on the side that opened onto the front lawn of the school; daycare rooms divided up by ages; one entire classroom devoted to supplies; one room set aside as the infirmary, with little divider walls to create cubicles for the sick children to have some privacy. Nikki peered into every room that was currently empty of people and made notes in the notebook she had brought along when she left her briefcase in the office. Everything at the Mission was clean and neat, but nothing looked like it had been new when the staff got hold of it.

She stopped short at the very last classroom at the end of the hall, startled by the sight of a familiar face. Max Keeler sat in the wide windowsill, reading to children perched on either side of her or sitting at her feet. Nikki searched the room for a few moments, looking for Tony Martin, Max's best friend and writing partner. Both were dark-haired and dark-eyed, with books forever in their hands. The two of them had been inseparable from the moment they met at Butler-Williams University. Nikki remembered Dr. Holwood bringing them home for dinner one night, to have them perform a silly skit they had written for the children's theater workshop at church. She had thought Max and Tony were meant for each other. Then again, Nikki scolded herself, she had been so sure she and Rich Thomas were meant for each other, and he dumped her for someone else his first year at Ohio State.

Why in the world did she think of Rich after all these years? Other than the fact, Pastor Wally had mentioned him, in a backhanded way.

"Where's Tony?" she asked, to get her mind off that subject.

"Tony?" Pastor Wally looked over her shoulder, through the window in the door. "Oh. Right. Usually, where you see one, you see the other. They look enough alike to be brother and sister." He sighed and winked at her. "Might as well be."

"Still not an item?"

"According to Joel, Max doesn't know Tony is a boy, and Tony doesn't know Max is a girl. They're hopeless. But at least they're hopeless together and they spend at least two days a week helping out with the kids. The kids love them, too."

"That's the important thing." She nodded. "But where's Tony? Is he sick today?"

"Nope. California. He has a writer-in-residence stint he's doing. Maybe the long separation will make them both wake up to what's under their noses."

"Pastor Wally, are you playing matchmaker?"

"Not much for an old man like me to find for excitement." He chuckled when she snorted and shook her head.

"You will never be old."

"There's old, and then there's old. This place keeps me young."

# Chapter Five

They turned around to head back down the hall and Nikki focused on the rooms they had ignored before. The first one was empty of furniture and people, except for a man in an khaki-green coverall, mopping the floor. The smell of pine and ammonia filled the air, strongly enough to make her eyes water. He stomped over to the bucket as Nikki and Pastor Wally looked in the door, and slammed the mop into it, splashing water onto the scarred tile.

"We're planning on turning this room into a coffee house. We figure it's next to the side door, keeps traffic away from most of the children. A nice place to relax for everybody. Let people stop in from the community, give them a good look at what we're doing without them feeling nosey. It'll provide some jobs, too, and our seniors will have some place to sit and read if they don't feel like doing crafts or playing cards in the other two rooms."

"Yeah, if we ever get enough money to fix this dump," the janitor said without looking at them. He finished wringing out the mop, then turned as he lifted it to start swiping at the floor again. He froze, his mouth falling open and his eyes widening.

Now Nikki knew why she had thought of Rich Thomas. She had glimpsed the man earlier, pushing that wheeled bucket down the hall. She hadn't really paid attention, but her subconscious had gone to work on that glimpse. She started to take a step back, then clenched her fists and forced her foot back where it had been.

"Hey, I know—" Rich raked a water-shriveled hand through his tangled, matted straw-colored curls and slopped the mop back into the bucket. "Nikki? Is that you?"

"Sort of." Her stomach twisted and her breakfast tried to come up her throat. She cast a reproachful look at Pastor Wally.

"Got to face him some time," the minister said under his breath, and gripped her elbow as if he thought she would flee down the hall.

"You could have warned me," she said just as softly. Gray slid between their legs and stood between Nikki and the approaching janitor.

"Half the time, it's like he isn't here. You forget he's around," Pastor Wally said, even softer.

"Whoa—where'd that beast come from?" Rich grinned and pretended to skid to a stop. He had a tooth missing on the upper left side of his mouth.

Suddenly, he wasn't the all-star athlete, president of the church youth group, future gym teacher, and the boy who broke Nikki's heart. He was just a janitor with bad teeth and dirty hair.

"He's mine. Gray, this is Rich Thomas. You've heard me talk about him."

Gray took another step closer and focused his unblinking gaze on Rich, who took a step backward. Nikki was delighted.

"Yeah—uh—what did you tell him?" Rich tried to laugh. "So, what are you doing back in town? I tried to look you up when I moved back, last year, and nobody was talking."

"Nikki works for the Arc Foundation now," Pastor Wally inserted smoothly. "She's here to evaluate us for that funding we need. I'm taking her on the fifty-cent tour."

"Hey, I could do that. Ain't nobody knows this place better than me. I spend most of my time on my knees, cleaning it."

"Well, I'm going to be around for quite a while," Nikki said, and managed to twist her arm free of Pastor Wally's grip without being noticeable. "I wouldn't want to stop you from doing your job."

"Hey, no—"

A door opened, two rooms down the hall. A little girl's heartbroken wailing echoed to them. Nikki winced, hearing echoes from her nightmares. Rich groaned and closed his eyes for a moment before he headed for the door. Nikki and Pastor Wally stepped back, and even Gray didn't hesitate to get out of his way.

"Should have known," Rich groaned, as he stepped out into the hall and saw the stick-thin, elderly woman leading a wailing toddler by the hand, down the hall, straight for them.

"I'm sorry, Rich, but when Aurora wants her daddy, she has to have her daddy," the woman apologized.

"Daddy?" Nikki whispered.

She glanced several times between Rich and the little girl. She had his straw-colored hair, frizzy curls wet with tears, and tangled. And his lung capacity, judging by the echoes her sobs raised. She wore pink shorts with a green daisy printed T-shirt and little red sneakers ready to burst at the seams.

Gray moved between Aurora and Rich and let out a soft whine. Nikki could imagine what the toddler's voice was doing to his sensitive hearing. The sobbing child saw Gray towering over her and gulped, coming to a dead stop. The sudden silence rang. Her glistening eyes got wide and she stared at the big dog.

"What's he—he'd better not hurt her," Rich stuttered. He took a step forward and Nikki caught him by the elbow, stopping him. She silenced him with a look and stepped up, to drop to her knees next to Gray.

"Hi." She wrapped an arm around Gray's neck, holding him still and putting herself between the child and the Akita. "This is Gray. I'm Nikki. If you hold your hand out, he'll shake hands with you." She held out her hand and said a silent prayer as the little girl studied her with those big, wet, unblinking eyes.

Aurora sniffed and rubbed her eyes and smeared glistening snot across her face. Finally, she hiccupped and nodded, and held out a wet hand. Gray dropped onto his haunches and raised his big paw, twice as big as the child's hand. He delicately pressed it against her palm. Aurora giggled and scampered back toward her teacher.

"Tickles!"

The other three adults let out their collective breaths. Rich stepped around Gray and dropped to one knee in front of the little girl.

"Rory, you know Daddy has to do his job. How am I supposed to get any work done if you keep yelling for me?"

"Want doggy." She scooted around her father, holding out both hands as if she would grab hold of Gray and never let go.

Nikki stood and took a tighter hold of Gray's leash as he retreated behind her legs.

"It's really kind of funny," Nikki said a short time later, as Pastor Wally led her into the gymnasium, where Firesong would do their fundraiser concert at the end of the week. "Gray's stood up to jerks with guns without flinching, and along comes a messy little kid and he nearly puts his tail between his legs." Her companion let out a disgruntled little woof. "Sorry, monster. I was ready to make a run for it, too. My ears were ready to burst."

"Just shows how smart Gray is. That little Aurora is... a piece of work, as we used to say when I was a boy." Pastor Wally hit the panel of switches next to the door, bringing up the big, dim lights that looked like barrels inserted in the ceiling, with wire cages to protect them from stray balls or anything else that might get thrown around the gym.

"What's the story?"

"You mean, where's her mother?"

"More like who's her mother? What's Rich doing back here, when he should be teaching?"

"Well, seems Rich forgot everything we taught him. He and Aurora's mother couldn't wait for the wedding." He paused, glancing sideways at her while Nikki digested that bit of news. "Turns out, neither of them wanted a wedding. Both their families were more than willing to help out, but the mother wanted nothing to do with either Rich or her daughter. She dumped the little girl on him and enrolled in another college. Rich had to come home and get a job. I couldn't exactly turn him or his mother down when he came looking for work, could I?"

"How come I don't feel sorry for him?" Nikki murmured. She leaned back against the wall and wrapped her arms tight around herself. She bit her tongue to keep from remarking that it probably wasn't Rich pestering Pastor Wally for the job, but his mother. Mrs. Thomas was hard to say no to. Sometimes Nikki had wondered if she had stayed with Rich longer than she should have simply because his mother was so much in favor of their being together. "He dumped me for — what was her name? Sue? Well, I made my choices, and he made his. Poor little Aurora has to pay, doesn't she?"

"He's doing the best he can. At least he didn't force Sue to get an abortion."

"Yeah." She took a deep breath, fighting the twisting sensation in her gut. "At least he didn't do that."

~~~~~

That afternoon, Nikki sighed in weary relief as she peeled out of her business clothes in the privacy of her attic bedroom, and slid into her jeans. Her faded jeans helped her relax better than a massage or soaking for an hour in a hot tub. She tossed her black linen slacks into the wicker dirty clothes hamper by the door and tumbled backward into her bed — remembering to duck at the last moment to keep from banging her head on the steeply angled roof. That was one of the few disadvantages of having the attic as her bedroom.

The Holwoods had understood Nikki's need for a special place all her own, that none of the ever-changing population of foster children could ever invade. Putting her private domain at the top of the house, with two flights of stairs and a door that locked between her and her temporary brothers and sisters, had made an invitation to her haven a treat to be earned with good behavior. Nikki had enough room to host slumber parties in middle school and high school. The bookshelves between the narrow attic windows and the gables were still full of the books she had loved as a child, neatly arranged by age and type. Her stuffed animals still sat silent and ready on the shelf running the width of the room on the inside wall, extending over the door. With her big brass bed tucked under the eaves and lots of quilts and pillows, and an old percolator to heat water for tea or hot chocolate, Nikki had spent many happy winter evenings up here, studying and listening to the wind moaning deliciously around her.

"Please, Lord, don't ever let me be so stupid again," she whispered as she lay and looked up the slanting roof to the skylight Dr. Holwood had installed for her twelfth birthday present. She had loved looking at the stars on warm, clear summer nights.

That brought back memories of Brock, both before and after she had run away from home to be with him. How many times had they gone out
~~~~~

to a field somewhere, stretched out and just watched the night sky and talked about their future? They had so many plans, so many dreams. She had truly believed Brock was her prince, the one to make all her dreams come true. She had been terrified and heartsick when she defied her parents to be with him. She had honestly believed she would feel even worse if she let him leave Tabor without her.

Nikki sat up abruptly, again barely remembering in time to duck her head. She had to get up and get moving and stop that train of thought. Brock was gone. She didn't doubt that under his shock and hurt, he was secretly relieved their daughter hadn't survived. Hadn't he told her plainly enough that he wasn't cut out to be a father?

That brought her thoughts back to Rich Thomas and little Aurora. Now, that was someone who should never have been allowed to reproduce. It almost served Rich right to be dumped by his girlfriend. Nikki knew she should feel sorry for him. He was going through exactly what would have happened to her, if Ringo hadn't used her as a human shield. And if Joan and Kathryn and the Arc Foundation hadn't moved heaven and earth to rescue her. Still, it was hard to feel sorry for Rich, when the sting of being dumped by him felt as fresh as if it had happened last week.

It happened in October, her junior year at Tabor High School, his freshman year at Ohio State University. Nikki had decided she would go to Ohio State, too. Dr. Holwood had gone down to the university for a conference and suggested Nikki tag along to visit Rich and look around the campus. He and Doria had approved of Rich Thomas: clean-cut, a member of Tabor Christian Church since infancy, head of the youth group, good student, and planning to be a high school gym teacher if his athletic ability didn't write his ticket for him.

Nikki had checked into her room at the campus hotel, grabbed her map and set off with Dr. Holwood's encouraging chuckle echoing behind her. She found Rich's dormitory without any trouble that Saturday afternoon, and nearly flew up the steps to the third floor. She knocked on his door and heard Rich say to come in.

Rather, she *thought* she heard him say come in. The door was unlocked, after all. She opened the door and found him on top of a girl straight from the swimsuit issue of *Sports Illustrated*. Her bikini underwear was very bright pink, lacy, and very definitely coming off. She was tanned and well-endowed, and didn't even have the decency to scream or try to cover herself when she saw Nikki in the doorway.

Rich swore at Nikki. She had never heard him use such words before. She yanked his class ring off her thumb and flung it at him, hitting him square between the eyes. Then she ran.

He didn't come after her. Nikki managed to cry out all her tears by the time Dr. Holwood came back from the conference to take her to dinner. She didn't tell anyone what happened. Her silence told her parents all they needed to know.

Brock had showed up three months later, while Nikki was helping out at the bake sale and hot chocolate table for Community Snow Days for Butler-Williams University. He came back five times to buy more goodies, and later admitted that he had tossed the cookies and cupcakes into the trunk of his car and forgot about them. His purpose had been to spend as much time with her as possible and impress her. He had impressed her — enough that she forgot all the promises she had made about purity and the dating rules discussed in the church youth group. She gave him her home phone number and her email address. Her world had been a bright, euphoric place for the next seven months, every time he had emailed to say he was coming back to town.

Gray reared back on his hind legs and thumped his forelegs down on Nikki's shoulder, knocking her backward into the mattress again. He washed her face with one long, wet swipe of his tongue. She let out a tiny shriek that turned into a groan, then a chuckle as she sat up again and pushed him away.

"Okay," she sputtered, wiping her face. "I get the message. Stop dwelling on the past and feeling sorry for myself." Nikki bent down, picked up her discarded dress shoe and waved it threateningly at him. The big dog didn't even blink. "I'm home, I'm doing something important, my life is going pretty good, and I'm out of my fancy clothes for the rest of the day. I should be happy, hmm?" She hunched her shoulders inside her green t-shirt and sighed. All she felt was tired.

She closed her eyes, and a moment later, there was a light knocking on her door. Nikki opened her mouth to yell for the person outside to come in, then paused. If it were her parents, they would have called through the door before they knocked. Why would Brandy or Davie or Danny come up here? They had no reason to follow her around the house yet.

"Who's there?" she finally asked after several seconds of silence. Gray sat down at her feet and looked at the door, but he didn't seem worried. Just interested.

"Open the door and find out," a young woman called. A few snorts and muffled laughter came through the wood.

"I don't know if I should." Nikki got up and went to the door slowly, despite the sudden racing of her heart. She should have known something sneaky was being planned, because Doria had asked her three times, yesterday and this morning, if she had any plans for the evening. Then Nikki had caught her hanging up the phone a little too quickly when she walked in half an hour ago.

Besides, the voice sounded familiar, but she couldn't place it with a name and face yet.

"Spoilsport," another voice said.

That one, Nikki recognized. She flung the door open and stopped short, staring at the four young women standing in the attic landing, grinning at her.

"You're being kidnapped," Max Randolph said. "Welcome home."

~~~~~

Victoria's was an ice cream parlor that sold novelty candy and gourmet hamburgers. The waitresses wore red and white-striped tops with puffed sleeves. It had been a fixture in the downtown Tabor area next to Silver's Candy Kitchen since the turn of the century. It also happened to be only twenty minutes of walking from the Holwoods' house. Nikki's four "kidnappers" walked her down Church Street amid a cloud of chatter and laughter. Gray was kept at home, much to Brandy's delight.

After Max Randolph was Dani Paul. Nikki's age, she was as quiet in person as she was hyper on stage, performing with Firesong. She wrote the words to the melodies her brother and cousins composed.

Third was Bekka Sanderson, one of Dr. Holwood's pupils. The two had been friends ever since Nikki could remember. Bekka's grandparents, who raised her, were just racist enough to dislike a black couple raising a white child. The Sandersons constantly teetered between their warring beliefs, either justifying snubbing Nikki and the Holwoods or awkwardly trying to make up for their un-Christian words and actions. Sometimes Nikki had been sure Bekka was her friend out of rebellion, and other times in recompense for her grandparents' inconsistency.

The fourth member of the group was Jeannette Marshall, Pastor Glenn's secretary. Nikki liked Jeannette but was more relieved than she liked to admit that the woman hadn't brought her four-year-old son, BJ, along for the outing. She hadn't been eager to get near the smallest children at the daycare center, and knew the presence of children near Mercy Grace's age would be the hardest part of her assignment.

"Pastor Glenn and Rita have him," Bekka said, when Nikki asked where BJ was, while Jeannette and Max were retrieving their order from the pickup counter. "They love playing grandparents. It's too bad they never had kids of their own."

"The whole church is their family," Dani said with a shrug. "Still, everybody should have a grandpa and grandma. BJ's a lucky kid."

"Heads down." Bekka hunched her shoulders, rested her elbows on the table and held her hands up on either side of her face. "The Ice Man cometh."

"You are so bad," Dani said, grinning, and mimicked her.

"What?" Nikki glanced around. Then she saw Arthur Montgomery
~~~~~

stalk through the talking, laughing patrons as if he walked through an empty room. He wore his usual perpetual scowl of disapproval.

She shivered, remembering the glares, the razor-edged comments directed at her and her foster parents by Mr. Montgomery. He had set himself up as judge of all that was right and good.

He had come to the hospital while Nikki was recovering from the accident and losing Mercy Grace. Not to console her as other members of the deacon board and pastoral staff had done, but to tell her she had gotten what she deserved for "flouting God's laws."

"Don't worry," Bekka said, resting a hand on Nikki's, when she turned her back to the man and hunched her shoulders without even intending it. "You won't run into him at church."

"Why?"

"He left the church. Wish he'd leave town," Dani added, glancing briefly over her shoulder at the man, who slapped some dollar bills down on the counter, snatched up a white take-out bag and stalked out without looking anyone in the eye

"When did that happen?"

# Chapter Six

"Near as we can figure out, he was trying to force Lisa and Todd to come live with him so he could control his grandchild's future, while also trying to prove Lisa was fooling around with someone," Max drawled as she and Jeannette returned to the table.

"Lisa?"

"His daughter-in-law. She's an artist—another point against her," Bekka said.

"I know who Lisa is. Katie told me she was doing the cover art for Firesong's new CD. Why would anyone think Lisa would fool around?" Nikki could only shake her head.

"Saint Arthur believes that any woman who went to college and has her own income and wears pants to church is the Whore of Babylon. I heard some of the gossip, when he was shouting at Pastor Glenn—"

"He yelled at Pastor Glenn?" Maybe the world was about to end?

"That's putting it mildly, unfortunately," Jeannette said, as she and Max settled down at the table again. "Don't ask, because I'm not repeating what I saw and heard." She mimed turning a lock at her lips.

"Tyler, the new director of Royal Community Theatre, and Lisa only met face-to-face the day the Ice Man made a scene at the Bluebird Café, but he insisted Tyler had to be her lover because he's a filthy, immoral actor. Uh, hello? Teacher at a Christian college for forever? He wanted Tyler thrown out of the church," Bekka said. "Pastor Glenn refused, even when he threatened to leave the church if he didn't get his way. So, he had to quit," she added, keeping her voice low so it could barely be heard above the talking and laughing and music in the restaurant.

"Guys, much as I love tearing down self-righteous jerks..." Max shook her head, her mouth compressed into a flat line but her eyes sparkling with repressed laughter.

"She's just too mature and nice for her own good." Dani sighed, looking up at the ceiling. Nikki snorted, muffling laughter.

"No, I'm not. I'm putting him in one of my new books as the villain, and the less talk there is, the less chance anybody will point that little fact out to him."

"If Tony were in town, he'd stop you," Jeannette said.

"If Tony were in town, he'd be doing it first," Max shot back.

"Anyway..." Bekka drawled, "you might meet Lisa at the Firesong concert on Friday. Although, she hasn't been feeling too well. Who would, with the Ice Man for a father-in-law?" She stuck her tongue out at Jeannette, who shook her head at her words, and fought not to smile.

"We really should be nicer. If we keep talking this way, we're stooping to his level," Jeannette said as she helped Max pass their orders around the table. "We kidnapped you for a reason, Nikki. We want to hear about the Arc Foundation and what it's going to do for the Mission."

"That's another link between us," Max added. "We volunteer at the Mission from time to time. We've kind of got a vested interest in finding out what you're going to do for the place. So… spill, kid."

Nikki was glad to. She gave them what the daughters of Quarry Hall referred to as the "second level public relations speech." It got deeper and more personal than the public face the Arc Foundation showed to the world at large.

Harrison Carter used his vast financial resources to fund many philanthropic activities, and his web of international connections to thoroughly investigate every organization that applied for help. Nikki had gone through a year of training at Quarry Hall, filling up the holes in her education, learning self-defense, investigative skills, and training with her companion/bodyguard to become an agent of the Arc Foundation and do that investigating.

"We're the eyes and ears and hands of the Arc Foundation," Nikki said, finishing her description of the grounds and facilities of Quarry Hall. "We go in first-hand and investigate everything and everyone that wants help from us." She paused to take a long pull at her peanut butter shake. "I haven't been involved very long, but I helped with a few intense situations when I was in training, and my first courier run got me involved in some small-town politics that turned pretty hairy." She grinned, thinking of the uncomfortable hours she had spent locked in a metal shed in the middle of nowhere, with the town's sheriff and Brooklyn in the next sheds. All three had prayed the roof off the place to escape before they died from the oven-like conditions in the sheds.

"I hope things are easier here with the Mission," Jeannette said.

"It's a worthy cause to get involved in," Bekka added. "What exactly are you going to do? Check the bank records, talk to the people in town, that sort of stuff?"

"Get involved in the Mission at every level." Nikki grinned. "Thank goodness, today was my only dress-up day. Tomorrow, I get to wear jeans and start poking into all the closets, looking at ledgers, talking with the kids. Then I'll do hands-on stuff and help with chores, cleaning, inventory, that sort of thing. It's standard practice to spend at least a month investigating places like the Mission."

"Why?" Dani wanted to know. "You don't think Pastor Wally's hiding something shifty, do you?"

"Never!" She flinched as her voice rose above the clamor of the half-full restaurant. "It's just... standard practice. Ninety-nine percent of the people working at places like this are exactly what they appear. Unfortunately, that one percent is what we have to watch out for. The way Uncle Harrison sees it, the foundation is doing God's work, with God's money. We have a responsibility to make sure God's money doesn't get used to benefit His enemies, even if it's done by accident or out of ignorance."

"Like, somebody using the place as a cover job?" Max asked. She grinned. "Something I should have the folks at the paper watching out for?"

"Oh, please." Nikki chuckled, glad her friend had turned it into a joke. "You keep the press out of this, Max. The less publicity Arc gets, the better. We make enough enemies as it—" The words died in her mouth and faded from her brain as she looked up and saw Brock standing by the railing that divided the register and candy counter from the dining area. He glanced over, saw her, and smiled.

That was the smile Nikki had always loved, the warm, delighted look that was eighty percent in the eyes. The smile that made her think she was everything good and beautiful in his life. It always made her heart lurch, so she couldn't breathe for a moment. That smile had convinced her it was right to defy her parents' rules and their expectations of her, and to turn her back on the things she had grown up believing, for his sake.

"Nikki?" Dani murmured, and turned to see where she was staring. "Who's that?"

"Brock."

"That's him?" Max leaned forward to get a better view. Brock frowned and colored a little when the entire table stared back at him. He turned away, much to Nikki's relief.

"Who's Brock?" Jeannette wanted to know.

"The reason I ran away from home four years ago."

"Well, you have to admit he's cute." Dani patted her hand. "Use the hormone overload excuse."

Nikki didn't know if she wanted to laugh or cry, but she was grateful for Dani's teasing. She settled for rolling her eyes and reaching to pick up the rest of her sandwich.

"Later," Bekka said. "He's coming over here."

That wasn't necessary. Nikki could see Brock following the hostess across the red and white tiled floor. He nodded to her, his smile a crooked little twitch of discomfort, and followed the woman to the little tables for two tucked up against the far wall. If he was far enough away not to hear their conversation, Nikki had no idea. She looked down at the potato skins on her plate, no longer hungry. What was Brock doing still in town?

"So, Dani, since you and Nikki are basically doing the same thing, working on funding for the Mission, why don't you fill us in on the plans for the concert?" Max said. "Nikki, they did tell you Firesong is getting regular gigs, and they even have a manager now?"

"I heard from Katie. I remember you guys leading singing in youth group and how excited you got when you had enough money for Andy's electric keyboard." Nikki tried to turn off her awareness of Brock. She gave Max a grateful smile and settled in to talk about anything and everything else.

Dani filled them in on the growing reputation of Firesong, which was made up of her Gibson cousins, her, and her brother, Andy. The people in Tabor Heights and surrounding cities now knew they weren't just another wannabe band. Firesong had concerts booked nearly every weekend now through the summer and were even scheduled to do a few music festivals.

"Of course, Mr. Danziger has other ideas for what success means." Dani rolled her eyes and groaned comically.

"Their new manager," Max supplied, before Nikki could ask. "He's a real go-getter. Dad would call him a shark. He knows people, so it's good for the band, but they have to be careful that he doesn't take over."

"He's been making noise about our upcoming CD. If things don't go his way..." She shook her head and summoned up a grin. "Listen to me — do I sound like some kind of whiny rock star, or what?" The others laughed with her.

"What's more important? Serving God or getting famous?" Nikki asked, almost as the question formed in her brain.

"According to Mr. Danziger, we have to get famous, first, then people will listen to what we have to say. Andy and the others think if we make God wait until we've made it, we'll keep Him waiting forever, because nobody really makes it. You know?"

"Speaking of Andy, what are your gorgeous brother and cousins doing?"

"Okay, let's see..." Max sat back and slouched a little in her chair and made a show of searching her memory. "Tom is the oldest. Remember Stephanie Avallone?"

"Vaguely. Her folks run the camp on Kelly's Island, right?"

"You'd like her. Perfect pastor's wife — though why she wants to marry a part-time musician who works on a farm, I'll never know."

"Tom Gibson is engaged? I heard about Andy getting engaged to Katie, but not about Tom."

"Married," Dani said with a grin.

"Hey, I just remembered. Guess who stopped by Quarry Hall last week, preparing for an Allen Michaels crusade this summer at the fairgrounds?" Nikki felt her spirits perking up. She muffled a chuckle when her friends gave her blank looks. "Kurt Green." She did laugh when Dani gave her a blank look. "Katie's cousin? You were best friends with Katie when you were kids, right?"

"Still best friends. Especially since she's marrying my wretched brother. Kurt's coming to town?" She shrugged. "Well, I guess he's grown up, since he's working for Allen Michaels."

Max and Bekka offered memories of church activities where they had run into Kurt, growing up. That left Nikki some time to sit and think and study Dani. And remember how Dani and Kurt sniped at each other when they were children and he was living with his Green relatives.

"Enemy aircraft at five o'clock," Bekka muttered, and nudged Nikki under the table.

She looked up—straight at Brock as he approached the table, his check in hand, on his way to the register to pay. She said a quick prayer that he would keep going, and found it denied as he went off course to step down to her end of the table for six.

"Hi, Nikki." Brock hunched his shoulders a little and glanced at the other four. His smile wavered just a little bit.

"Hi." She clasped her hands in her lap and wondered what she was supposed to do now. Introduce him to her friends? Ask him to join them? Show some interest in his life? "What are you still doing in town?" slipped from her lips before she could stop herself.

"Actually..." He let out a breathy chuckle, which sounded weak enough to draw a throb of pity from her, just for a moment. "I'm looking for a job. My parole officer is working with the missions group sponsoring me and they're letting me settle here, so..."

"In Tabor?" Nikki's sandwich turned to lead in her stomach.

"Uh huh." His smile lost a few degrees of steadiness. He glanced at the other four. "Know anybody who needs a good accountant? Business analyst? Numbers cruncher?" He only waited a few seconds, not long enough for anyone to answer. "Well, it was worth a try. Uh, I'll probably see you around, Nikki. Nice meeting all of you." Nodding, he turned and hurried over to the register.

"He didn't meet any of us," Bekka pointed out under her breath.

To Nikki's relief, nobody asked her what had just happened, but she could almost hear the questions rolling around in their heads. Then their waitress came to start clearing away plates and asked if anybody was interested in dessert. She couldn't help wondering if everybody said no because of that little scene with Brock, and not because they weren't hungry.

They went for a walk through downtown Tabor when they left Victoria's, instead of going back to the Holwoods' house. Nikki kept quiet, glad to let someone else do the leading for a while. It felt odd to go any length of time without Gray at her side. She felt almost naked. She kept turning to look for him, especially when they walked across the bridge over the Metroparks road. They paused to look down at the long stretch of trees and asphalt road, and the faint glimmer of moonlight and starlight on the water of the river and lakes in the distance. Gray would like to go for a long romp through the Metroparks.

"This was fun," Bekka said, as they neared her apartment building, and she prepared to leave their group. "Let's plan on getting together a couple more times while you're still in town, Nikki. You said a month, right?"

"At least."

"Great. Maybe I'll see you when I'm working at the Mission."

"I'll definitely see you there when I'm not at Tri-C," Dani added. "I'm technically Jill-of-all-Trades, so if you need a pair of hands, give a yell."

It was another twenty minutes before Bekka actually went upstairs and the other four walked on. They stood in the light from the doorway, throwing out ideas for getting together again, comparing schedules, talking about their work. Nikki, Dani and Max continued up Span to Church, and Jeannette split off from them to go pick up BJ at Pastor Glenn and Rita's house. Nikki liked the feeling she had of being part of the group, of having a place and a history with the others. She found herself wishing, just for a few minutes, that she could stay in Tabor. It was home, after all. Her various jobs for the Arc Foundation had kept her moving; face one need or crisis, take care of it, clean up the mess, move on. Wouldn't it be nice if she could settle somewhere as a stationery agent for Arc?

That thought stayed with her after she got home, and Max and Dani got in Max's car to drive to Homespun, where Dani had parked. She was thoughtful, wistful, as she unlocked the front door to go inside.

*Wednesday, April 2*

The next morning, Nikki worked at the front desk, helping to sign in the children brought in for the daycare center. There was a simple, efficient security system where the children had numbered tags pinned to the back of their shirts. The parents dropping them off had a matching number and they had to hand in the tag before they could take their child out of the daycare. As Claire explained to Nikki during a lull, even in Tabor there were shattered marriages that got nasty when it came to the children. The system had been instituted after one near-disastrous incident when a father who had been denied custody came directly from the court building and tried to take his son from the daycare. Fortunately, the teacher in that room was a friend of the mother's and knew the battle over custody was going on. Another worker might have just assumed that since he was the boy's father, he had the right to take him. The teacher had delayed the father while Pastor Wally called the police. That sort of situation would never have a chance to happen again.

Nikki was impressed, and glad to be impressed by the caution and responsibility exhibited by the Mission. These were her friends, her church, her hometown being tested. She wanted them to be worthy of the Arc Foundation's help.

Once the incoming traffic slowed down, the next stop was the kitchen. The children who came before 7a.m. got breakfast. The daycare and the senior center both provided lunch and sometimes dinner, depending on how late participants stayed at either end of the spectrum. Plus, the Mission packed up box meals to take to housebound members of Tabor Christian, whether infirm or handicapped, new mothers home from the hospital, or people sent home to die in familiar surroundings. Nikki tried not to feel self-conscious as she poked her head into ovens and refrigerators and looked behind the curtains under the sinks to inspect the cleanliness. What did she really know about such things? The Carters and Joan had answered her protests of inadequacy with one simple instruction: pray for clear vision and insight and listen to her gut instinct. If something felt wrong, Nikki was to investigate further and get advice from experts. If she felt it necessary to call in the Health Department, she should feel no shame. If the place felt right to her, she shouldn't worry that she had missed something. The representatives of the Arc Foundation were told to always depend on the leading of the Holy Spirit—even in something so mundane as a kitchen's hygiene standards.

Nikki spent the rest of the morning in the kitchen, helping and listening to the friendly, easy chatter of the workers. There was one main cook, Joe Horse, who had been the cook when the Mission was still an elementary school. He had been a friendly, graying, wizened old black man when Nikki was ten and eleven years old. The only change now was that his close-cropped hair and beard were pure white. He regaled her with stories from school, shared memories, and directed his ever-changing staff of volunteer workers through their chores.

The only time Joe lost his contented smile and stopped humming his endless string of tunes was when Rich came in to mop up a spill from a broken bag of sugar. Nikki supposed it was because he took nearly twenty minutes to get from his previous job to the kitchen. He slouched into the room, pushing his little bucket on wheels, the waves created by his too-rough movements slopping pine-scented, steaming water on the dull green tile floor.

"Yeah, where is it?" he muttered, and didn't even look at Joe for directions. He also didn't notice Nikki standing at one of the worktables, cutting up a long tray of freshly baked cookie into bars.

Nikki looked at Rich, in the same coveralls as yesterday, with his hair tucked up under a Yankees cap, and wondered if he had washed Aurora's hair. His little girl needed new shoes; anybody could see that. Was he that hard up for money? Or was his daughter just going through a growth spurt that he couldn't keep up with?

Joe tugged aside the garbage can that had been put over the sugar to keep people from walking through it and went back to chopping celery for the big pot of chicken soup for lunch. He didn't watch Rich slowly sweep up and then mop up the spilled sugar. His silence and the tight hunching of his shoulders made Nikki wonder what bothered the usually garrulous man.

"Him, he's no good," Joe volunteered, after Rich finished his work and the rattling of the bucket's wheels faded down the hall. Nikki wondered if he would have said anything if there had been any other workers in the kitchen at that moment. "All he cares about is getting in a girl's pants—and look what it got him. Poor little Aurora. That sweetheart deserves a better daddy."

"It looks like he's trying to take care of her."

"Yeah, only because his mamma won't take no laziness from him." Joe scowled into the steam of the ten-gallon stockpot as he stirred the dry noodles into the mixture. "That boy, he could have made good, but he didn't think. What's wrong with kids today, they think they can just go sleeping around and making babies without looking ahead of themselves?"

"We're stupid." Nikki almost laughed when the little black man turned sharply and stared at her, his bushy white eyebrows raised. "I ran away from home to be with my boyfriend. I got pregnant without getting married first."

"Yeah, but you, you're doing good work now. Where's your baby?"

# Chapter Seven

"In heaven. I wanted to keep her, but..." Nikki tried to smile despite the ache of tears pressing at her eyes. "Well, I guess God had other plans."

"Yeah, but you'd have her right with you if you could, wouldn't you?" He relaxed back into something close to his previous cheerful self when Nikki nodded. "I bet you'd marry the daddy and be a good mamma, if you could."

"If I could," she said, simply to short-circuit another series of questions.

Her words and his echoed in her heart for the rest of the day, though.

At lunchtime, Nikki took Gray outside for a long run around the block. She felt sorry for him, exiled to sit in the open doorway where the kitchen opened onto the parking lot, while he watched her work. Health regulations forbade dogs in the kitchen.

"My Gway doggie!" Aurora shrieked and bolted from the group of toddlers playing on the swings and teeter-totters, as Nikki and Gray came around the playground side of the building. She laughed and flung herself at the big dog. With a canine sigh and a reproachful glance, Gray sat down and let the little girl embrace him with grape sucker-sticky hands. At least she wasn't crying and suffering a runny nose today.

"She sure does love your pooch," Rich said, stepping over from a doorway to join Nikki. He grinned at Aurora, who was trying to climb up on Gray's back. The toddler was unable to get a grip in his thick, glossy fur. "Maybe I should get one for her. Keep her busy at home, huh? They make good watch dogs?"

"The best." Nikki smiled at him. She was glad he thought about things like safeguarding his daughter and making her happy. It proved Joe's words wrong; Rich was making good, despite his mistakes.

He had to be a good father. He was taking time from his many duties to check up on Aurora when her class went outside to play, wasn't he? The Mission was a big building and Rich was the only full-time janitor. From comments she heard earlier, there was always something to be cleaned up, something that needed fixing, some old equipment that needed to be coaxed into continuing to work, to avoid the expense of replacing it.

If the Arc Foundation decided to underwrite the Mission, Nikki knew thousands of dollars worth of equipment would be replaced immediately. She had already noted half a dozen places where the tile in the floor had been broken and patched with colors and patterns that didn't match, as a stop-gap measure. Windows were boarded up when they were broken, instead of being replaced. Some doors were chained shut because the locks were so old and stubborn they couldn't be relied on to stay locked. The kitchen needed to be enlarged, according to Joe. It needed a walk-in freezer and refrigerator, instead of making do with the half dozen units donated by people from church who had bought themselves new ones. The restaurant-quality dishwasher was the only good-quality piece of equipment, and had been donated four years ago, new, by the family that ran Rick's Bakery.

Maybe Rich could have a staff of janitors under him, giving him more time to spend on his daughter. He probably worked from sunrise to sunset, which explained Aurora's tangled hair and the way she clung to him and demanded all his attention when she did see him. Poor little girl, denied her father's company because he was working so hard to take care of her. With better pay and more staff, Rich could work more reasonable hours.

"What are you smiling about?" Rich asked, yanking Nikki back from her thought chain of ideas and dreams.

"I'm just glad to be home and doing something important."

"Yeah?" He grinned and leaned a little closer. "I'm kind of glad you're home, too. Things just weren't the same without you, Nikki."

A thrill tightened through her chest. When was the last time Rich had talked to her with that soothing, low tone of voice?

Then she remembered—the day he said good-bye and headed off to Ohio State University. He had told her he would miss her and made her promise not to date anybody while he was away. Unbidden, the stark, too-sharp image of him on top of that nearly naked co-ed in his dorm room filled her mind. He hadn't made any promise to stay faithful to her, but that never occurred to her until now, years later.

"Come on, Gray. No more lazing around. We gotta get our exercise in and get back to work." She stepped briskly over to Gray's side and reached to lift Aurora off the patient, suffering dog.

The little girl fell to the grass before Nikki could touch her, but fortunately, she burst out laughing instead of crying. Gray jumped to his feet and scurried around behind Nikki before the toddler could get up and reach for him again.

"Maybe I could borrow him some night when Mom is busy, huh?" Rich stepped over, picked up Aurora, and slung her up to sit on his neck astride his shoulders. The little girl giggled and held on tight to his greasy, grimy collar.

"Gray doesn't do diapers or bedtime stories." Where, she wondered, was this repartee coming from, and just why did her heart insist on skipping a beat whenever Rich grinned at her in that particular way? He was slime. He had cheated on her and yelled at her for walking in on him when he was indulging in pre-marital sex. He had gotten a girl pregnant without marrying her.

*Look who's talking,* that quiet voice in her heart shot back. *You grew up believing that you would only sleep with the man you would marry.*

*But Brock and I were planning on spending the rest of our lives together. We just never bothered getting married,* Nikki argued back.

Sometimes she couldn't decide if she was going crazy, or she had a guardian angel whispering into her head. One thing she did know after all this time: Nikki would only get into trouble if she ignored the promptings of her revived conscience.

"Do you ever see Aurora's mother?" she asked, and nearly laughed when Rich jerked, his mouth dropped open for a few seconds, and he flushed dark red. "Is there any chance of you two getting back together? Little girls need their mothers."

"Haven't seen her for more than a year now, since she dumped Rory on me and took off, and I don't care if I ever see the selfish — she's out of our lives, okay?" He jiggled Aurora, prompting more giggles from her.

"This isn't the way we were raised, Rich. You were the leader of the youth group, for heaven's sake! You knew better. What does the Bible say about being joined, one flesh, with the person you have sex with?"

Nikki flinched and felt her stomach drop. What did that say about her and Brock? Did that mean they were joined, married for all intents and purposes, even if they hadn't signed a contract?

"Yeah, well, things are different when you get out into the real world. You know that. You've been out there."

"I've been out there, and I did a lot of stupid things, and the stupidest was turning my back on how I was raised. Gray, come on, we have to get back to work." Nikki snapped her fingers and turned to leave.

Gray growled, a second before Rich grabbed hold of her arm just above the elbow. Tight.

"Nikki—"

"Gray doesn't like people touching me without permission. If you don't let go—" She waited, glaring at the grimy hand gripping her arm, until Rich released her.

"I know we've got a lot of garbage between us that should get cleared up. Will you at least talk to me?" He flashed her that charming smile that had calmed the minor political and personality skirmishes in their youth group when they were in high school. Rich had been the leader, the smart one, with so much potential he had been held up as an example for the younger children in their church.

Nikki wondered, briefly, how many members of their youth group had been disillusioned, maybe even turned their backs on church and God, when they heard how the All-American clean-cut boy had fallen away from the very principles he preached to them.

"Not now," she said. "I have work to do. I think getting the Mission hooked up with the Arc Foundation funding is a little more important than our personal grievances." She stepped back, just in case he tried to grab hold of her again.

"You're absolutely right. How about going out for dinner? Or coffee? The Perk-and-Perch is a great little place, over on Main. Ever been there?" He grinned a little wider when Nikki shook her head. "You'd like it. Tonight?"

"I don't know. Let me think about it." She turned and forced herself to walk, when she wanted to run. Nikki felt Rich's gaze on her until she turned the corner. The pressure of his gaze alternately warmed her and chilled her.

What was she doing, letting that jerk get close again? She had sworn off him — she had sworn off all charmers for the rest of her life. Hadn't she?

Still, it was nice to know Rich was sorry and he admitted he was wrong about what he had done.

What if she hadn't caught him with that girl in his dorm room, and had gone to Ohio State University like she had planned? Would Rich have dated her exclusively? Would he have talked her into pre-marital sex? Would she have married Rich when they graduated? Would she have a little girl like Aurora right now? Would she have been able to ignore Brock, if Rich hadn't broken all the rules and her heart?

"Nikki?" Brock's voice startled her so she stumbled, just as she rounded the corner and approached the side entrance into the Mission.

At this side of the building, the door was only steps away from the sidewalk and the street. Brock stood on the opposite side of the street, smiling at her. He looked tired and hot, and his sport jacket was slung over his shoulder.

Gray settled down at Nikki's feet and just watched. No protective stance, no growling, no staring at Brock. Nikki felt betrayed, and the next moment mentally slapped herself for that.

"How's it going?" He glanced both directions, then headed across the street. The traffic was nearly non-existent in this part of Tabor, now that the Mission was no longer a school. The largest building directly across the street was a dormitory, and then a number of athletic buildings and administration offices for the university.

"Fine. What are you doing?"

"Looking for work. This is a nice little town." He looked around and took a deep breath, smiling a little more, as if he had never smelled such good air before. "This is a great place to settle down. That's what I should have done before, instead of dragging you into my mess."

"You didn't exactly kidnap me. I went willingly enough," she admitted. Why did Brock have to look at her like he used to, all warm and sweet and protective? He didn't have the right.

"Because I wasn't honest with you. I'll never forgive myself for what I did to you. I made you choose between me and your folks and God. I was a pretty selfish jerk back then."

"I thought you were Prince Charming."

Where, she wondered, were all these stupid admissions coming from? Why was she getting soft with both men who had hurt her so badly? What was wrong with her?

"Yeah, well, Prince Charming could fix everything and put it back the way it was. Ah, look, would you mind if I stopped by later?"

"I have work to do, Brock. That's why I'm back in town."

"Not here." He gestured at the former school building. "I mean, if I came by the house. Maybe we could sit and just... talk. Clear things up between us." He let out a snort of laughter. "Maybe you should take a good swing at me, to make up for my hitting you."

"That's stupid." For some reason, she had to grin at the suggestion.

"Yeah, I've been that a lot lately. Look, I have a lead to follow up. Can I call you?" His eyes lit up when Nikki nodded without even considering the consequences. "Good. Then I'll talk to you later. See you, Gray. Take care of her, hear me?"

The big dog let out a snort that could have been agreement or disgust. Nikki couldn't tell. She stayed where she was, in front of the door, and dropped to one knee to stroke Gray's back as she waited for Brock to vanish down the sidewalk. He headed into the business district of Tabor. That bothered her, but where else was he supposed to go to find a job?

Why had he chosen to stay in Tabor? She knew she definitely didn't want to explore that question very far. She might not like the answers she got.

~~~~~

Brock understood why Mandy Gordon told him he'd better hurry if he wanted to apply for work at the *Tabor Picayune*. He saw the rental trucks parked in front of the newspaper office and in the parking lot on the side of the building, as he crossed the bridge over the Rocky River. The newspaper was moving. His landlady had mentioned that Andrew Coffelt, the publisher had been lamenting the problems his newspaper had suffered with their recently departed accountant. The man had put the books into a tangle, so that the part-time accountants who handled individual functions such as accounts payable, accounts receivable, and payroll, couldn't be sure if they were working with actual figures.

He reached the front door in time to see two men stagger around the
~~~~~

customer service counter at the front of the office with an old wooden desk between them. Brock pulled the door open and stood back. They thanked him with grins and nods and slung the desk into the nearest rental truck. He followed them back into the office. Two women were working at the front counter, both on the phone. Both were dark-haired. The older wore a jacket and skirt outfit in stripes of hot pink and lime that made Brock's eyes ache. The younger one wore jeans and a Butler-Williams sweatshirt with the sleeves rolled up to her elbows. She looked slightly familiar, but he couldn't place her right away. The older one's expression reminded him of his least favorite elementary school teacher. Miss Carr had constantly given the impression that everyone was wasting her time and no one would ever get the right answer, unless they cheated. This woman's tone of voice got sharper and her expression more wrinkled and sour as she nodded and kept trying to interrupt whatever the person on the other end of the phone was saying.

Brock turned and looked at the younger woman, to see she had hung up the phone. She glanced sideways at the older woman, rolled her eyes, and turned to him, putting on that polite face of someone who dealt often with the public.

"Can I help you?"

"Yeah, thanks." He pulled out his battered leather folio to get a copy of his resume. "I'm looking for a job." He stepped up to the counter.

"So you're following through," she murmured. One corner of her mouth quirked up when he just shook his head. He guessed he looked as confused as he felt. "I was with Nikki the other night in Victoria's."

"Oh. Right. One of her friends from before. I thought you looked familiar." For two seconds, he considered just giving up and walking out.

"So you're for real about getting work and staying in town. That's a point in your favor. What job are you looking for?"

"Uh... accounting?" His face heated when he realized just how stupid that sounded. "My landlady, Mrs. Gordon, said there might be an opening."

"Well, if Mandy sent you, that's another point in your favor."

She held up a finger, gesturing for him to wait, and stepped over to one of four desks pushed up against the sidewall of the half-emptied front room. From the piles and clutter covering the desks, they were being used as a dumping ground while the office was being emptied out. Brock waited, watching the woman who was still on the phone, breathing heavily through her nose and holding the phone out from her ear about four inches. He could just make out an angry male voice.

"Here you go." Nikki's friend returned to the counter and slid several sheets of paper stapled together across the surface to him. Her hand stayed on it, and Brock got a chill up his spine as he met her gaze. He imagined if Nikki had an older brother, he would give him the same look this still-nameless friend of hers gave him now. Warning sat at the top of the list of all the meanings in that look. "Just don't break her heart again, okay?"

"Swear." He held his hand up, palm out, and waited until she removed her hand from the papers.

"There's an empty desk around the corner, if you want to fill it out now and leave it." She pushed open the gate that separated the reception area from the rest of the office and gestured at a freestanding divider beyond the catchall desks.

"Thanks. Umm, I didn't get your—"

"Maxine, what are you doing, wasting this nice man's time?" The other woman had finally gotten off the phone. Brock was pretty sure the caller had hung up on her, though he wouldn't put it past her to be worked up enough to slam the phone down on her end.

"She's helping me, thanks," Brock said, and stepped through the gate. He braced himself to be grabbed by the arm and yanked back. He grinned at Max, turning his head where the other woman couldn't see. He remembered now who she was. Nikki had talked about her friends, and he remembered Max Randolph's name quite clearly.

"Helping you with what?" She followed him over to the desk. "I'm responsible for the front desk. Despite this chaos we're going through. She's only here to help me. And I must add, you're doing an awful job, Maxine, leaving me out of the loop."

"When was she supposed to interrupt that very important phone call to clear things with you?"

From the corner of his eye, Brock saw Max settle down at another desk on the far side of the office area behind the counter. She flinched and glanced over her shoulder at him and grinned, crossing her eyes. He hoped he had made a friend by standing up to this officious, sour-faced woman.

"You're applying for work?" She reached for the paper, her eyes lighting up with interest, and Brock slid it out of her reach.

"Sorry, but I'm on kind of a time crunch. Could I fill it out? I'm sure you'll have plenty of time to look it over after I've left."

For about five seconds, she just stood there, eyes wide—Brock swore they spun around a few times—as she tried to process his words, probably trying to decide if he was flattering her or cutting her down. With a snort and a smirk, she stuck her nose up in the air and turned on her heel to head back to the front counter. He guessed she had decided to be flattered. Definitely not his intention.

The moving crew made four more trips past him, carting filing cabinets minus their drawers, while he filled out the basic information on the job application form.

"What a beautiful day!" an older man chortled, coming in the front door. "How is everyone on this lovely, warm afternoon? Everybody eager and ready to settle into the new building?"

Brock turned to see a white-haired man in a light gray, three-piece suit stroll around the counter and flip the gate open. He carried a crisp Stetson that matched his suit, in one hand, and a large, string-handled carryout bag in the other. From the way it swung at his side, it was heavy.

"Hello there. And who might you be?" The older man rocked back on his heels when he swung around the corner past the divider and saw Brock, just turning over the page of the application.

"He's applying for an accounting job," the woman called, sounding brisk and a little too happy to share such mundane news.

"Brock Pierson," Brock said at the same time.

"Really? Max?" He turned to the desk where Max had been working on what looked like text on a large computer screen.

"Mandy Gordon sent him over, Mr. C," Max said, barely glancing over her shoulder.

"Hmph. Mandy Gordon doesn't know what she's talking about," the older woman said, and turned back to whatever papers she had spread out on the counter.

"Mustn't let personal grievances cloud your judgment, Myrna," Mr. C said. He held out his hand to Brock. "Andrew Coffelt, publisher. I must say, your timing is lovely. How about we take care of your interview right now?"

"Ah—sure—that'd be great." Brock hurried to shake Mr. Coffelt's hand and gather up his folio, jacket and paperwork, when the man gestured for him to follow him down the hall to the back of the long, narrow office building.

# Chapter Eight

"Just ignore Myrna," Mr. Coffelt added, when they had passed out of the front of the office area, down a hallway and past several empty offices. They came out into a large room full of people dismantling computers and emptying out desks into crates. "She considers herself an authority on Tabor Heights history, and one of the first families in the area. She's been peeved with Mandy for years, since Mandy renovated several houses that Myrna claims belonged to her family and are historical treasures." He chuckled as he led Brock into the last room in the long row of rooms, which turned out to be the combination lunchroom and kitchen of the newspaper office.

"Myrna wanted the houses restored to their so-called original splendor and made available for historical tours. However, she wasn't willing to put up a single dollar or talk her cronies in the historical society into buying the buildings from Mandy. She seemed to think Mandy and her husband were striking at her personally when they refused to donate the houses to the historical society. Then she got even more upset when a search of the records showed Myrna's great-grandparents lived in one of the houses, but never owned any of them." He shrugged and looked at the take-out bag in his hand as if he hadn't seen it before. "Sometimes I think my Angel is right, and I'd forget my head if it wasn't attached. Excuse me." He chuckled, set the bag down on the table, and stepped back into the other room, full of reporters and desks and chaos. "Lunch is here!"

When he returned, he gestured for Brock to follow him to another office off the main newsroom. In moments, he was seated at the denuded desk, with Brock settled in a chair facing him. The people passing by the door only glanced in on their way to get their lunch.

"I think I should lay everything out on the table before we get into an interview, Mr. Coffelt." Brock took a deep breath and hoped his face didn't give away the racing of his heart.

He liked this place, just from the brief encounters with the people here. Just like he liked the whole town of Tabor Heights. He imagined himself working here, making friends, going to ball games with the sports reporter, even deftly sniping at Myrna, who wouldn't even realize she was being put in her place. He wanted a place to belong. Belonging demanded honesty. Even if he ran the risk of losing that possibility of belonging.

"Do you know Nikki James?"

"The Holwoods' girl. I do indeed. Nice girl. I saw her around town the other day, I do believe. What about her?" Mr. Coffelt sat back in his chair, resting his elbows on the armrest.

"Do you know her story? How she ran away a few years back?" Brock waited until the man nodded. "I'm the guy she ran away with. She got her life back on track, and I've paid my debt—a little prison time—and I'm getting my life on track. I'm here in town to win her back, and to make a new life. I'm planning on attending Tabor Christian and..." He shrugged. "Just doing whatever I can to make things right."

"That's quite a lot to lay on the table. I'll give you that." He tipped his head to one side and studied Brock, his eyes narrowing.

It was an effort for Brock to sit still and endure the man's scrutiny, and keep meeting his gaze. *Please, God, I'm depending on You. Help me make things right with Nikki. Let me find a place here so I can stay. Please?*

"I like honesty," Mr. Coffelt began, when the silence had dragged on so long that Brock could make out individual voices in the other room as the office workers talked over their lunch. "Mandy Gordon is a good judge of character. How'd you meet her?"

"Open Doors prison ministry sent me to her."

"My church supports that ministry, and I'm on the outreach board, so I have a general idea of the requirements. Another good recommendation. You do realize I'll have to run a check on you, what sent you to prison, and if your parole officer and counselor believe you're trustworthy when it comes to a business's financial records."

"Yes, sir." Brock flinched when a couple drops of sweat that had been gathering on his hairline ran down into the corners of his eyes.

"Call me Andrew." He chuckled softly when Brock blinked and shook his head. "I listen to my gut a lot, and so far it likes you. Let me ask you something... I heard Nikki travels for this foundation she works for. If her work takes her on the road, settles her in another state, do you plan on picking up roots and following her?"

"I guess," he said slowly, "that would depend on how well I fit in here. And if Nikki ever lets me back into her life and her heart. I'm here to win her back. That might mean staying put, here where the people she knows can keep an eye on me. And maybe trust that God will bring her back to me, if that's what He wants for us," Brock added, his heart thudding at triple speed. "I liked this town when I was first here, before I took Nikki away. I can see myself staying here for the rest of my life." He thought of Paul's words a little more than a week ago, warning him that Ringo's former supporters might come after him for revenge. *Please, God, let me have a long life here, and not bring trouble on these nice people.*

"Uh huh. That's honest enough." Mr. Coffelt nodded slowly. "Well, let's talk, shall we? Just how much accounting experience do you have?"

~~~~~

It was good to get home at the end of the day, peel off her clothes, and take a long, hot shower. Nikki liked getting involved in every aspect of the work she investigated at the Mission. She liked helping Joe with the cooking and packing up meals to go out into the town. She liked helping Claire sort through the supplies in the communal art closet and decide how much longer the different colors of construction paper and tempera paints would last, and whether they could go another week before re-ordering. It made her heart ache a little, to realize how much scrimping and careful calculating went into such simple things as art supplies and making sure there were enough toys for all the children when they went out onto the playground. She had run up and down the long central hallway several times, helping to track down the single bicycle pump in the entire building, so that three different teachers could pump up the balls their children were using. That wasn't right, Nikki decided. What was so expensive about a bicycle pump that the Mission couldn't have one in every classroom? Or maybe the question should be: Why couldn't some of the wealthier, successful businessmen in the congregation of Tabor Christian stick a crowbar in their wallets and make sizable donations, or even just buy needed equipment outright?

Aurora had ambushed her with giggles and tight-wrapped arms two times when Nikki went into the little girl's classroom. She held those memories tight in her heart, even though it caused a painful little throb. Would Mercy Grace have been a giggly, wiggly little girl, so eager for affection? Would the two little girls have been friends?

"You're awful quiet," Doria said, as she and Nikki worked on the last stages of putting together supper and guided Brandy, Davie and Danny through their homework.

"Long day."

"The Mission is a good place. It's too bad it hasn't grown as quickly as this town needed it to."

"I wondered a few times today how things would have turned out if I could have volunteered there when I was in school." Nikki slid the dish of pickles out of Davie's reach and waited for the boy to reach for it anyway. She tapped his hand, prompting giggles from all three children, and moved it another five inches. "Maybe if I had seen some of the hurting little kids and that lady who came in today... I might have thought a little harder before I did some stupid things."

"What stupid things?" Brandy demanded.

"What lady?" Doria asked, overriding the uncomfortable question. She and Nikki shared a smile.

"She was all bruised up — her boyfriend beat her — and she had three little boys with her." Nikki took a deep breath. "Looks like they all had
~~~~~

different fathers."

"Ah. Looking for money or shelter?"

"Escape. If she was the only reason I was sent here, I'm glad." She stepped back over to the stove and stirred the rice in the frying pan. "Pastor Wally wasn't quite sure where to send her. I called the shelter for battered women Arc set up over in Toledo two years ago. She and her boys are safe and the police have an arrest warrant out for the boyfriend."

"If he's her boyfriend, why'd he hurt her?" Danny asked in an uncharacteristically soft voice. Nikki wondered what he remembered of the life he led before he and Davie were taken by Children's Services.

"People are mean, sometimes. They say they love someone, but that doesn't stop them from hurting them," Doria said. "Are you almost finished with your homework?"

Dr. Holwood came through the front door at that moment and all three children leaped from the table to run to greet him.

"Answers that question," Nikki said with a grin.

*Thursday April 3*

That morning, after the drop-off traffic had slowed, Nikki was surprised to see Officers Todd James and Mike Nichols saunter into the lobby of the Mission. She was still in the office with Claire, checking the attendance sheets and watching her new friend struggle with the accounting program on the computer. The two policemen saw her and took up identical poses in front of the office door, hands on their hips, shoulders hunched, glaring at her. She stifled a chuckle and hurried to get up from behind Claire's desk in the office and go out to meet them.

"You, little girl, are in a heap of trouble," Mike said, pointing a long, calloused finger at her. "Get over here," he added, when she paused just out of arm's reach.

"Didn't do nothing," she grumbled, then burst out laughing and opened her arms. All three laughed as she hugged first Mike, then Todd.

"Why didn't you tell us you were home?" Todd said, holding her by her shoulders after he hugged her, and shook her twice. "Why'd we have to see you walking down the street this morning?"

"Why didn't you turn on your siren and pull me over?" she shot back.

Mike laughed and Todd blushed. He had pulled that trick on her when she was fourteen and had punched a bully picking on two kindergarteners on the way home from school. The bully had been all bluster and mocked Nikki, holding a hand against his bloody nose and telling her she would get thrown into jail for punching him—until she addressed the officer as "Uncle." Then the boy had gone white with terror and looked like he would burst into tears.

"Can I assume you know each other?" Claire said, coming out into the lobby.

"Just checking on our favorite delinquent." Mike froze when Gray strolled around the corner of the office and tipped his head to one side to look up at the two officers. "What in the world is that?"

"My bodyguard and bully repellant," Nikki said, fighting not to laugh.

The last few parents dropping their children off for the day hurried into the building then. Mike and Todd stepped out of the way and waited while Nikki and Claire went through the sign-in routine. Then she took them into the cafeteria where they could sit down and she gave them the short version of what had brought her to town. They were duly impressed and pleased when she took them through the sniff-and-introduction routine with Gray.

"Looks like you made good," Todd said, nodding, as they walked through the lobby to leave. "Glad you're home, kiddo. At least for a while."

"Just stay away from that loser, Rich Thomas, okay?" Mike added.

"That's going to be a little hard, considering he works here." Nikki decided to be flattered rather than insulted by the warning.

"Yeah, but we've seen a couple hundred guys like him. A real slouch, getting by on what he can con out of others. Then a nice girl comes along and he cleans up and does his Mr. Straight-and-Narrow routine and traps her in a moment of weakness. We don't want him hurting you again, okay?"

"I don't want him hurting me again, either. Besides, it'd take a week to de-grease him." She shuddered, which got chuckles from her adopted uncles. They parted with hugs and warnings not to cause trouble.

"What's the story with those two?" Claire wanted to know, when Nikki returned to the office to try to help her with the recalcitrant computer program.

"They saved my life when I was a baby, and I'm named for them, so they're my honorary uncles. That's the short version," Nikki added as the final parent-and-child scurried through the door, dropping shoes and jackets and other bits of necessary gear in their hurry.

"Uh huh." Her eyes twinkled and she stood up to take care of the extremely disorganized family. "I want the long version later."

~~~~~

At lunchtime, Nikki took Gray out after they ate, instead of before. Aurora's classroom was having a picnic on the lawn in front of the school and Rich sat in the shade of the front step. He wasn't looking at Aurora, who giggled with three little friends, pelting each other with potato chips. He looked up and down the front sidewalk, fidgeting and tapping both
~~~~~

feet out of synch. Nikki felt an odd jolt through her chest when he saw her and immediately jumped to his feet. Was he watching for her to show up?

"No," she murmured to Gray, and slowed her steps a little. What would make Rich think she would come back this way? He was just keeping watch over his little girl, spending some time with her, and looking around because she was otherwise occupied.

"Hey," Rich said, stepping down the front walk to meet her halfway.

"Nikki!" Brock called from the corner where he had just appeared. He wore the same sport jacket as yesterday, but different pants and shirt, and it looked like he had a slight burn from yesterday. Nikki suspected he had spent the entire day walking from business to business, looking for work. Then she wondered why she paid so much attention to his appearance. It wasn't her job to look after him anymore. She wasn't his girlfriend and decorative distraction on business calls.

Then she glanced at Rich, who stopped and jammed both fists into his hips and watched Brock hurry across the lawn to catch up with her. Rich's hair was a tangle, as usual. He had several strips of five o'clock shadow where he hadn't been very careful with his morning shave. And now that he was closer, she caught the distinct aroma of old sweat. If he couldn't figure out how to operate a washer, couldn't his mother at least make sure he had clean clothes? Or maybe the problem was that his mother took the "tough love" approach, refusing to clean up after him when he wouldn't pay attention to rules of basic hygiene?

*Stop it*, she scolded herself.

"Great news!" Brock blurted. He nodded to Rich but focused all his attention on Nikki. "I got a job. At the paper."

"At the *Picayune*?"

"What'd they hire you for?" Rich blurted. "They wouldn't hire me, and I grew up here."

"I didn't know you were a reporter." Nikki winced at the nasty bite in Rich's voice.

"Not." Brock grinned and jammed his hands into his pockets. "Accountant. Your friend, Max was working the front desk when I walked in yesterday and she knows Mrs. Gordon, my landlady and... it just all fell together. Got to admit, it's a little weird when God answers your prayers so fast."

"Yeah. Weird," Nikki murmured.

*How could Max do that to me?* she raged for a moment.

Then again, she hadn't exactly told Max, or anyone else in Tabor, that Brock wasn't to be encouraged to stay in town. But Max should have known better. What was Max thinking, helping Brock find an excuse to stay in town?

"Hi, I'm Brock Pierson." He held out his hand to Rich, who stared at it a moment as if Brock offered him a snake to hold. Or couldn't he remember what it was like to shake hands and what it meant?

"Rich Thomas," he finally answered, and shook, tugging free of Brock's grip just quick enough to be an insult.

"I know you." Brock's smile faded. "I know I've heard your name somewhere, even if I don't know your face."

Nikki panicked, wondering what she had told Brock about Rich. It probably hadn't been kind. Had she made Brock laugh a few times, telling him about some of the stupid things Rich had done? Her face got hot.

"So, what are you doing here?" she asked, to keep Brock from remembering.

"Well... you're about the only person I really know in town. I figured, I had to share the good news with someone."

"Good news?" she choked.

"Hey, if you're pestering Nikki, you better stop right now," Rich blurted. "She's here on business. I don't want some math geek making trouble for her, got me?"

"I got you." Brock nodded and took a step back. "It's nice to know you're watching out for her. Especially after what you did to her in college. Kind of paying your debts. I believe in paying debts."

"What I--?"

"When do you start work?" Nikki broke in. She prayed she didn't sound interested, but she couldn't let Rich work up to a bluster.

"Monday. I was wondering if I could take you out tonight to celebrate?" He gave her that crooked, hopeful grin that used to make her laugh, and feel like she was the most important person in the world to him. So long ago.

"Celebrate?" She choked on the dozens of things she could say — most of them nasty. What made Brock think she'd want to *celebrate* his ability to stay in Tabor? She didn't want him here, not while she was in town, and certainly not after she went on to her next assignment.

"No such luck," Rich said. "Nikki's going out with me tonight. You can have her tomorrow."

"Have her?" Brock's eyes narrowed. "Who are you to tell her what she can do?" He turned to Nikki, questions in his eyes.

"Rich did ask me out first," she hedged. "But tomorrow is the Firesong concert. I have to be here for that, work behind the scenes."

"Then take her out Saturday," Rich said. "If Nikki doesn't have things to do here for the Mission. She's a really important lady." He jammed his fists into his hips and stuck his chin out. On anyone else, Nikki would have been impressed by his belligerence. On Rich, it just looked immature.

"Saturday's out," Brock said, sparing her from echoing him by asking Rich what he thought he was doing, saying when she could go out with someone. "I have to drive to Columbus to meet my... counselor."

Nikki had the distinct feeling he had been about to say "parole officer."

"Counselor? You got some mental problem?" Rich said with a grin.

"Not anymore. And it's more a matter of my soul than my head." He looked Rich up and down again, then shook his head. "Some other time, then. Guess I'll see you in church. You take care, Nikki." He grinned down at Gray, who infuriated Nikki by thumping his tail on the sidewalk a few times. "You keep watching out for our lady, Gray." Then he turned and hurried down the sidewalk.

"Church?" Rich groaned. "What's with this guy?"

"Like he said, it's his soul, not his head." Nikki muffled a groan, when it occurred to her that Rich's reaction probably meant he hadn't been to church since he left for Ohio State. She looked down at Gray. He whined and stood up and walked away. Good enough for her. She turned to follow him, but Rich's voice stopped her.

"Hey, so what time do I pick you up tonight?"

"Oh." Did she really want to go out with Rich? Then again, what if Brock had heard the uncertainty in her voice and decided to check up on her tonight? She hadn't really lied to him, but that was how it would look.

"It's not really a date, you understand? I'll meet you at that coffee shop you mentioned yesterday. Perk-and-Perch, right?"

"Yeah." Rich grinned wide enough to reveal a second missing tooth.

Nikki wished she could go home and hide in her room for the rest of the day. Dating old boyfriends was not what she had in mind when she returned to Tabor. Especially not just to avoid Brock. Why had he decided to settle here?

# Chapter Nine

"Probably because of you," Doria said, when Nikki told her what had happened at the Mission that afternoon. They were washing the dinner dishes while the children played outside, with Gray and Dr. Holwood supervising.

"Me?" Nikki nearly dropped the glass baking pan she was drying. "I did not encourage him. Not a bit. I didn't even look at him or talk to him during the trial, and I certainly didn't write to him when he went to prison."

"Maybe you should have talked to him, at least once. Brock's determined to make up with you. If you'd written to him, you could have settled things, at least."

"What was I supposed to say to him, Mum? My life is great now, Ringo killed our baby, don't ever call me?"

"When did Mercy Grace stop being just your baby?"

"Huh?" Nikki stopped short and thought back over what her foster mother had said. She didn't like that little smirk Doria wore. It usually meant she knew something and she wasn't about to tell Nikki, but make her learn the truth the hard way.

"You said 'our' baby, but until Brock showed up here, you always referred to Mercy Grace as 'my' baby, 'my' daughter." Doria rinsed the broiler pan and pulled the strainer plug in the sink.

Nikki had to think about that. Was that all it took, for Brock to show up and say he was sorry, and suddenly she wasn't her own person anymore? What right did he have to suddenly move in on the pain she had survived and turned into a victory?

Or was it the feeling that she wasn't alone? That could be good and bad. Nikki enjoyed being alone, just her and Gray, driving for hours at a time when they took care of errands for Arc. But she all too vividly remembered the feeling of peace and contentment and safety, knowing Brock was always there. Believing — mistakenly — that he always put her first as soon as he got his "errands" out of the way. Life with him had been one long adventure, constantly moving, traveling, new places and people every week — and Brock always the constant, steady part of her life.

"Nikki?" Doria prompted, when the dishes were dried and put away, the sink scrubbed, and still she was silent.

"Mum, why is he here? It has to be more than just me..."

"He's a Christian now, and he wants to do what's right. He feels responsibility for you."

"I made my own choices. They were stupid and they were wrong, but I still chose what I did."

"Well, Brock obviously doesn't feel that way." She glanced at the clock over the sink. "You'd better get going. Are you going to change before your date?"

"Mom, it's not a date." Nikki wished she could laugh. Why had she agreed to meet Rich?

~~~~~

Nikki got to the Perk-and-Perch five minutes late. She expected to find Rich pacing and growling. He had been a stickler for schedules and promptness in high school. But he wasn't there. She waited until ten after, then went inside, thinking she would find him waiting there, already halfway through one of the gloppy, heavy pastries full of fruit and cream she had seen through the big display window of the coffee shop.

Nothing. No Rich, and hardly any other customers, either. The coffee shop was only one-quarter full, probably because it was a Thursday night. The narrow storefront had the coffee bar, ice cream and pastry counter down one side, a series of four-man booths down the other, and a handful of two-man tables scattered in the floor space between them. It was dimly lit, with art prints haphazardly hung on the dull brown cinder block walls. Nikki ordered an iced cappuccino and took a booth where she could see the door. She pulled her notebook out of her purse and made notes of things to investigate tomorrow at the Mission and questions to ask Pastor Wally and Claire that she had thought of on her walk home.

Rich came in at nearly 7:30, when she was considering heading home. He slid into the booth without an apology, just a grin, and leaned forward to try to kiss her. Nikki jerked back out of reach and wished she had brought Gray with her. What did Rich think he was doing? Was that his way of apologizing for being late?

"Great place, isn't it?" Rich gusted. He raked one hand through his hair—dripping wet, which meant he had taken a shower. Nikki was grateful for that. "I come here a lot to unwind. Even bring Rory, when Mom can't take her."

Nikki tried to imagine Rich babysitting a toddler in one of these booths. Especially one as wriggly and easily distracted as Aurora. She couldn't visualize the boy she had dated in high school putting up with the fuss and noise and inconvenience. Well, maybe he had changed. She knew she had.

She watched him as he placed his order. He fidgeted, unable to stand still at the counter. That was a change, too. The Rich she had known in high school had been calm, confident; nothing made him uneasy. He had
~~~~~

never showed when he was worried or upset, and even when he got angry with people for breaking rules or showing up late, he didn't bark at them. This Rich in front of her acted like he lived on espresso. Maybe being a father had changed him. Or losing his scholarships. Or finding out he wasn't a spiritual giant.

"Don't you go to church anymore?" she asked, when he returned to their booth with his clunky mug of coffee and a paper plate with a drippy, gooey pastry balanced on top of it.

"Church?" For a second he paused, staring at her as if he didn't understand the word. Then he nodded and slid into the booth, banging the plywood frame. "Sure. Yeah. All the time. Rory loves it. Mom wouldn't hear of us missing. Why?"

"Well, you seemed kind of shocked when Brock mentioned seeing me in church."

"Yeah, who is that guy, anyway? He sure seems to think he owns you. Did he follow you to town or something?"

"No. He came here to talk to my folks, and I just happened to arrive at the same time for my assignment." She frowned and tried to hide it by sipping at her drink. After all this time, hearing the stories of other sisters at Quarry Hall and her own adventures, Nikki knew there really was no such thing as accidents. Not for those who trusted in God to direct their lives.

"Yeah, this Arc place. Weird place you work for."

"No it isn't!"

"Hey, didn't mean it like it sounded. Just that I don't know anything about this place that's going to dump tons of money on the Mission. So tell me about it, okay?" he said with a placating little gesture and that smile that had been part laughter, part mischief when they were in high school. He had been able to lead the youth group with that smile.

It was either tell him about Arc or let him ask more questions about Brock, and Nikki certainly didn't want that. She gave him the same information he could have found on the foundation's web site or in the dignified, lovely brochures Sophie had recently redesigned. Rich seemed duly impressed by the power and resources the Arc Foundation had at its disposal.

"So, things are going to really change when you guys take over, huh?" He tipped back his cup and drained it.

"We aren't going to take over. We provide resources so worthy endeavors can continue what they're doing. Just because places like the Mission have a hard time making ends meet or expanding doesn't mean they're doing anything wrong."

That response was nearly straight from the web site, too. Nikki wondered if she should be proud or amused by her response. She certainly had learned her lessons well.

"Then what are you guys doing here, looking into everything, if you're not going to take over? Why can't you just get them to fill out some papers, and hand the big guys a check every couple months?"

"This money belongs to God. We're responsible for it, how it's used, how organizations will change once they get it. Stewardship doesn't end when Elizabeth writes the check." Nikki wished she had brought Gray, though she doubted dogs were allowed inside the coffee shop. She wanted to know what his reaction to Rich would be right at this moment.

"Stewardship. Haven't heard a word like that in a long time." Rich leaned back in the booth and grinned at her. "Got to admit, you got into the big time, Nikki. Bet your folks are proud of you. Arc wouldn't happen to have any jobs for a guy like me, would it?"

"You have a daughter to take care of," slipped out of her mouth before she could think of another reply.

"Well, heck, yeah. That's why I want a better job. You don't think I want to spend the rest of my life mopping floors and fixing things and living behind my mom's house, do you?" He chuckled and reached across the table and took hold of her hand. His fingers had grime around the nails and the skin felt cold and stiff.

That was honest dirt, earned keeping the Mission clean, Nikki scolded herself when she flinched at the dark stains. But she didn't like the feel of his hand; that had changed, too. Rich used to have warm, supple hands. Too deft, sometimes. How could she have forgotten the one really big fight they had gotten into, when he had tried to slide his warm, gentle hands inside her shirt while he kissed her goodnight? He had apologized with tears so effectively, Nikki had pushed it to the back of her mind. She hadn't even remembered it when she caught him having sex in his dorm room. She remembered it now, though. Rich certainly had changed — and she was a hypocrite. She had fought him because of a tiny little touch, had been horrified, sickened and infuriated to see him so intimate with someone else. But she hadn't put up a bit of struggle when Brock seduced her on a fine July evening and convinced her to run away from home with him the very next day.

"Nikki?" Rich squeezed her hand. "You okay? You look like you're a million miles away."

"Just... thinking."

"Guess so. Anyway, what about it? You think you could get me a great job like yours, traveling around the country and helping people? I saw that notebook computer you were working on this afternoon, and your cell phone. Top of the line equipment, huh? Nothing but the best for God's work, right?"

"You have to go through a lot of training. And you wouldn't be sent out on the road. Not with a daughter to support. Road jobs are..." She refused to tell him that positions like hers were dangerous. She wasn't about to tell him that her first job out of training, a simple courier job, had ended up with her being left to die in a metal shed in the middle of nowhere. "Road jobs are for people who have no real ties. No husbands or children, hardly any family. The Arc Foundation and Quarry Hall are sometimes the only family any of us have." She was a daughter of Quarry Hall and a representative of the Arc Foundation. That meant almost as much to her as being a forgiven child of God.

Rich continued with more questions about Arc before she could think of a prevarication, try to guide the conversation into another area. What kind of jobs were there for someone with a child to support, then? What kind of training could he get? He admitted without a bit of shame that he hadn't finished college—could Arc pay for him to get his degree? He devoured his pastry, got up to get a second dessert, never offered to get her anything, and continued with his questions.

Nikki led the questions back to the Mission, trying to answer with illustrations from the Mission's needs. She didn't like this cross-examination, though she understood Rich's curiosity and concern for the Mission. This was his livelihood, his only means of providing for Aurora. He couldn't want a bunch of cold, corporate strangers taking over and changing things.

She almost laughed when, directly on the heels of that thought, Rich asked about changes in the staff. Would Arc hire more janitors? Get high-tech equipment? Install security systems? Expand the facilities? More staff? Maybe better toys and decorations for the daycare rooms? Now he sounded like an anxious father, and that pleased her.

Realizing that sent a little jolt through her. *Why* did she like this facet of him? Because she hadn't liked the nosey side of Rich Thomas, or some other reason?

"It's been a long day," she said, drawing back when Rich tried to take hold of her hands again. She didn't like the feel of his hands; they made a lie of his words and his face and the memories of their dates so long ago.

"Heck yeah. I bet you did more work than ten other people at that place." Rich chuckled and picked up his fork to scrape at the sticky residue from his chocolate swirl cheesecake. "You're one important lady, Nikki. I'm proud of you."

"Thank you ever so much, kind sir," she murmured. He laughed louder, sounding like the boy she used to know.

"It's really great to see you again. Kind of makes me think I wasn't wrong to come back to Tabor after all. You know..." He shrugged. "You think maybe we can patch things up between us?" he said on a softer note.

"Patch?" Nikki's mind flashed to Brock, who wanted to make up with her.

"You have no idea how good it was to see you the other day. Like I was being given a second chance. Tabor's a great place to grow up in, but I really thought I was stuck here. No hope. Then you walk in, and it's like God said I could have a second chance. What do you think?"

"I don't know..." The smart answer was that she wouldn't be in town long enough to start up a serious relationship. How much did Rich have to do to make up for breaking her heart? He had betrayed God far more than he had betrayed her, turning his fine words and standards and the Bible studies he had led into lies by having sex with a girl he wouldn't marry.

*How much,* that quiet voice in her heart whispered, *does Brock have to do to make up for what he did? And who gave you the right to judge him?*

"It's him, isn't it?" The warmth left Rich's voice, making it sharp and hard. "That Brock jerk. The one who's following you around town. You've got a thing for him, don't you?"

"Brock? You've got to be kidding. We're—over. Long over and done with." She reached for her empty mug to take it to the rack holding a bus pan over the garbage pail. Rich caught hold of her hand, gripping hard enough to hurt, and keeping her in the booth.

"What does he want from you? Who is he?"

"That's none of your business!" she said, louder than she intended.

"Yeah? Who does he think he is, talking about me making up for what I did to you? What did you tell him about us?"

Nikki lifted one foot, ready to kick him under the table. But no, she couldn't. Rich wasn't threatening her. He was just upset. He wouldn't hurt her. Not physically, anyway. The kicks Vincent had taught her were to save her life, not take revenge for broken promises when she was a junior in high school.

Still, Rich made her so mad...

"Brock is the guy I fell for when you betrayed me and slept with that..." she half-whispered, until she almost choked on the word she wouldn't speak. Nikki liked the shock that widened Rich's eyes and made him loosen his grip. "I ran away to be with him. He took good care of me. Better than you could ever do. But what we did was wrong. Just as wrong as you messing around with that stupid blonde in your dorm room. At least I didn't break any promises to anyone who loved me, when I was with Brock." She jerked herself out of the booth and deposited the mug in the pan and hurried out the door.

"Nikki!" Rich followed on her heels. "Sweetheart—I'm sorry."

Those words so rarely came from his mouth, they stopped her short on the brick sidewalk.

Maybe Rich had been knocked down enough to learn he could be wrong. He had never been wrong in high school, other than a few attempts to touch where he wasn't allowed. He had never needed to apologize. He was the model Christian young man. Until he went away to college.

If Nikki could cast aside what she believed in so easily, how could she condemn someone else for it?

Besides, what did Rich think when she agreed to meet him here? Maybe she had done it to hide from Brock, or even hurt him a little, but Rich had most likely felt encouraged when she accepted this pseudo-date.

"It's been a long day," she repeated, unwilling to apologize and all too aware of it.

"I'm sorry. Really." Rich jammed his hands in his back pockets, hunching his shoulders and bowing his head and looking at her from under his ragged brows with his patented comical-repentant look. She recognized it, but instead of getting angry, she sputtered a chuckle. Rich grinned. "It's been eating at me for years, you know. The look on your face when you walked in on me and Sue."

"Aurora's mother?" she guessed.

"Yeah. It was stupid. It was wrong. But I just felt so guilty... I thought I could experiment a little, fool around, and nobody would ever know. I figured you wouldn't get hurt. Maybe I was just so mad that you weren't there. But that wasn't your fault." He took a step down the sidewalk, heading down Main toward Sackley. Nikki let him guide their walk, mostly because it was on her way home anyway.

"Then I guess I started feeling mad. Why should I feel guilty, you know? Nobody would ever know. And the more mad I got, the more time I spent with her. And she was... beautiful. A lot of fun. And you weren't there, to keep me on the straight and narrow." He flashed a toothy grin at her, making a joke out of it.

Something twisted inside Nikki. So now this was *her* fault? Rich needed her influence to be a good Christian boy? Sure, she had heard about lots of "good Christian boys" and girls, for that matter, who stumbled and fell away from their upbringing the moment they walked through the doors of college. Who did he think he was, to put responsibility for his sins and stupidity on her?

"Then you walked in on us—I swear, that was the first time we had sex."

"You kept having sex until she got pregnant," Nikki pointed out quietly as they reached the corner and turned right on Great Street.

"Yeah. And I wanted to marry her. I mean, it's the right thing to do, right? Rory needs two parents. But she's a selfish little... she couldn't care less about our little girl. Since I didn't have any money to hand over to her, she just dumped our baby on me and took off. Never looked back. Just breaks my heart." He shrugged and they walked for a few dozen yards in silence. He gave her a sideways glance. "Rory really likes you. A lot."

Nikki wondered where he got that idea. The little girl seemed more enchanted with poor, longsuffering Gray than with her. Then again, Rich was Aurora's father. She probably told him lots of things she wouldn't tell strangers. But how much exactly could a two-year-old say?

They didn't say much else as he walked her home. The walk wasn't very long, just twenty yards up Great to Church, a block-and-a-half down Church to the Holwoods' house. Nikki was relieved to see the lights on in her foster father's study at the front of the house. Rich had never felt comfortable around her parents; especially because Dr. Holwood had been their Sunday school teacher in high school. He wouldn't try to stay long. She suspected she could invite him in and he would refuse.

"So... see you in church?" Rich asked, as Nikki stepped up onto the wide porch.

"Sure. Do you go to the Singles class?"

"Nah. It's nice and all, but there's really no place for single parents, y'know? I take Rory to the nursery and I slide into the back pew for the service. That's about it." He shrugged and his smile grew more crooked. There was a catch in his voice. "Some folks just aren't very forgiving, when it comes to guys trying to make good on their mistakes, y'know?"

"Yeah. I know." For a moment, she was tempted to tell him about how far her mistakes had gone with Brock. She wanted to tell him about Mercy Grace, but only for a moment. Her dead child was none of his business.

"Well." He looked over at the lighted window with the shade drawn down. There was a wide shadow that had to be Dr. Holwood at his desk. "See you Sunday."

"Sunday," she echoed.

# Chapter Ten

Doria wasn't waiting when Nikki stepped into the house. She grinned, realizing she had fully expected her foster mother to be there, just like she had been after all Nikki's first-time dates in high school. Nikki glanced through the sheer curtains over the narrow window next to the door. Rich sauntered down the sidewalk, hands jammed in his pockets. He almost swaggered. He must have enjoyed their pseudo-date more than she had.

"Back already?" Dr. Holwood rumbled, accompanied by the creaking of his massive wooden swivel chair as he got up.

"Already." She stepped down the hall and leaned into the frame of the open door. "Not waiting up for me, were you, Daddy?"

"I'm a whole lot more relaxed about your safety and activities when you're not here." He winked at her as he reached to get a book from the floor-to-ceiling shelves along one wall of his office. "When you're under my roof, you're five years old again."

"Thanks for not treating me that way."

"I'm learning a few things in my old age." He nodded toward the lopsided, faded, gold brocade chair sitting across from his desk. He settled back into his chair and opened his book and flipped through a few pages while Nikki took her perch in the other chair. "Did you find out what you wanted?" he said after a few moments of comfortable silence.

"Find out?"

"I seem to remember when we got the whole story out of you, you vowed never to have anything to do with 'that jerk-face slime Rich Thomas' if he was the last man left on the face of the Earth."

"Oh." She grinned and slouched a little. "He's changed. I've certainly changed. Who am I to criticize others?"

"Who are any of us? All have sinned and fallen short of God's glory. Only the sinless can throw stones — and point fingers."

"Is that your lesson for Sunday?" Nikki grinned, taking out what little sting there had been in her mumbled words.

"No. Someday, though." He leaned back in his chair and folded his arms across his chest. "What's on your mind?"

"Why is it easier to — why do I want to give Rich a chance, but I want to run Brock out of town? I didn't do anything to Rich, and he hurt me. Brock and I did wrong together. It should be easier to forgive him.

Especially if he's a Christian now, like he says. I mean, Daddy, I went out with Rich tonight just because Brock wanted to take me out. Did I want an excuse not to go, or did I want to hurt him?"

"Maybe both. I never claimed to be an expert in the way women's minds work." He winked at her, effectively defusing the gasp of disgust about to escape her. "I think you still need to forgive yourself. How can you forgive him for lying to you, using you, ordering you to abort your child, when you can't forgive yourself?"

"That sounds like far too easy an explanation."

"Hmm. Maybe. You've been through a lot in the last few years and you've grown a lot, and your life has gone in a totally different direction than you ever intended. I'm proud of you. Your mother is proud of you."

"But you wish I had taken a less exciting road?"

"We love all the children who come through our home, but God gave you to us. You were our little girl from the moment Todd and Mike put you dripping wet and shivering into your mother's arms. We want you to be happy and safe. We wanted you to make the right choices in life and to give your heart and soul to Jesus first above everything."

"I hurt you so bad when I turned my back on everything," she whispered.

"Yes, you did. But we got over it. Love heals all wounds. But sometimes there's a scar that won't go away. A reminder. Like a broken bone that twinges when the weather changes. We will always love you, Nikki, and we'll always pray for you and forgive you, and you will always have a home with us. But you're not the young woman you could have been. Maybe God let you stray to put you through this pain and make you a stronger person to serve Him. Who knows? We won't know all the answers until we stand before the throne on judgment day."

"So I should forgive Brock and Rich and myself and just go on with my life?" Nikki asked with a crooked little smile. "Easier said than done, Daddy."

"It's always easier. But I think you can do it. You've got more motivation than most of us, if you think about it. Your baby is watching you. I'm fully convinced that those who have gone ahead are aware of our struggles and pains. Live to make your child proud."

"Especially since she's the only one I'll ever have?"

"You don't know that. The doctors only said the damage *might* reduce your chances of carrying to full-term, not that you'd never have another baby."

"Why would I want to get pregnant again and risk killing another baby?" All the sweet, tired relaxation that had seeped into her body rolled away, like a receding tide.

"Who says you'll get a chance? Something you're not telling me about

Rich? Has he finally come to his senses?"

Nikki shuddered. Picking up with Rich again would be like going back to high school and erasing all the intervening years.

If only she could.

"I guess it's too soon to know anything." Nikki got up and stepped around his desk to brush a kiss across his cheek. "I'm heading up to bed. Thanks for being here."

"I'll always be here, baby girl," he rumbled, and caught hold of her arm, to bring her down low enough to kiss her forehead.


*Friday, April 4*


"Now that's a bear!" The light baritone voice was accompanied by a rattle and clatter that echoed in the old school's hallways.

The morning drop-off rush had just ended. Nikki debated whether to go look for Rich to start setting up the gym for the concert that night, or trust he was already at work. She turned and saw a low, squat figure emerge from the darkness of the hallway leading to the gym. She flinched, seeing a human head on the shape and nearly turned to go back to the Mission's office. Then she looked at Gray, who just stood there at her side, unfazed. Grinning, she reached over and hit the light switch for the hallway.

The shape turned into a man in a wheelchair, who raised his arms defensively over his head and squeaked, "Bright light! Bright light!"

"You are definitely too big for a gremlin," she said, muffling laughter at the reference to the very old, slightly ridiculous movie. "I've been warned—you must be Tommy."

"And if that's your bodyguard, you must be Nikki." Tommy gave his wheelchair a hard shove and glided down the hallway toward her. He made a show of wiping his long-fingered hands on his jeans and held out one hand to shake. "Nice to finally meet you."

"I'll take your word for it." She met his grin and decided she would enjoy verbally and mentally sparring with Tommy, who had a steady comedy career along with working at the Mission. She admired him for getting a degree in early childhood education and getting himself around so well, just as much as pursuing his comedy career. Claire had shared with her several handfuls of Tommy's mental bombs, to warn her how her brother would zing her out of nowhere and attempt to turn her brain into a rubber ball, to go bouncing around the room.

"Uh huh. You really have been warned about me." He gestured at Gray. "I don't suppose you rent him out in the winter, to pull cars out of ditches?"

"Just about as often as you put chains on your tires."

"Oh, be still my heart. You're my kind of girl." He fluttered his eyelashes at her, making her laugh.

Why, Nikki wondered, did guys have such naturally thick, long lashes? Tommy was rather good-looking, rugged, with wide, well-developed shoulders and thick, blue-black hair, square jaw, and upper body build of someone who spent long hours on weight machines. Claire had shared that an injury in childhood had put him in a wheelchair. She didn't say what had happened to their parents, but it had been Claire and Tommy against the world since she was a college freshman.

"Somehow, I don't think I should take that as a compliment," she returned.

"Smart girl. I'm guessing you're here to start setting up for tonight?" He gestured back down the hall to the open doorway of the stage area of the gym.

"Just to check it out."

She looked over her shoulder for Rich to show up. The silence from the gym was a bad sign. He should have been at work already, pulling out carts of chairs or at least unfolding the bleachers that ran down the sides of the gym. Joe had warned her when she stopped in the kitchen that Rich would vanish if there was hard work to do, until he had been summoned a dozen times and someone else started the task. Then he would grumble about other people trying to steal his job from under him.

"Well, I can help a little bit." Tommy tipped back on his main wheels and pivoted around, then streaked down the hall to the gym door.

She had to hurry to catch up with him, a little amazed at how fast he could move.

Nikki figured out the stubborn old metal latches that held the bleachers folded up against the walls and got both sets pulled open. Tommy used a bungie cord to attach a cart of folding chairs to the back of his wheelchair and dragged it out of the storage room to the gym while she did that. They had gone back for another cart of chairs by the time Rich sauntered in with his shoulders hunched, hands in his pockets. His one-piece suit was unbuttoned to his waist and hung off one shoulder, revealing a faded and stained T-shirt that featured an overly endowed woman falling out of her string bikini.

"What do you think you're doing?" he snarled at Tommy and gestured around the room. "No stupid gimp is gonna—"

"We're under a deadline," Nikki said, and fought to keep her expression neutral. She didn't like the hot feeling of satisfaction she got at the shock on his face when she stepped into view behind Tommy.

"Nobody said nothing about any deadline," Rich grumbled. "What?" he snapped, and glanced down at himself, finally reacting to the pointed glare she gave his clothes. "Oh. Sorry." He fumbled with the buttons as he crossed the gym to the doorway of the storage room. "What's the big deal about setting up chairs, anyway? Nobody's gonna be sitting for long."

"People pay for seats, they get seats." Tommy sounded entirely too cheerful. He whipped his chair around and headed into the storage room.

Rich grumbled and put very little room between rows. People would have their knees digging into the backs of the people in front of them. Nikki went behind Rich and re-adjusted the rows of chairs as soon as he slammed them into place. She was relieved when Claire called over the PA system, asking Rich to go to the four-year-old room to clean up a mess. She would get the job done faster by herself, without cleaning up after Rich's slapdash job.

"Let's hope it was a major mess that'll keep him really busy until lunchtime," Tommy said. He tipped his head to one side and fluttered his eyelashes at her in mock innocence, when Nikki gave him a narrow-eyed-measuring look. She couldn't help it—she had to laugh.

~~~~~

Firesong showed up midway through the afternoon, to set up for the concert that evening. For a while, it felt like old home week, chatting and laughing with Tom, Jim and Jason Gibson, Dani Paul and her brother, Andy. Pastor Wally, Claire and Tommy joined them, with the tickets, cash boxes, and a team of volunteers who would be handling admissions and monitoring all the entrances into the Mission, acting as security. Katie Green showed up with dinner for everyone, after they had finished hauling in all the equipment and instruments and put everything in place.

Gray got up from his place at Nikki's feet, growling loudly enough to be heard through the laughing and teasing through the meal. She looked where his muzzle pointed. A man in a navy blazer and dark red shirt sauntered through the doorway of the gym with a sneer evident on his narrow face. He shook his head, freezing when his gaze intersected Nikki's. Instantly, his expression shifted to cheerful, and he clapped his hands three times as he continued into the room.

"Okay, people, this is great! How are we all feeling tonight, huh? Ready to wow the old home gang?"

Tom got up to make introductions. The newcomer was Troy Danziger, and he had just contracted with Firesong to be their manager and get their next CD produced professionally. Nikki debated sharing with Dani what she had seen, and Gray's reaction to the man before he had even entered the gym. She had learned long ago to trust her gut instincts when they contradicted people's words and reputations. Even more important, she had learned to trust Gray's reactions to people and situations. If Gray didn't like Troy Danziger, then she wouldn't either. The problem was conveying that information to Dani, who certainly hadn't
~~~~~

had to depend on Gray to stay safe and alive several times in the last year. Nikki regretted not re-establishing contact with her childhood friend when she settled in Quarry Hall. If she had spent time with Dani in the last two years, she wouldn't have hesitated to warn her now.

Would it do Firesong any good, even if she could warn them? They had a signed contract with this man.

Nikki put her reservations aside to think and pray about later. They had to finish hooking up the sound system and assigning everyone to their posts for the evening. In one hour, the doors would open and the audience would start pouring in. The Mission and Firesong needed the public relations boost from this concert even more than the money it brought in.

She looked for Kurt Green but didn't see him until after the concert. The crew scurried around the gym to clean up and then ranged through the Mission, emptying the wastebaskets in the bathrooms and cafeteria. She and Kurt waved to each other but didn't stop to talk. She was going one direction and he was going another. She assumed he had caught up with Katie somewhere during the concert. She had money to gather up and rough tallies to make for the evening's proceeds. Of the refreshments, only ten cans of soda, four mini bags of chips and two packs of cookies didn't sell. Nikki had calculated that they needed to sell only half of the supplies to break even, so they had made a tidy profit just off food. She helped Pastor Wally wheel away the garbage cans that had been set up by each door into the Mission to collect freewill offerings, to lock up in his office to be counted in the morning.

~~~~~

Brock hung around after the concert as long as he dared, watching Nikki at work. She amazed him, shifting easily between directing the concert workers and taking directions from the husky older man and the strawberry blonde woman who seemed to be in charge of everything. A few flickers of jealousy nipped at him when he saw her joking with the young man in the wheelchair. He scolded himself that he didn't have any right to feel jealous or possessive, or to feel threatened by Nikki's friendship with or affection for anyone else. He had certainly forfeited any claim on her heart—but that was going to change. No matter what it took. First he would prove to Nikki that he had changed. Then he would prove to her that he still loved her, and maybe loved her in a better way, with a purer heart, than when they had been together. Then he would earn her love all over again.

He headed for the doors of the lobby in the center of the building, then paused for one last glimpse of Nikki before making the twenty-minute walk back to his rented room.

"Can I help you with something?" A graying, stocky man paused in crossing the lobby. Brock had seen him stop to talk with Nikki several
~~~~~

times during the cleanup.

"Sorry. I was just... looking around."

"You look like a man waiting for someone."

"In a way." He gestured at Nikki, chatting with a teenage boy as they pushed a cart loaded with garbage cans down the hallway from the cafeteria to an open door by the back of the gymnasium. "I'm here because of Nikki."

"You work for the Arc Foundation?" He chuckled and held out his hand to shake Brock's. "Sorry, I should really introduce myself. I'm Glenn Carson, pastor of Tabor Christian."

"Brock Pierson." He saw that flicker of recognition in the elderly minister's eyes and was relieved when the man didn't flinch or pull his hand away. "You know who I am, then."

"I spent a lot of hours praying with the Holwoods, then talking with Nikki, when she was in the hospital."

"I'm not here to hurt her. I want to make things right."

"How do you intend to do that?"

"Pray?" He shrugged. "I plan on joining your church, for starters. Mandy Gordon said you have a counselor at your church. I was thinking of making an appointment, once I got some things taken care of."

"Uh huh. You must be the new boarder she mentioned." Pastor Glenn's smile widened and he nodded. "How about coming over to the church some time next week, and you and I have a talk?"

"I'd appreciate that. A lot."


*Saturday, April 5*


Saturday, Nikki spent most of her time in one of the children's rooms. Being the weekend, when a lot of parents didn't work, attendance numbers dropped and classes were combined. The outer door into the largest children's care room stood open and the children were allowed to play outside since there were more than enough adults around to supervise. Nikki stationed herself outside with Gray, who immediately drew little Aurora to giggle and climb all over him. It bothered her to see the little girl at the daycare. Rich didn't work every day, did he? Shouldn't he spend more time with his daughter? Where was he?

Asking Aurora did little good. The little girl laughed and gave up tormenting Gray in favor of climbing into Nikki's lap. She rocked back and forth until Nikki caught on that she wanted to be bounced.

"She's not really a talker," Max said, emerging into the sunshine.

Nikki wondered how long her friend had been listening to her try to get some answers from Aurora. Maybe it was silly. What kind of vocabulary did a two-year-old have? She couldn't base her judgment on the foster children her parents had watched over the years. Some were so damaged by abuse or trauma or neglect, they wouldn't talk no matter their age.

"Guess I sound kind of silly, huh?" She breathed a sigh of relief when Aurora crawled out of her lap to toddle off and pester someone else.

"Nah. You just think all kids should be smarter and better behaved than they are." Max settled down on the grass next to the doorstep where Nikki perched. "So, how's the inspection coming along?"

"Oh, the inspection is fine. If I didn't know Pastor Wally, the miracles he pulls off with his shoestring budget would make me suspicious."

"We get a lot of donations—food, clothes, supplies and help. So..." She cocked her dark head to one side and studied Nikki a moment. "How's everything outside the inspection?"

"Dandy."

"That was sarcasm if this actor's daughter ever heard it. Anything I can help with?"

"Yeah. Tell me how to keep from strangling you?" Nikki tried to grin. "Me?"

An argument over the play kitchen set up on the lawn pulled them both to their feet. It was several minutes before the shrill cries and tears calmed and the children went looking for toys they didn't have to share.

"That's always a problem on Saturdays," Max said as they headed back to the doorstep and shade. "Too wide an age group. Kids play differently at different ages. So, what did I do?"

# Chapter Eleven

"You got Brock a job," Nikki said.

"Not me. He was there filling out an application and standing up to Myrna, which automatically made him one of the good guys. Mr. C. came by and what was I supposed to do? He was in his jolly, I-love-everybody mood. Introduce Brock to him as the guy who ruined your life? Brock was asking about the accounting job that Mandy told him was available. The walking financial disaster ran out on us last week—which was an answer to a lot of desperate prayers, so—I don't know—timing is everything."

"Yeah, but whose timing are we talking about? Mine or Brock's or Mr. Coffelt's?"

"How about God's timing?" Max shrugged. "I talked with Brock, just a little bit, after he came out from talking to Mr. C. He sounds awful sincere and he's sorry for hurting you. He was asking about a church to attend, how he thought he'd go to ours, but he wanted to know what else was available. He also told Mr. C. about being in prison. Gotta admire a guy for being that honest."

"If he tries to hide anything, he knows it'll all come out eventually."

"Maybe. So why's he staying in town anyway?"

In halting words, Nikki told her about meeting up with Brock when she first came home and taking him to Mercy Grace's grave. It was easier talking with Max about such things because she knew all the ugly details. She and her parents had come to see Nikki when she was in the hospital.

Aurora came back and cuddled up in Nikki's lap while she was still talking. The little girl didn't demand to be rocked, but leaned against Nikki, a warm weight faintly scented with bubble bath and peanut butter. And fell asleep.

"Mercy Grace would be just a little younger," Nikki murmured, gently shifting the child to a more comfortable position.

"Who would she look like?"

"Huh?" Her voice cracked a little.

"Empty arm syndrome," Max said. "We've had some girls come through here, suffering from post-abortion trauma. The what-ifs. The guilts. Dreams about their baby that was never born. Hearing a baby crying in the night. Even years, decades after they aborted and thought they were free and clear. Even the girls who refused to believe a baby was anything more than a blob up until a month or two before birth. A lot of them keep picking out kids in the crowd, walking past playgrounds and schools. They think, my kid would be that age. Or they wonder who the baby would look like, her or the guy. Aurora isn't Mercy Grace."

Nikki's voice caught in her throat. She would have protested, but the sympathy in Max's grave voice stopped her. Was that what was happening? Had she just been too busy the last two years to think or feel her way completely through her loss? The counselors at the hospital and her adopted sisters in Quarry Hall told her the effects of her loss could crop up far in the future, with no warning, triggered by something she couldn't even be fully conscious of even after it happened.

"I didn't abort," she finally said.

"I know. But you still blame yourself, right?"

"Oh yeah." Nikki took a deep breath. It ached in her lungs. "So, when did you get a counseling degree?"

"School of hard knocks. I think about how things would be if my mom took the easy way out and aborted me and pursued stardom. She chose to keep me and sacrifice her career. She met Dad and they settled here in Tabor... and here I am, trying to pass on some of my hard-won wisdom."

"Oh, thanks very much." They exchanged slightly teary grins. Nikki sighed and cuddled Aurora closer. "Still, you can't help wondering..."

"I know." Max wrapped an arm around her shoulders and shook her. "So, am I forgiven?"

"Oh, I guess so."

"You're ever so wonderful. I better get those two apart before —" She leaped to her feet and dashed to the knot of children at the far corner of the lawn, where a few yelps turned into a tussle on the ground.

Nikki was glad for the excuse of Aurora on her lap to keep her seated. She watched Max disperse the combatants. She had probably had lots of practice with her two younger brothers.

Despite herself, Nikki thought back to what Max had said about Brock. She was both impressed and disturbed that Brock would so readily offer information about his past to Mr. Coffelt. It wasn't something he could keep secret, but why tell people at the beginning of the process? Wasn't he ashamed of what he had done?

Maybe the problem, she mused, was that she was too much ashamed of what they had done together. Was she afraid of what people would say and do about her, if they learned about her past connection with Brock?

Shouldn't she be proud of him, facing his past and paying for it, and getting on with his life?

"No," she whispered to Aurora, the sweaty little head resting on her shoulder. "I don't care what he does anymore. I try not to hate him, but I can't let myself care."

A hollow, sharp little thud deep inside made a lie of her words.


*Sunday, April 6*

Sunday, Pastor Glenn spoke about angels. Nikki didn't realize Rich was in the pew behind her until he spoke after the closing prayer. All her family's friends at church had to come by and say hello and welcome her home. Nikki couldn't have seen Rich, because of all the people around her. Then the prelude music faded into the first hymn, the congregation stood to sing, and the stragglers hurried to their seats as the service began.

She did see Brock, though. Sitting near the front, not looking around. He sat with Mrs. Gordon, which made sense, Nikki supposed. She liked the garrulous, plump woman, and told herself she was being ridiculous, feeling betrayed by the help she extended to Brock. It was Mrs. Gordon's living to rent apartments and houses, and her mission as a Christian to help newly released prisoners get acclimated to society again. Nikki could only hope Mrs. Gordon didn't know she was the reason Brock had come to town and decided to stay.

Nikki forgot all that when the service ended, the organist played, and she heard Rich's voice.

"Sheesh, you'd think Pastor Glenn would stay away from the trendy topics." Rich grinned at her when she turned to stare, as if delighted to have startled her.

"Oh, don't be ridiculous, Richie." Eleanor Thomas slapped her son lightly on the arm, then turned all her bright-eyed attention to Nikki. "It's so nice to see you home, Nicole. You'll be joining us for dinner, of course?"

"Uh—" Dinner with Mrs. Thomas was the last thing Nikki wanted. The woman had started planning her bridal shower and picked out a china pattern for her after Nikki had dated Rich twice.

"Mom, I didn't ask Nikki to come with us yet." Rich guided his tiny mother out into the flow of traffic down the side aisle of the church. For a few moments, the Thomases were separated from the Holwood household. Nikki was grateful. She liked Mrs. Thomas, really, but she was just a little too "correct" for Nikki's taste. She insisted on calling her Nicole and had moaned and apologized to Nikki for months after she found out about the breakup with Rich, and why it happened. Besides, no one over fifty had a right to be skinny and darkly tanned all year round, and not a gray hair or wrinkle to be seen.

"So, can you come?" Mrs. Thomas asked, appearing out of the crowd in the narthex. She was good at ambushes like that, Nikki remembered.

Doria met Nikki's gaze and smiled in sympathy. Nikki paused, despite her better instincts. Her politeness immediately separated her from the rest of her family.

"Sorry, but I've already got plans." Nikki said a silent prayer of thanks that she was riding to Fairlawn with Xander and Hannah. They were to meet with Joan for lunch and discuss legal matters for the Mission and what she had seen and done in her first week there.

"Oh." For a moment she was silent, and the flow of traffic moved them out into the main hallway. The congestion broke up as families headed out the doors or down halls or stairs. "Aurora will be so disappointed. She just adores you, Nicole."

"I think she's sweet," Nikki said to be diplomatic, instead of voicing what she really thought. How in the world could Aurora let her grandmother know how she felt about someone she had just met?

"Well, why don't you help Richie get her from the toddlers' room, so she doesn't cry. And you have to plan on dinner next Sunday. No, wait — next Sunday is Easter. So the Sunday after that."

"I'll think about it. All depends on my schedule. I have reports to make, and I might need to go back to Akron for meetings. I have a lot to do while I'm here in town."

Suffering through a fancy, dry dinner at the Thomas house was not high on her list of priorities.

"Goodness, you'd think you were heading out of town again." Mrs. Thomas chuckled indulgently, as if Nikki's hedging were ridiculous. "We certainly know better, don't we?"

"But—"

"Come on." Rich looped his arm through hers and deftly guided her down the stairs to the basement, which held the nursery and younger age Sunday schools and the church kitchen. Immediately, the noise level and congestion cut back by two-thirds. Nikki breathed a sigh of relief. When she tried to tug her arm free, Rich held on tighter.

"So, what'd you think of that sermon?" he asked as they stepped into line with all the parents waiting to pick up their children.

"It was great. Pastor obviously did a lot of research."

"But angels are so trendy. Next week, he'll probably talk about Pokemon or the *Twilight* series. Yuck!" He chuckled, ignoring a few frowns from the couples ahead of them.

"Pastor debunked all the trendy garbage people believe about angels. Weren't you listening? Angels are servants and warriors and messengers from God, not all that sticky-gooey New Age spirit guide garbage. They don't guide us to higher levels of awareness, and they certainly don't teach us how to become gods. That's a lie straight from the Garden of Eden."

Nikki shuddered, recalling a story Megan had shared the last time she had been home at Quarry Hall. The older girl had run into a group of people living in a monastery situation who had fallen under the sway of a so-called angel. It was a nightmare of mind control that had nearly taken Megan's life.

Aurora saw Nikki and Rich and raced to the door, screaming with delight. Neither of them could say anything for several moments, as they gathered up the little girl and her scattered shoes and craft papers. Aurora wouldn't let her father carry her but held out her arms for Nikki. There was a curious pressure in Nikki's chest that had nothing to do with the child's negligible weight in her arms as they headed back upstairs and out to the parking lot. She rather liked it.

"Heck, who believes in angels, anyway?" Rich said with a chuckle.

"I do."

"Oh, sure, you wear one around your neck as a good luck charm?" He leaned forward as if he could see down the high neckline of her dress. Nikki fought an urge to deck him with a strong right hook. She had to hold wiggly Aurora with both arms or risk dropping her.

"I don't believe in luck." She took a deep breath, pushing aside the mix of awe and glee and quite sensible terror that came over her when she remembered her few close encounters with supernatural powers. "I do believe in God's hand on our lives. He sends His angels to shelter us."

"Aw, come on—"

"I've seen angels. I've seen people come from nowhere and heard them give instructions to my friends when we were in trouble. When I asked about them later, only a few of us saw them or heard them. One saved my life. I should have been killed in a car wreck, but he pulled me out before the explosion. Witnesses say I fell out, but I know someone pulled me out. I felt arms around me. I heard a voice, comforting me. Someone held my hand. He was there in my hospital room when I woke up. He held my hand when Mercy Grace died." She blinked hard against tears and flashed a smile for Aurora. The little girl understood her tone of voice, if not the words, and watched Nikki with a wrinkled brow, and her mouth pursed into a pout.

"Yeah, well, if you think..." Rich looked away, clearly uncomfortable with the conversation. He led the way to the distinctive, bright yellow and purple spot of movement that was his mother. "So, who's Mercy?"

"Mercy Grace was my baby. The accident that made her be born prematurely eventually killed her. She'd be two in June, if she had lived."

"Heh. Like a little sister for Rory, huh?" He tweaked his daughter's nose. She squealed and hid her face against Nikki's shoulder.

"I don't think—"

Then they reached Mrs. Thomas's car. The woman swooped over to them, snatched Aurora away, and settled her into her car seat with practiced ease. Before she could insist again on Nikki joining them for dinner in two weeks, Nikki made her escape.

She felt curiously hollow as she hurried across the rapidly emptying parking lot to join her family. Something felt odd, even wrong, but she couldn't put her finger on it.

Her adopted sisters at Quarry Hall teased her that she thought too much, analyzing everything when she should just try to go with the flow sometimes. Nikki didn't think so. She had to try to understand. She had gotten into trouble because she hadn't thought things through far enough, or long enough.

Now, what had bothered her about that innocent walk through the church and out to the parking lot? Rich's comment on Mercy Grace and Aurora being sisters? Mrs. Thomas's insinuation that Nikki was staying in Tabor a long time? Or Rich's refusal to believe in angels or take them seriously?

~~~~~

"Vincent is going to do some recon in the next few weeks," Joan said, after she, Xander, Hannah, and Nikki had discussed the concert and what Nikki had observed so far at the Mission.

"Recon? As in?" Nikki glanced at Xander and Hannah. They both shook their heads, indicating they were just as lost as she was. She had driven down to Quarry Hall with them and would have expected them to give her some advance warning, after all.

"Checking out the landscape, security options, assessing the neighborhood." Joan leaned out of the booth at the back of Max & Erma's and looked around the half-full restaurant before continuing. "There's been some activity in Ringo's former network."

"And you think Nikki is in danger?" Xander said. "Wouldn't it be smarter to just bring her home to Quarry Hall?"

"They're not after her, as far as we can tell. You did hear Ringo died in prison?" She folded her napkin and put it on the remains of her salad. "It's looking more and more like murder, rather than random violence. Either revenge or punishment for getting caught, or someone he messed over in the past getting even, taking advantage of him being separated from his muscle."

"Are they after Brock? He wasn't involved in the murder, was he?" Nikki didn't like the flutter of panic that wove through her. She flashed back to the kitchen and that night Ringo had shot Brock for trying to protect her.

"No. Definitely not. Records show Brock refused all attempts at contact, even reported it whenever someone from his old life tried to get through to him. No, what worries us is that some of Ringo's old crew have fallen off the grid. And there are rumors that Brock might be called back to witness against some who haven't gone to trial yet. The defense attorneys are trying to paint him as having a whole lot more authority and
~~~~~

inside knowledge than he really did, and they're trying to get his deal with the DEA thrown out."

"And those invisible men are going to come after Brock to silence him?" Xander guessed.

"He was just a numbers cruncher, an accountant and a front man," Nikki said. "I mean, yeah, I was oblivious, but I would have noticed if he was doing things like actually selling and making deals. Brock was there just for window dressing and to keep the records straight. He didn't do Ringo's business for him."

"You know that, I know that, the DEA knows that." Joan reached across the table and rested her hands on Nikki's. "You and I both know that the world doesn't care when the truth conflicts with what it *wants* to believe. I know this won't be easy, but you should probably warn Brock that his past is about to catch up with him."

"Yeah, you're right. About it not being easy." She sighed and closed her eyes a moment. She had wanted some excuse to urge Brock to get out of town and give up his trying to get back together, so why did she hesitate to take advantage of this development? "I'll warn him, but I doubt it'll do any good. He didn't go into Witness Protection like he should have."

"Why not?" Hannah asked. She shook her head. "That was stupid. Sorry. Forget I asked."

"What?" Xander said.

"I'll explain it to you later."

Nikki laughed with Joan and Hannah at Xander's comical exasperation, despite the cold, hard knot of apprehension in her chest.

When she got home to Tabor that evening, she wrote a note to Brock, telling him what Sophie and Joan had found out and their theories and warning. He was supposed to start work the next morning, so she knew she could leave it at the boarding house for him and avoid all chances of running into him. That would have to do. If Brock chose to believe the warning and act on it, or not, she had done her part. She just hoped he wouldn't think that she actually cared about him.

She didn't, did she?


*Tuesday, April 8*


Lisa Montgomery came into the Mission that morning to resume working with the children. Nikki sat in on the morning session with the kindergarteners, fascinated as Max and Lisa guided the children through making up their own stories. Lisa made lightning sketches on a dry erase board to illustrate what the children said happened in the rambling, sometimes disjointed adventures.

"I've missed them so much," Lisa said with a slightly teary smile, when Nikki and Claire walked her to the door, just before lunch.

"We're just glad you're feeling better," Claire said, squeezing Lisa's hand. "How are things with...?"

"We have a counseling session this afternoon, when Todd gets off work." She glanced at Nikki and blushed. "Sorry, we're leaving you entirely out of the loop."

"I heard a little," Nikki admitted. "I'm just glad you're able to get back together with your husband. Mum and Daddy have been worried about you." She muffled laughter when Lisa's expression turned puzzled. "I keep forgetting you switched your faculty adviser after I left town, so we never really met... Dr. Holwood is my foster father."

"Oh. You're that Nikki. Okay." Lisa managed a smile and nodded. "You work for the Arc Foundation with Anne, right?"

Nikki and Lisa stood in the doorway for another twenty minutes, chatting about mutual friends, before Lisa headed for home. Right now she lived over Rick's Bakery, but as part of their reconciliation, Todd insisted they switch residences. He would move into her apartment and she would take the cottage on Kiln that he had rented. Nikki knew the house, when Lisa described the little cottage and admitted she and Todd had wanted to live there since they were engaged.

"He isn't being pushy about it, but if we're switching places, he wants me to move in before I start showing." Lisa shrugged slightly and rubbed her hands over her stomach in a gesture Nikki knew too well. "For some reason, he thinks I won't be able to climb those stairs in another month."

"All that exercise will be good for you," she offered. "But I wouldn't tell him, if I were you. Take advantage of it. It'll make up for the 2a.m. feedings."

"You talk like you've had some..." She shook her head. "Blame hormones or something. I guess it takes a wild imagination to be a cartoonist."

# Chapter Twelve

"Experience?" Nikki couldn't breathe for a moment. She nodded. "I lost my baby at seven months, if that's what you're referring to."

"I can't imagine—I mean, I've imagined it. When things were the worst for Todd and me and I was sick and... I imagined what it would be like. But to go through it for real..." Lisa reached out and wrapped her arms around Nikki for several heartbeats.

Lisa came back while Nikki was helping Joe in the kitchen, putting out the soup-and-sandwich dinner for the senior center. She carried a canvas grocery bag that looked heavy and put it down on the counter in the kitchen, waiting until Nikki was free.

"Maybe this is crazy, and maybe it's presuming a lot, but I just have this feeling that you need to see these. And maybe you could pass them on to Anne, next time you go down to Quarry Hall, since she's kind of gone through this with me, but..." She gestured at the bag.

"What is it?"

"My book." A tiny laugh escaped her. "Actually, a lot of books."

They settled down in the cafeteria to talk, and Lisa explained. She pulled out a collection of ring binders and sketchbooks and bound pages that came from her publisher.

Lisa made her living doing a cartoon strip, *PK,* detailing the adventures of a pastor's family. A series of *PK* comic strips would be published in a book by a publishing house separate from the syndicate that distributed the comic strip to Christian magazines and newspapers. Lisa explained that it started out as an idea for a single book, to come out in October in time for Pastor Appreciation Month. The editor had expanded the idea to include three books of reprints of what had already been published in the last two years, and then three books of new, continuing story lines.

Nikki didn't get to read until that evening, after the children were in bed and the household was quiet around her. The galley proofs were for one storyline Lisa felt important for Nikki to read. In it, the pastor's oldest daughter and her husband were Lisa and Todd's alter egos. Lisa had been going through terrible pain and distress at the time she created the storyline. The publisher loved it because of the gritty reality and pain. The couple were in an accident at the height of a terrible disagreement. The husband had been killed, and the pregnant wife lost her baby. Nikki found it hard to read when she got to that part.

As far as she knew, Lisa Montgomery hadn't known anything about her life, the foolish and rebellious choices she made. She didn't know how Nikki got involved with a man involved in the drug trade, let him romance her out of her values and beliefs, and ran away with him. She couldn't know how pregnancy had jolted Nikki into turning back to God, her struggle to regain her faith, and how she had fled Brock to keep from being forced to abort.

How could Lisa know about those last horrid days? Ringo's men hunted her down, sure she had gone to the authorities to turn them in, and she had become a prisoner where once she had been a pampered decoration and unwitting tool. There was no way Lisa could know Nikki's daughter had died as a result of that car chase and accident.

Tears kept filling Nikki's eyes and she had to continually stop and wipe them with the edge of her nightshirt and try to keep reading. Nikki ached with the girl in the story, named Katie, as she suffered through the accident, reliving her arguments with her husband and crying for the child who would never rest in her empty arms.

Nikki cried harder when in a series of panels, Katie dreamed visits from her lost baby. How many times had she awakened herself, reaching for her baby? She had dreamed of Mercy Grace as a toddler last night, most likely triggered by seeing little Aurora Thomas at the Mission.

Gray sat next to Nikki on the floor of her room, his heavy head resting on her thigh as she leaned against her bed and read. The big dog whimpered when Nikki stopped several times to choke back sobs. A few times, he even got up and licked tears away before she could tug on the hem of her nightshirt. Nikki was glad he was there when she got to the end. She wrapped her arms around his neck and buried her face in the thick ruff of fur, as she had done many times since he chose her to be his person, and let the last tears come.

Had she been wrong? Was there still so much that needed healing, deep inside? Nikki thought she had healed enough to go out on the road and serve, ministering to those in need. How could she think she was even partially healed when the ache rose up this strong, as strong as the day she woke in the hospital and realized her baby wasn't safe inside her anymore?

She thought she had forgiven Brock, but maybe she had been fooling herself. She didn't hate him, but there was still an ache, still a quiet voice wailing deep inside.

"I admit it," she whispered to Gray. "Sometimes when I wake up in the middle of the night, I still wish he was there. I really need him to hold me. I thought he loved me. I thought I loved him. It should be over, but..." She took a deep breath and swallowed down the words.

They echoed through her heart and mind, though.

Brock seemed to think things could be made right. That was pain in his eyes, when he looked at her. Longing that Nikki recognized from her own mirror during those aching times of healing at Quarry Hall.

"He can't—we can't go back to the way things were," Nikki whispered, as if verbalizing it would make her heart accept it as fact.

She looked down at the book lying closed in her lap. Katie had assured her dream-baby that despite all their anger, the hateful things they had said to each other, she truly loved her baby's daddy and she knew he still loved her. Things could never be the same again, but she held onto the belief that things would have been made right if they had just tried harder and a little longer. The out-of-control truck had taken that from them.

"Totally different," she said, shaking her head.

And yet...

When she crawled into bed, Nikki fully expected to dream of Mercy Grace again, brought on by the cartoon strip. When she woke in the morning, though, she couldn't remember a single shred of dream. Somehow, she was disappointed, when common sense told her she should have been relieved.

*Wednesday, April 9*

Vincent was waiting on the front steps of the Holwoods' house when Nikki got home that afternoon. She didn't even see him, hidden in the shadows, until Gray sped away from her. There was only one person who could get her companion to race away from her like that, and she wasn't surprised to see Vincent emerge from the shadows as Gray reached him. He was slim and elegant like always, with his shaved head and trim goatee, and his cocoa-toned skin letting him blend into the shadows around the house. The security chief for the Arc Foundation was down on one knee, giving Gray a brisk rubdown when Nikki came up the sidewalk.

"I'd ask what took you so long, but I'm guessing you've been playing invisible and checking out the neighborhood the last few days," she said.

"You'd think so, but I've been trying to pick up the trail where our missing men vanished." Vincent gave Gray one final hard rub and shoved him away. "So, how have you been doing?"

"It hasn't exactly been like I expected."

"Never is, short-stuff." He slung an arm around her shoulders, drawing her in for a one-sided hug. "You up for a walk-through of the neighborhood?"

"Would it matter if I wasn't?" She tried to make her voice and expression sour, but failed utterly when Vincent tipped his head back and laughed.

While they walked up Church Street and the side streets, then to the Mission and around the central business district, he filled her in on the new information that had trickled in since she had spoken with Joan on Sunday. Little was new, and it only expanded on the useless details. Vincent asked more questions than he answered, pumping Nikki's memories of the encounters she'd had with Ringo's henchmen over the two years she had been on the road with Brock. Even fragments of what she considered useless information might turn out to be helpful in predicting who might come after Brock, their approach, and what they might do when or if they showed up in Tabor Heights.

Vincent entertained her family with stories of training the Arc Foundation's dogs during dinner that night. Nikki knew better than to relax and think she had escaped one of his punishing workouts — "refresher courses," he called them. She was proven right when Vincent responded to Davie's question about what else he did besides train dogs.

"I teach self-defense." Vincent tipped his head in Nikki's direction. "Has she shown you all the neat Bruce Lee moves I taught her yet?" He pretended to be dismayed when the boys responded with gleeful negatives. "Okay, Nikki. You and me. Back yard. One hour."

"What if I don't show up?" she retorted, deciding to play the game rather than resist and disappoint the children. Besides, her parents were trying not to laugh. Better to treat it as a game than a punishment.

"I know how to find you." He waggled his eyebrows like a melodrama villain.

~~~~~

"Thanks for seeing me on such short notice," Brock said, following Pastor Glenn into his office at the church that evening.

"Not at all. My wife has a short meeting right now, so the timing is perfect." The husky, gray-haired pastor smiled warmly and settled down at the table in a corner of his office. He gestured at one of the other three chairs, inviting Brock to sit. "So, what did you want to talk about?"

"I want to start out right here. This town means a lot to Nikki, and considering what harm I could probably do..." Brock shook his head, licked his lips, studied his hands folded in his lap. "Do you know the whole story, of what I was doing, how I almost got Nikki killed?"

"The bare bones. Just enough for her parents to ask for prayers for her safety, and then what happened when she was found and brought home."

"I romanced her into leaving town with me. I got her pregnant, and then I nearly got her killed when I started working for the good guys and my job turned ugly."

"Drug dealers, I heard," Pastor Glenn commented in a soft,
~~~~~

emotionless voice that encouraged Brock to continue. "Before you turned your life around, I mean."

"Yeah, that's a nice way of putting it. I never really handled the — the exchange of merchandise. I was the front man, the one who paved the way, made a nice, clean, trustworthy image. I used Nikki to convince people we were good folks. Who could look at a girl like her and think there was anything dirty going on behind the scenes?" Brock swallowed hard, forcing back the thousands of passionate, hurting, pleading words that wanted to pour out. They were meant for Nikki, not this kindly man who looked like he would be more comfortable in a flannel shirt and jeans, chopping down trees or building barns.

"Why do you feel it necessary to confess to me? Shouldn't you talk to her parents?"

"I have. I think they forgive me. I want to make things right, you know?" He looked down at his hands, clenched so tight the knuckles were turning white. "I became a Christian in prison. A lot of it was due to Nikki, the things she said, how miserable she was when she did wrong things to make me happy. It was real for her. It meant a lot to her. For the first time in my life, I really started thinking about my soul. Heck, I was raised in church, but it never made any sense or meant anything to me until I saw how the life we were living hurt her." Brock swallowed hard. "I'm here to make a new life for myself. This is Nikki's home. This is where her heart is, no matter where she goes. I couldn't think of anywhere else I'd want to be my home."

"And you want the truth out in the open, right from the beginning. That's commendable."

"So, I have a job here. So far, so good. But I figure, I better keep busy, you know?" He tried to smile. It only moved one corner of his mouth. "To stay out of trouble, and get to know people, too."

"Then I would recommend joining a Bible study, for starters. We have one on Tuesday nights and another on Thursday." He chuckled. "Well, actually, we have Bible studies almost every day of the week, morning, noon and night. But those two will provide you with mentors. Men who are solid rocks in our church, in our community. I suggest you start there, make friends, build a network. Make a place for yourself. Set down roots."

"That's great. If you don't mind..." Brock shrugged, ducked his head. "Maybe I'll join both. It's not like I have anything to do in the evenings. Having friends. Decent, honest friends. Yeah, I'd like that more than anything. Almost anything." He forced himself to meet Pastor Glenn's gaze.

"There's nothing wrong with admitting that we're empty and in need of help and healing," he offered gently.

"That's me. All over. But what I was thinking of when I came in here...

is there any place where I can—like—I don't know, do some volunteer work? Community service work? I'm basically an accountant. After everything I did, I think I'm pretty good at picking out the dirty tricks other folks are playing. I can find all the loopholes. I figure I can use it to protect people, too. So, can you use me?"

"Actually..." Pastor Glenn nodded, eyes half-lidded as he thought. "If you're considering becoming a member, I think there are places we can use you. If what I have in mind materializes... maybe you'll be able to prove yourself to Nikki, while you're at it."

~~~~~

Red and blue lights flashed at the same moment Nikki launched herself backward to avoid Vincent's low roundhouse kick. That curious, there-but-not-there sensation kicked in, so she reacted without thinking or even feeling. She twisted in mid-air, landing on her hands to curl up and somersault across the grass. Brandy, Davie and Danny cheered as she landed on her feet and only staggered a little.

"You want to tell me what's going on here?" Officer Mark Donovan blurted, leaping from the driver's seat of the police cruiser that had pulled up on Stephen, parallel with the Holwoods' backyard.

"We're learning how to beat up the bad guys!" Davie crowed.

"No, we're teaching you how to *avoid* getting beaten up by the bad guys," Vincent corrected. He pulled out a handkerchief from his pocket and wiped the sweat from his shaved head. "Let me guess, officer. Some friendly neighbor called and said a big, ugly black man was beating up on a poor little defenseless white girl, and you should get over here and save her from a fate worse than death?"

"What's that?" Brandy wanted to know.

"Liver and onions for dinner for a week," Nikki said, earning a chorus of "ewwws" and gagging sounds from the children. "Get on inside. The lesson's over." She didn't wait to see if they obeyed but crossed the neighbor's yard with Vincent right behind her. From the clatter of feet on the back steps and the creak of the door, they had obeyed.

With the falling of dusk, she had thought the impromptu little demonstration and refresher lesson in the back yard would have been partially hidden from prying eyes. Obviously, she had been wrong.

"That you, Nikki?" Mark stepped off the sidewalk, meeting them halfway across the grass.

Nikki hoped the lack of lights turning on in the surrounding houses meant the neighbors were out—hopefully at church at prayer meeting or youth club activities—and the ones who had called the police were too ashamed to signal their presence.

"Yep, it's me." She glanced over her shoulder at Vincent. "Mark Donovan—Vincent Howard. Vincent is my teacher. One of my teachers."
~~~~~

"What's he teaching you? How to be a tackle dummy?" Mark offered a crooked grin, so Nikki knew they weren't in too much trouble.

"How not to be one." Vincent offered his hand and the two men shook. "Nice to meet you. Sorry about scaring the neighbors."

"Yeah, well, I knew it was too quiet of a night."

"Before you ask, I'll be heading back to Akron in another half hour or so."

"Vincent..." Nikki didn't know if she should feel ashamed, amused, or relieved. If he didn't feel the need to hang around, that meant he felt confident in her situation. A few more moments of thought, and she knew it was ridiculous to think that anything could drive him away. Certainly not a faintly embarrassing situation with nosey neighbors.

"It's okay, short-stuff." Vincent nodded to Mark, who grinned back at him. "Just a warning, Officer Donovan. I plan on coming back a few times, just to make sure my worst-ever pupil stays in practice."

"Just as long as you let the neighbors know you'll be putting on some martial arts demonstrations whenever you show up, that's fine."

Nikki bit her lip to keep from blurting that she hoped Vincent didn't have to ever show up again. That was just the kind of challenge he loved. She wouldn't put it past him to return every other day, just to irritate her. A moment later, she laughed, because she was glad of that certainty. It was good to have people she could depend on, for support and teasing and embarrassment and laughter.

*Thursday, April 10*

"So... what's with you and Rich?" Dani said, as she helped Nikki inventory the closet off of the gym that held furniture and tools dating seemingly from the Civil War.

"Nothing, I hope." Nikki straightened up from digging through a box that looked like it held nothing but scraps of wood and dust. She slapped her hands together and stepped away from the cloud she generated. "I went out with him last Thursday, but..."

"It's complicated?"

"Major complicated." Nikki thought about what a snot Rich had been during the setup and cleanup for the Firesong concert, and then his complete turnaround on Sunday. Probably all show for his mother's benefit. And what exactly was she going to do about Mrs. Thomas, who seemed to think Nikki had come back to Tabor Heights to stay? "Then there's the whole baby problem," slid out of her mouth before she thought about what she was saying.

"Aurora's adorable, but yeah, I can see how you wouldn't want to get stuck with someone else's responsibility."

"Huh?" Nikki thought her heart would leap out of her chest. Dani didn't know about Mercy Grace, did she? For a few seconds, she couldn't breathe. How could she call Dani her friend, and not have confided in her about that pain and shame? *What kind of a wimp am I?* she wondered, even as tears prickled at her eyes.

"Hey!" Dani caught hold of her hands and led her over to a bench splattered with a dozen different splotches of paint. "What's wrong?"

"Nobody knows, do they?" She wiped at her eyes with her clean wrists and leaned back against the wall for a few moments. "Arc does a fantastic job, keeping things quiet. I was terrified of the gossip when I came home, but..." She sighed. The Bible was right when it essentially said that a person's sins would catch up with her. How could she salvage this moment with Dani, and be honest with her?

"Knows what?" Dani sat down next to Nikki.

"You heard about the big mess, when I was trying to come home?"

"Yeah, you broke up with Brock and left him, and then his boss kidnapped you to use you as a shield when the cops were closing in."

"Brock was working for the DEA, getting evidence to use against Ringo. It turns out all the witnessing Mum and Daddy did when he was here did have some effect. Delayed, but..." Nikki closed her eyes and wrapped her arms tight around herself. Her breath caught in her chest for a moment, painfully tight. "I was pregnant, and Brock ordered me to abort, so I left."

"Good for you," Dani whispered.

# Chapter Thirteen

"He knew I wouldn't abort. He did it to make me leave, before I got hurt. But Ringo decided a mother and baby would be the perfect disguise. There was a fight and Brock nearly got killed and an accident and... I was seven months along. My baby lived for a little while." Her eyes opened and she took a deep breath. "I named her Mercy Grace. She's buried at Quarry Hall, in the willow garden."

"Okay. Makes sense."

"It does? Because I can't stop thinking about Mercy whenever I see Aurora. And it scares me, every time she grabs onto me. Which doesn't make any sense."

"I'm taking psychology classes right now. It's classic transference—" Dani flashed a crooked grin at her. "At least, I think that's the term. But I think you're afraid you're substituting Aurora for your baby." She licked her lips. "And maybe you're drawn to Rich because he offers an instant family?"

"I hope not." A gasping laugh escaped Nikki. The last thing she needed was the emotional, egocentric roller coaster Rich Thomas could put into her life. "Does that sound like sour grapes?"

"Sounds like common sense. Rich is a creep. He was always good at hiding it, until he got away from the people who kept him in line. Now that he's shown his true colors, why make the effort any longer?"

"And the last thing I need in my life is a man complicating it and distracting me. I have so much work to do." She levered herself up from the bench, feeling stiff and achy from the weight of her memories.

"Yeah, but it's good work." Dani followed her back to the boxes they had been digging through. "And I made that decision a long time ago."

"What decision?"

"Stay away from romance and dating and all that gook. It just sidetracks you. There are better things in life to worry about."

"Uh huh. Then how come you're maid of honor for Katie and your brother?"

"That's different."

"Uh huh." Nikki smirked just a little. She welcomed the chance to move the focus of conversation off herself and onto Dani. If she got a chance to tease, all the better.

"They're family. Katie's always been like a sister to me, and..." She let out a fake scream and swung her hand around, as if she would hit Nikki.

Grinning, they settled back to work for another twenty minutes in silence, broken only by the sound of discards landing in the ashbin set outside the closet door. Nikki blinked back a few more tears as she considered how easily that revelation had gone. The last few days had been harder than she thought. At least Brock hadn't come to confront her about the note she left for him.

She concentrated on the Firesong concert. That had been the high point of her assignment, so far. It had been fun catching up with old friends. She thought about the innocent fun they had together, in school and church and summer camp. It still amazed her that Tom Gibson was married and Andy Paul was going to marry Katie Green, of all people. Not that Katie wasn't wonderful, but that Andy would fall in love with his sister's best friend. Nikki was delighted — and relieved — to be invited to the wedding. Katie had insisted as soon as they ran into each other before the concert. It had only been a few years since she had run away with Brock, but Nikki felt as if an entire lifetime had gone by and everyone had changed. She was afraid to discover changes that hadn't been for the good.

"Is Katie feeling all right? She looked kind of tired, dark around her eyes, when I ran into her at the concert," Nikki said, after they hauled a sawhorse with a broken leg out into the hall.

"Lots to do to get ready for the wedding, I guess."

"Yeah, probably." She grinned as they headed back into the closet for the other sawhorse. "I just about screamed when Kurt walked into Quarry Hall a couple weeks ago, and we realized we knew each other. I was shocked he remembered me at all."

"Kurt wasn't that much of an oblivious, arrogant jerk."

"Hmm, maybe. But it sure seemed like he didn't know I was alive. If all the girls our age weren't in love with Kurt, they were in love with Andy."

"Yeah? So you had his initials on your book covers, instead of Andy's?"

"I had both, depending on which class it was, and which one smiled at me in church that week." Nikki shook her head. "We were such stupid kids when we were that age."

"True. But at least I got smart and decided not to let guys mess up my mind and my life at an extremely early age." Dani froze for a moment and her eyes widened. "Oh, sorry. That was a stupid thing to say. I wasn't criticizing you. I mean, honestly, you had such rotten deals, first Rich and then Brock and then..." She wrapped an arm around Nikki's shoulders. "We're good just like we are. God has given us work to do, and we don't need anybody but Him, right?"

"Right." Nikki managed a tight smile, and a sharp, decisive nod.

*Friday, April 11*

Nikki came out of a second supply room, the existence of which seemed to have been forgotten by most of the Mission's staff. Her knees ached from kneeling on the cracked tile floor, her hands stung from paper cuts, and she was coated in a layer of dust from digging in the corners. She had done as thorough an inventory of supplies as she could. She had an idea of how to calculate the rate of use of supplies, and how expenses would go up as the Mission expanded its outreach and facilities. In the last week, she had managed to meet every teacher and staff member — paid and volunteer — and got an estimate from them of how much they used and planned to use in the future. Nikki had a good idea of how much should be in there, based on the careful record of expenditures Claire kept. Whether the actual inventory matched estimates would be a telling point. Rich had dropped a number of complaining hints about the practice of "borrowing" equipment and supplies from the Mission and "forgetting" to return or reimburse. Nikki hoped he was wrong. Theft, especially by staff, was hard to track down and had proven a reason for the Arc Foundation not to support some supposedly worthy endeavors.

And whenever Harrison Carter and the Board of Directors decided not to become involved in an organization or operation, investigations always seemed to follow. Too many times, those investigations had revealed shady dealings and sometimes downright illegal activity that had been hiding handily behind the front of benevolence. Nikki hated the idea that someone might try to do the same with the Mission.

She frowned as she thought of Rich Thomas and his far-from-subtle allegations. He made a point of looking for her every day and spent too much time, in her opinion, talking to her. Usually offering advice that usually started with, "You know what you should do, you should ..." She didn't need his hints about stealing to sense his restlessness and bitter spirit. It made sense, actually. He had a bright future only five years ago, but he had no degree now. No training. He wanted to start a sports program at the Mission, but right now there wasn't enough money for equipment, let alone raising his salary for increased duties. And he made it clear that being a coach entitled him to far more money than a mere janitor. Nikki ignored his unsubtle hints that he expected Arc to finance the program *when* it took over, not *if*. No matter how many times she emphasized that Arc would partner with Tabor Christian, not take over, Rich wouldn't listen. Quite frankly, Nikki saw more problems with his proposal than the lack of money and equipment, though it was a good idea and in line with his talents. First, Rich didn't have his degree, and no training working with children. And second, it was more time spent away from his daughter.

That led to thoughts of Aurora herself. Nikki did love the little girl and the toddler seemed to reciprocate—which was good, because Rich had asked her to babysit twice in the last six days. Nikki accepted the first time he asked because Brock called to take her out to celebrate his new job, and it was a convenient excuse to say no without lying. The second time, she hesitated too long to say no, and Rich took it as a yes. Nikki seriously thought about Max's comment about empty arm syndrome. Was she replacing Mercy Grace with Aurora? That wasn't healthy.

Getting a break from Rich and Aurora made her thankful Friday had finally come. Tonight Nikki had a fun evening planned, dinner and movie and girl-talk with Max and Bekka. Dani was out of town with Firesong, and Jeannette had a mother's group activity.

Gray, who had wisely taken up his post out in the hall away from the dust and clutter, now raised his head and whined. Nikki pulled her thoughts back to the present. How long had she been staring blindly at her clipboard? Then she heard the tight male voices. They kept low and urgent, which signaled trouble to her. Ringo had been that way, almost purring before he shot Brock.

That was Brock's voice, she realized with a prickling sensation up her back. What was he doing here? She hurried around the corner, into the lobby. Brock stood in the doorway to outside, and Rich blocked his way with the bucket and mop handle.

"I don't care what you think," Rich growled. "You're not coming in until you tell me what you want with her."

Nikki felt sick. She glanced at her watch, only quarter after twelve. The scenario was easy to guess. Brock had walked over from the *Tabor Picayune* to see her on his lunch hour, and Rich decided to play sentinel. He had been trying to inch his way into being her assistant the last few days and had intervened a dozen times already when other people wanted to talk with her. Nikki thought her last talk with Rich, saying bluntly that he had no authority and she didn't want him to "protect her," had finally sunk in—but obviously not.

"You were looking for me?" she asked, as Brock opened his mouth to retort.

"Yeah. Mr. Clean here seems to think I need a hall pass." Brock moved to cross the lobby to her. Rich hesitated and missed thrusting the mop handle in his way. Nikki had the oddest feeling he had tried to shove the stick between Brock's legs to trip him.

"I told him you were busy and he wouldn't go away," Rich grumbled.

"It's break time." Nikki tried to think of where she could lead Brock where they wouldn't be alone, but could still talk without being overheard. The noisy cafeteria a few dozen steps away might be the perfect place.

"He's got no business wasting your time."

"Why don't you let Nikki decide for herself?" Brock snapped. "I'll bet you didn't give her any of my messages the last few days, did you?"

"Messages?" Nikki hated how her face got warm. She didn't like Brock getting angry when it came to her. Not through fear, but because for so long, making him happy had been the focus of her life.

"Hey, I'm a busy guy." Rich jammed the mop back into his bucket and slowly wheeled it down the hall. "Not your secretary."

*Since when?* she wanted to snap at him. If he insisted on getting involved with everything she did, knowing every detail of her schedule, then he had better accept some responsibility with it. Especially if he accepted messages from Brock for her, and yet neglected to deliver them.

Nikki and Brock stayed silent, not looking at each other until Rich vanished around the corner. Then she gestured for him to follow her to the cafeteria. They stood in the doorway, where they could be seen by more than four dozen children and fifteen workers, but chatter and thuds of chairs made it impossible to be overheard.

"So... what did you want to see me about?" she asked and clasped the clipboard to her chest. Gray settled at her feet. His tail thumped three times against the door when Brock reached down to stroke his head.

"I still want to take you out to celebrate." He smiled, and it took away all the dark clouds in his eyes.

"Brock... I'll celebrate you getting your life back together. I'm glad you're a Christian now," Nikki said slowly, struggling for words and calm. "But don't ask me to celebrate your being able to stay in Tabor."

He was silent. Too quiet. Watching her with nothing in his eyes. Just like he had the day she told him she was pregnant.

Then he nodded and looked away and blinked hard. Had her words hurt him? Nikki had thought she could never do anything to hurt Brock, that he was too strong, too confident, and his life hadn't been wrapped around her, like her life had been wrapped around him.

So much had changed. Loss and her year of training and the jobs she had taken for the Arc Foundation had taught her and made her grow. Nikki knew now, if she ever gave her heart to someone, he would have to belong to Christ first and then she would come next in his life and everything else would be after her. She couldn't take a man who put his job and security ahead of important things—like inconveniently timed children.

Would she ever be able to forgive him for that?

"Okay." Brock sighed. "I can understand that. You feel like I'm invading. Makes sense. But Nikki, how can I show you I've changed unless

I'm where you can see me?"

"You don't have to prove anything."

"Yes, I do." He reached out to tuck a sweaty strand of hair behind her ear with the same lazy, graceful tenderness that had won her heart so long ago. She had been a silly child, thinking physical tenderness meant a loving heart. Nikki froze, hating the melting sensation inside, the sudden pang of longing for what was gone—and Gray's lack of reaction. He was supposed to protect her, wasn't he?

"There's nothing left between us. You don't owe me anything."

"I stole two years of your life. I hit you. I endangered your life because I worked for Ringo—I'll owe you forever."

"No—"

"I want to owe you," he murmured.

Nikki imagined she could feel the hurt and longing in him, digging down into the ground. As if he were growing roots. He would never leave Tabor as long as she considered it home.

Was he making it his home because it meant so much to her? To haunt her? Or did he really mean what he said? Why was he doing this to her? He couldn't really mean it, that he wanted to make up for everything that had happened to her.

Nikki thought maybe she was starting to believe him. She had braced herself to be approached by Brock after church on Sunday, waiting for some kind of speech on how he had endured the service just to prove himself. But he had said nothing, done nothing. No one had said anything to her about his presence, either. Maybe that had started to convince her; he had gone to church for himself, and not to prove something to her.

Nikki wished she hadn't trained herself to analyze and question everything. What had happened to the girl who accepted what people told her because she wanted to trust and believe everyone?

She knew what had happened—he was standing in front of her. With aching in his voice and regret softening his eyes. Except for that single tender touch, he stayed away from her.

Nikki knew she should be angry, just to defend herself, make herself strong. But something sweet and heavy and sad inside smothered the feeling. If Brock moved any closer, if he tried to kiss her... she thought she might let him.

"What would Mercy Grace think if I didn't at least try?" he asked.

"Huh?"

Nikki flinched. Her mind flashed to Lisa's cartoon strip, and the dream sequence of the baby's ghost begging her mother to forgive her father. Did Brock have to be dead for her to completely forgive him?

"Our little girl is in heaven, and I don't want anything bad between us when we finally see her someday." Brock forced a smile, but his eyes glistened with pain. "I hope she looks like you."

"If you're trying to guilt trip me —"

"Whatever works, whatever it takes..." he offered with a shrug, ducking his head and looking away for a moment.

"You haven't changed. In some places. Which is good... I suppose." Nikki felt too tired to hold onto the shreds of her hurt. One counselor had suggested she held onto her anger to fight the guilt she felt. He told her that when she could finally forgive everyone involved — Ringo, Brock, Angelo, Marcus — she could forgive herself and get on with her life.

"So will you go out with me? At least once?"

"Okay," she whispered. Then, louder, "But not tonight. I have plans with my friends."

"Saturday?"

"I'm working here. As usual."

"Toughest nine to five job I've ever seen." He smiled a little wider.

"Worth it."

"Yeah, I'm learning that." He tucked another strand behind her other ear and brushed her cheek with his thumb before drawing away. "Sunday? Just sit around and talk? Or walk around town and see all the places you used to tell me about."

"That sounds nice, but..."

"But what?"

"Well, Sunday is Easter. Daddy and I have all these plastic eggs filled with candy for the kids, for an egg hunt. And Mum's corsage. And Easter dinner and..." She shrugged. It startled her a little to realize she wanted to invite Brock to join her family for dinner, but she couldn't. That would give him the wrong idea.

"I forgot. Glad you reminded me." Brock tried to smile, but the corners of his mouth trembled just a little. Seeing it made her ache for him. "I volunteered to go to the City Mission and help serve dinner, hand out care bags."

"Oh." Funny, but now she was disappointed. Nikki wondered if it would help to bang her head against the wall a dozen times when she got home that afternoon. Something was definitely loose inside her brain and causing short circuits.

"Rain check on the walk?"

"That sounds good."

The funny thing was, Nikki realized later, she really did like the idea.


*Saturday, April 12*


"The guy's a jerk," Rich said as he handed Aurora over to Doria

Saturday night.

Some emergency had come up with a cousin in Mansfield and he had to drive his mother down to visit. He had been so apologetic, stumbling over himself when he called to ask for help, Nikki didn't have the heart to say no.

But Rich wasn't worried about his cousin right now. He was angry about something. Nikki had the feeling she had come in on the middle of a conversation, or even an argument Rich was having with someone on the way over to the Holwoods'.

"Who?" she asked, and wished her mother hadn't whisked Aurora off to the kitchen to get some fresh cookies. Nikki didn't want to be left alone at the front door with Rich in this mood and only Aurora's backpack for protection.

"Brock," he sneered. "Guy thinks he can tell everybody else how to do their jobs. Criticizes how I mop the floor! He goes walking around and looking at everything like he owns the place. Next thing you know, he'll be telling Claire and Pastor how to do their jobs. Thinks he's smarter than everybody."

Nikki bit her lip to keep from telling Rich that Brock was indeed a great deal smarter than him. She had seen him go through ledgers and pick out errors everyone else had missed, and calculate rates of interest in his head, faster than other people could use calculators. Rich had trouble keeping his checkbook balanced, according to his adoring mother.

"Why's he after you?" Rich demanded. "You ran away from home with him, but why's he here? You left him, didn't you?"

"That's none of your business."

"You slept with him."

"I said, that's none of your business."

"What happened to the good little girl who promised to save herself for marriage?" he growled and reached to grab hold of her shoulders.

Nikki sidestepped, twisting free before he even touched her, and shoved Aurora's backpack against him. She startled him with that trained move, shocking the anger from his eyes for a moment. She almost laughed.

# Chapter Fourteen

"What happened to me? Why don't you sit down and analyze what happened to you, first? How dare you judge me? You were the one who made me *promise* to not date anybody, and then I find you —" She choked on the filthy euphemisms for sex that tried to burst from her lips.

"You ran away with this guy because you were jealous?"

A guffaw burst from his lips — just before Nikki sealed them with her fist. Rich dropped the backpack and stumbled backward, barely catching himself before stumbling off the porch steps. He clamped both hands over his mouth, but not before she saw the spurt of blood. Her knuckles ached sharply and Nikki suspected she would find the skin cut from his teeth. She refused to look, though.

"Where'd you learn that?" Rich mumbled, backing down the steps.

"The same place I got my head and my soul straightened out. It's probably been too long for you to remember, Richie," she drawled, forcing sarcastic sweetness into her voice just to keep from screaming at him. "Remember what Jesus said? Remove the board from your own eye before you try to help someone else remove the speck from their eye. Take a good long look at the mess you made of your life, and clean it up, before you criticize someone else. You know nothing about what Brock's gone through. You don't know anything about his training or his talents or what he can do. The Mission would be lucky if he helped out." She bent quickly and snatched up the dropped backpack. "Don't you have to go pick up your mother?"

"Yeah." He hunched his shoulders, glaring at her from under his brows for several seconds. "Uh — thanks for taking the kid. I'll meet you before church to get her stuff, okay?"

"That sounds good." Nikki braced herself in the doorway and watched as he stumbled down the walk to the driveway and got into his rusty, cherry red Escort.

She remembered riding in that car when it was new, feeling proud and important, sitting in that front seat. Now the car looked pitiful. It was just as beat up and badly tended as Rich's life. What was wrong with him?

"What's wrong with me?" she whispered.

Doria was busy with Aurora in the kitchen. From the laughter, it sounded like Brandy had joined them. Nikki hurried up the stairs to her room. Gray emerged from the side hallway and followed her. She barely waited for him to come inside, almost shutting the door on his tail.

"Where were you when I needed you against that jerk?" she grumbled.

Gray gave her a mocking canine look and she grinned, knowing what it meant after all this time together. He hadn't even appeared in the doorway because he considered Rich no threat. And he was exactly that. No matter how blustery Rich got, no matter how red his face or how loud his voice, he wasn't a danger to her in any form. What had happened to the boy she had daydreamed about sharing the rest of her life?

"Lord, please help Rich straighten out. Knock him flat, like You had to knock me flat. Some of us are denser than others... Please help me forgive Brock. I'm still holding onto anger. I'm still blaming him, deep inside. I keep saying that what happened was as much my fault as everyone else's," Nikki whispered, dropping to her knees in the middle of the floor. She wrapped her arms tight around herself. "But do I really listen to myself? Please help me forgive him. Please help me be a friend to him. Please help me trust him. Lord, I used to love him. Way back at the beginning, I prayed he would be a Christian and stay here in Tabor, and now I've got what I prayed for. And now I can't stay."

She shivered, hearing the bitter laughter trying to break through her voice. The longing in those five words. Did she really want to stay in Tabor?

"Please, Lord, I don't know what's going on in my head anymore. Or my heart."


*Sunday, April 13*


"So, how about going out to dinner with me?" Rich greeted Nikki, when he met her in front of the church that morning.

"Can't." She tamped down another flare of anger. The service was about to start, and she had been standing out here with Aurora, waiting for him, for nearly half an hour.

At least the little girl was too busy chattering at her plush bunny to notice her father's arrival and the tension flaring in the air. She kept putting the toy as big as her head in and out of the Easter basket Doria had put together for her at the last minute. It wouldn't have been nice for Aurora to have nothing to do, no basket to fill, when Brandy and the boys scrambled around, hunting for their Easter baskets and then ran around outside in the dawn chill, hunting for all the plastic eggs Nikki and Dr. Holwood had hidden for them.

"You are always busy. What's wrong with you?" Rich snapped, stomping one foot so hard his battered loafer nearly came off.

"What's wrong with you? It's Easter. I'm spending it with my family. Don't you have plans with your mother?"

"Oh. Yeah." His face twisted as he visibly fought anger and embarrassment. "Hey, Rory, ready to go?" He bent and scooped up the little girl, putting her astride his hip with enough force to knock the basket out of her hands. "For Pete's sake, can't you shut up just once?" he blurted, when the little girl let out a wail and tried to leap from his arms to retrieve her treasures. "I should have left you with your grandmother last night."

"Wasn't your mother out of town?" Nikki said quietly.

"No. Where'd you get—" Rich let Aurora slide down to the ground again. "Oh, yeah. Look, things changed at the last minute. And Rory was so excited about staying with you, so I figured, what would it hurt?"

"Nothing." She swallowed down the shiver of uneasiness that crept up from deep inside. "But considering our past, I think focusing on honesty would be good for both of us."

"Oh, come on, Nikki..." He raked both hands through his hair and turned around once, as if searching for inspiration or help from the parking lot. He nearly tripped over Aurora, on her hands and knees, picking up her scattered treats. "Why do you have to keep picking on me?"

"I'm not. Look," she said, holding up a hand to stop him. Judging from his expression, he was ready to argue long and loudly. "I have to get inside. The service is starting. My folks are holding a seat for me. Bye, Aurora." She hurried to pull the door open and enter the building and get away from Rich and his daughter as quickly as she could. If Aurora even noticed she was gone, Nikki had no idea.

She was able to lose herself in the service, enjoying the special music. Tears came to her eyes when Pastor Glenn called out the traditional greeting, "He is risen," and the congregation called out, "He is risen indeed!" Nikki was able to forget for minutes at a time that she had ever left home. This scene could have been the last Easter service she had spent at home, before she ran away with Brock. She blinked away tears when the longing to be able to turn the clock back and avoid all her bad choices nearly choked her. By the time Pastor Glenn finished his sermon and the praise ensemble broke in with a rousing, acapella version of *Easter Song*, her spirits had risen again. She easily traded greetings with old friends as her family left the sanctuary.

It was good to see Lisa Montgomery walking with her husband, Todd, and wearing a delicate lily corsage. Nikki looked around, half-expecting to see Mr. Montgomery looming in the background, glaring at his unwanted daughter-in-law. But he was nowhere to be seen, reinforcing the report from Max and others that he had indeed left the church because things weren't done his way. She breathed a sigh of relief. Her spirits drooped a little when it occurred to her that if he had been in the church, he would have lectured her that she had no right to be there in church on such a holy morning, tainting it with her sinful presence.

Nikki tried to shake off those thoughts. It was easier than she thought, because Brock was nowhere in sight. She wondered if he was enjoying his morning of serving at the City Mission, helping the homeless people who would attend the service and meal. Maybe the Mission could do something like that next year. If the Arc Foundation provided funding, of course.

"Hey, I was hoping you didn't go yet." Rich startled her, appearing from seemingly nowhere when Nikki reached the parking lot. "You're ticked at me, aren't you?"

"What makes you think that?" Nikki barely managed to keep the sarcastic bite out of her voice. She really did want to know if Rich had any idea of his thoughtless, selfish actions and how he treated other people.

"Look, I can see you might be mad at me. I mean, yeah, I could have left the kid with my mom, since she wasn't going out of town."

"If you weren't out of town with your mother, why did you need to leave Aurora anywhere?"

"I just needed to blow off some steam with the guys, that's all."

"You could have just said so, instead of lying."

"Yeah, well, I figure you might tell me to grow up and think about Rory instead of having a good time with the guys."

"Do you think you need to grow up?"

Rich just frowned and stared at her, visibly confused by her question. The thickness in her throat could have been laughter or an angry shout.

"Where's Aurora right now?"

"With Mom. Thanks for saving my neck, by the way. I was able to find some place that was open and had some flowers. Mom was really pleased."

"I'm glad." Nikki hoped Mrs. Thomas never figured out that the nudge to give her something for Easter had come from her. She didn't want to encourage the woman to think there was something between her and Rich. Then again, Rich had most likely taken credit for Aurora's Easter basket of treats and toys. She suddenly felt very tired.

"So, you think you can get away this afternoon? After you take care of the family stuff," Rich hurried to add, when she opened her mouth to say no.

"That 'family stuff' will take all day. Look, I have to get going. They're waiting for me." She gestured across the parking lot, as if there was a car waiting for her. Actually, when the weather was nice, the Holwoods made it a practice to walk to church. They were all probably halfway home. She would have to hurry to help with Easter dinner. "See you at work tomorrow," she added, and set off across the parking lot.

If Rich said anything, she didn't hear him. Nikki didn't look back. She wove her way among cars to keep him from seeing where she went and that she was on foot when she left the church parking lot.

That did it. She definitely needed to go to Quarry Hall, just to get away. To visit her baby's grave, definitely, but to walk the birch tree ally and sit on one of the bridges that crossed over the ponds and take some time to think.

Nikki knew better than to ask the Holwoods to go with her. Doria had gently nudged her several times to break the habit, the need, to visit Mercy Grace's grave. Nikki thought she had done a great job so far, almost two weeks in Tabor without going back. Besides, it was Easter. She needed to at least stop in at Quarry Hall and say hello to whoever was home.

After lunch, the children happily played with their toys and compared treats they had found in the eggs they gathered. Doria settled down at the computer to download all the pictures she had taken of the fun and the children in their new clothes. Dr. Holwood had a phone call that sounded like it would keep him busy for a while. That left Nikki at loose ends, and she decided now was the best time to go and take some of the potted lilies she had bought yesterday just to decorate the house. But she didn't want to go alone.

For several seconds, she thought of walking up the street to see if Brock was home and invite him. Mercy Grace was his daughter, after all. No, he had gone to the City Mission and probably wasn't home yet. Besides, wouldn't that encourage him, make him think she cared?

"Well, maybe care more than I do. Because I guess I care a little. Enough for him to bother me," she said to Gray as she reached her attic bedroom to change from her dress to jeans, a t-shirt, and sneakers. "Am I going a little crazy, do you think?"

Gray snorted and bobbed his head. She laughed.

"Who should I ask?" Nikki sat down and toed off her moccasins. "Maybe the better question would be, who knows? It'd make Mum happy if I didn't go by myself. Of course, she'd be happier if I didn't go at all. Mum really thinks I should just let go, but I can't. Not all at once."

The question of who knew—who wouldn't ask uncomfortable questions at the worst time—helped narrow down the field. Max would be busy with her family, or on the phone with Tony, working on their latest book. Why they couldn't do that through email, Nikki didn't know. She suspected maybe Max was more attached to Tony, emotionally, than she was aware, and she needed to at least hear his voice while he was out of town doing his writer-in-residence gig.

Nikki couldn't think of anyone in church who knew about all the details of her accident and losing her baby, and who didn't have obligations or family events to keep them busy. Except for maybe Dani

Paul.

"You're a life saver," Dani said, when Nikki called and proposed a drive to Akron. "Tom and Stephanie are over at her folks' place, Andy is over at the Greens' and Kurt was making noises about coming over to jam with Jim and Jason. Aunt Betty and Uncle George left about ten minutes ago to put flowers at the cemetery. Save me!"

Dani drove over to the Holwoods' house in fifteen minutes. Nikki waited in the driveway with the Jeep, and Dani jumped into the front seat. Gray and the lilies were in the back seat. They drove through McDonalds' to get shakes, and they sipped and chatted about Firesong and what Nikki wanted to do next at the Mission, on the drive down to Akron. When they turned down Portage Trail, they both fell silent.

"Whoa," Dani murmured, as Nikki's Jeep pulled up in front of the wide wrought iron gates of Quarry Hall. She sat forward and studied the rolling lawns and the sprawling, gray-gold stone house far in the distance. "This is seriously high class."

"It's... a stretching experience." Nikki reached into the compartment between the seats and pulled out her remote control to open the gates. She wondered if Vincent was in the house today, or if he was out running his mysterious, personal errands. She decided she had been too much out of touch with the residents of Quarry Hall, which made no sense because she was only an hour away.

"Stretching?" she asked, as the gates swung open.

"We have our rooms in the servants' quarters, and we help with the cleaning and cooking. And when Uncle Harrison and Aunt Elizabeth have VIPs come from out of town, we put on our party clothes and help entertain. And act like innocent, elegant, high-class hothouse flowers." Nikki fought not to laugh. "Who are trained in hand-to-hand combat and put our lives on the line to defend the innocent and abused."

"Stretching." Dani shook her head as the Jeep rolled up the long driveway. "We're here for more than just a family visit at Easter, aren't we?"

"You're one of the few people who know about Mercy Grace." Nikki tipped her head toward the potted lilies sitting on the back seat. Gray crouched on the floorboards with his head resting on the seat between the pots. For some reason, the big dog liked the smell of the lilies. He had sat guard over them almost around the clock since Nikki brought them home from the greenhouse, except when he was called away to accompany her.

"How come you're not bringing your folks here?"

"Mum thinks I'm just reacting to Brock showing up, trying to win me back. She says I should let go. My baby's soul is what counts, and that means she's not here." She nodded toward the connected buildings of the stables and the low, sprawling garage, and pulled to the right into the parking area. There were no cars for visitors. The garage doors were down, so Nikki had no way to judge who was home by which cars were there.

"You don't agree with her?"

"I do. It's just not that easy walking away. I've been here for every holiday since the accident, and I've always put flowers on her grave. I can't just stop now. Just because Brock might follow me," she added, her voice softer.

"If he's causing trouble—"

"No, he's not." She managed a smile and put the Jeep into park.

Nikki decided to show Dani the house after the visit to Mercy Grace's grave. She took Dani around the outside, along the perimeter of the half-acre of vegetable garden that was in the process of being planted. They carried the potted lilies in silence, walking along the path that looked over the stair steps of the landscape, going down to the national park lands far below. Gray loped ahead of them, disappearing over a slight rise in the landscape.

The entrance to the willow garden was guarded by two rough-cut granite pillars and surrounded by a tall fence of the same sandstone that comprised the house. The silence wrapped around Nikki, soothing her, startling her with the realization that she had been nervous about bringing Dani here. Gray waited in the shadows, lying beside the brass plate for Mercy Grace's grave. Dani held her pot, waiting until Nikki put hers down.

"Hi, honey," Nikki whispered, kneeling as she put down the second pot. She brushed her fingers over the plate. "Mommy's here."

She was grateful that Dani waited in silence. Somehow, that made it easier to get up from her knees after only a few minutes of thinking and forcing down the choking lump in her throat. Gray pressed against her side as they left the willow garden and she gladly twined her fingers through his thick fur.

When she and Dani made it into the house, after a brief tour of the gardens and grounds, Joan, Anne, Sophie, and Jennifer were waiting in the Great Hall with refreshments. Nikki laughed when she saw the lamb-shaped cake surrounded by green-dyed coconut and jellybeans. It was a joke between her and Joan that Harrison Carter was bound and determined to make up for all the childhood treats and fun that her sister had missed. Again, it struck Nikki that she was grateful their mother had tried to kill her when she was a baby. She had grown up with parents who loved her, while Joan had been dragged around the country with their psychotic, terrorist mother, until she escaped at age fourteen.

The Carters were out of the house for the afternoon, so the girls sprawled in the Great Hall and ignored ***Ben Hur*** on the TV, followed by

*The Ten Commandments*. They chatted and laughed, devouring the lamb cake and jellybeans with big glasses of milk. Nikki didn't even think about Dani feeling uncomfortable until they were already settled in. Her friend seemed to hit it off with everyone, and didn't stare for even a minute at Jennifer, who wore a scarf turban-style over the stubble of her hair. It had been shaved off for surgery to correct injuries sustained in her last mission for the Arc Foundation.

Overall, Nikki was more than pleased with how that afternoon had turned out. She would try to wait three weeks until she came down to visit her daughter's grave again. Then four weeks after that, then five. Until maybe she wouldn't have those nightmares at least once a week, when she heard Mercy Grace crying and couldn't find her daughter, no matter how many doors she opened and halls she ran down.

*Monday, April 14*

Nikki met Bekka's roommates, Kat and Amy, when they showed up to help move Lisa from her apartment over Rick's Bakery to the cottage Todd had rented on Kiln. It was almost comical how the two girls wouldn't talk to Todd, much less look at him. During trips to the cottage, Bekka explained. Amy and Kat were in roller coaster relationships and at the moment were in their "all men are dogs" phase. That could change in a day, depending on whether Amy's regular boyfriend, Joe showed up with flowers or if one of the dozens of boys who wanted to date Kat showed up at their apartment on his knees. Both girls had been heartily in support of Lisa leaving Todd and suing him and his father for emotional battery and false advertising.

"False advertising?" Nikki didn't know if she should laugh.

# Chapter Fifteen

They reached the cottage then, and Bekka waited until she had parked the Jeep and they gathered up their first armloads to carry inside, before she explained. The door was open because Lisa's sister-in-law, Lindsey, had taken the afternoon off work to stand guard and organize what everyone hauled over. The two brothers-in-law were helping Todd haul Lisa's big furniture pieces over, and then haul his furniture back to the apartment.

"They figure that Todd promised one thing and delivered another, when he was dating Lisa and asked her to marry him. The problem is, Lisa broke up with Todd a couple of times over the very problems that are at the root of the troubles they're fixing now." Bekka nodded at the open door. "Kind of like someone buying a bowl with a big crack in it, knowing there's a big crack in it, and then suing the manufacturer when it leaks."

"Love makes us blind—or we want to be blind because we think we're in love," Nikki offered.

"Yeah, well, there are a bunch of things I wish I hadn't seen." She crossed her eyes at Nikki when they reached the door and stepped inside.

Kat and Amy showed up with their carload, along with two more of Lisa's sisters-in-law, by the time Nikki and Bekka got their car unloaded. They stayed to help unpack and generally organize the other two carloads, and by then Todd had showed up with the rental truck and the big furniture. The next trip had the apartment emptied, and when Nikki and Bekka brought the Jeep's load into the cottage, they decided to help set up a picnic dinner in the living room. Nikki kept careful watch and she approved of the smiles Lisa and Todd shared, the tentative touches, and the way he looked after her and hurried to take any load she tried to carry. She also returned the bag of ring binders and galley proofs—and was relieved when Lisa said she wanted to talk about the whole "baby issue" but that it would have to wait until later. She had deadlines to meet, and a house to settle into.

Nikki was pensive on the quiet drive home. She remembered the few short days of dreaming about settling into a little house and decorating the nursery and the idyllic life she wanted to have with Brock. Then he had come back to their hotel from a week-long trip away—which, she learned during the trial, had been to meet with his DEA contacts and pass on the first batch of information—and her dreams had been shredded by his reaction. He hadn't told her right away to abort, but it was clear he didn't want their baby. He never accused her of deliberately getting pregnant, but he did blame her for being careless with the over-the-counter contraceptives she used.

Looking back, Nikki wondered if Brock had deliberately picked fights with her to drive her away. He couldn't be honest with her about the work he was doing, either the drug dealing work for Ringo or the information gathering he was now doing for the DEA. He couldn't pack her up and send her home to Tabor without making Ringo suspicious. Especially if Nikki put up a fight about going home.

"He had to drive me away," she whispered as she pulled up in front of her parents' home. Nikki blinked hard against tears she had promised herself she would never cry again. Tears for Brock Pierson and the relationship they had once shared. She sat there in her Jeep until the ache in her chest faded and the tears dried, leaving her eyes feeling hot and scratchy.

*Tuesday, April 15*

Tuesday afternoon, Nikki was surprised to see Todd James and Mike Nichols, in uniform, saunter into the lobby of the Mission. She sat in the office with Claire, sipping iced tea and proofing the newsletter that went out to the volunteers and people who donated regularly to the Mission. The two policemen saw her and gestured for her to come outside. A tiny shiver of apprehension went down her back as she hurried to get up from behind Claire's desk in the office and go out to meet them.

"Got a problem. The Chief sent us over personally to check with you," Mike said as the three of them stepped out the door. They stayed in the shade of the big entryway of the former school.

"The Chief?" she echoed.

"Got some complaint about a guy who's hanging around the Mission, harassing people and spying on you," Todd said, taking up the conversation. "Said you were in some kind of danger from this guy. Considering the source, we figured ... well, we weren't too worried until we checked into the guy and found out he's a convict."

"Brock." That shiver sank into her gut and turned into a knot. Who would make a complaint against Brock, and how had they found out about his past so quickly?

She wished she hadn't let him join her, when she took Gray for a walk around Poe Lake at lunchtime. The day was so bright and warm, the air smelled so good, and her thoughts from last night were still uppermost in her mind. When Brock caught up with her, carrying a paper sack of what was obviously his lunch, and he smiled as if seeing her was the highlight of his day, how could she refuse? They had talked about the chaos of the newspaper staff as they settled into their new office and the friends he was making. He had mentioned Pastor Glenn was giving him a project to do for the church, but he hadn't gotten the call yet. She was genuinely pleased that he was getting involved in the church and had come back to the Mission in a good mood that Rich Thomas's sulks couldn't dampen.

"Brock was released on good behavior," she hurried to say, feeling slightly irritated that she had to defend him to her adopted uncles. She wondered if Rich had seen her walking with Brock and had filed the complaint against him. She wouldn't have been surprised. "He worked with the DEA and helped clean up a drug ring, and he's a Christian now." She shook her head, slightly dizzy from all the thoughts and suspicions and regrets swirling through her head. "Uncle Todd, what's going on?"

"So you know the guy?" Mike said. "Nikki, honey —"

"He's straightening out his life."

"What's he doing here, stalking you?" Todd asked.

"He's not stalking me!" Nikki caught a glimpse of movement around the corner of the doorway. Gray growled and headed for the door that was propped open to let in the fresh air, but she leaped and caught him by his collar, stopping him. "Brock got a job at the *Picayune* and he's renting from Mandy Gordon."

"On your street."

"Mrs. Gordon has been helping released prisoners for years. Where else is he supposed to go? He's following the rules."

"You're defending him pretty strongly, for being terrified of him," Mike observed, his concern wrinkles softening.

"Who lodged the complaint?" Not that she really needed to ask.

"Not allowed to say."

"I can guess." She sighed and dropped to her knees to get a stronger hold on Gray. The big dog wasn't trying to get away from her, but Nikki needed to hold him.

Besides, it was clear that he disliked Rich and the feeling was mutual. Gray wouldn't bite him, but she wouldn't mind seeing her big bodyguard knock him to the floor, sit on his chest and maybe terrify some manners into him. That afternoon when she thought Rich tried to trip Brock with the mop handle flashed into her mind. What kind of damage could he do to Gray with that mop handle? She didn't want to find out.

"Whoever lodged it is worried he's trying to make trouble for the Mission because you're here. Said this Brock guy stops by almost every day, looking in windows, walking up and down the halls, poking his nose into everything, asking all sorts of questions," Mike admitted.

"You could say the same about me," she sputtered.

"So you don't mind if the guy is here?" Todd asked.

"What are you going to do? Run him out of town? Yes, I mind ... but not as much as I did when he first got here." A tiny smile surprised her as it curved her lips. "He's trying to prove he's changed. He feels like he owes me... Could you just record that I'm not worried, and I know he's no threat to anyone else? For heaven's sake, I walked around the lake at lunchtime with the guy."

"Yeah, we know. Saw you. Good thing you had a chaperon." Mike winked, and Nikki was horrified to feel the heat of a blush wash across her face.

The blush returned when she came back into the office later that afternoon, just before closing time for the daycare, and found Brock standing behind Claire at her desk, studying the computer screen from over her shoulder. For a moment, Nikki just stood there in the doorway. Her face felt so hot she thought the temperature of the office could go up five degrees.

"Hi," she finally said, startling them both. Brock stepped back from Claire, putting more than arm's length between them. "What are you doing here?"

"Pastor Glenn sent him over to help us clear up this mess with the accounting program," Claire said. "Isn't that great?"

Brock went very still, watching Nikki. Did he wait for her to denounce him?

"Pastor Glenn sent you?" Nikki swallowed, forced herself to relax. She trusted her pastor's instincts; or was it his sensitivity? "This is the project you mentioned you were waiting to hear about?"

"I told him I wanted to get involved and help out and use my talents and..." Brock spread his arms, indicating the entire Mission. "Here I am."

"Great. How are things going at the *Picayune*?"

"Getting there. Claire's explaining the computer program —"

"Trying to explain," the woman broke in, laughing. "We were so glad to have this program donated, we should have known something was fishy. It's a beta test of a program that isn't even out on the market yet — that's why we got it free. This thing is never going to sell if it works this badly and the manual is so hard to untangle."

"I haven't really investigated that far," Brock added with that deprecating little smile and a glint in his eyes that meant he was interested in the challenge. "I have this feeling, though, that we'll have to start from scratch. Maybe go back to paper records, and if we try computer programs again, get a different program."

"Can I have a witness?" Claire chirped.

"Uh, Claire... I think Nikki needs to see me about something." He stepped around the desk and headed for the door. "Be back in a minute."

"Okay. The problem will still be here when you get back."

Nikki followed Brock around the corner, down the hall toward the gym. It was quiet and dark now. Not even echoes of splashing water or thuds of a mop handle on a metal bucket. That was strangely comforting.

"I'm sorry," Brock said. "I had no idea Pastor Glenn was planning on sending me here."

"It's okay." She grinned at his surprise. Truth to tell, she was just as surprised at how calmly she seemed to be taking this. Maybe because of last night's revelation, and the prayer she had prayed Saturday night, turning over to God everything concerning Brock and her past pain. Nikki had no idea how long the peace and confidence was going to last, but she was going to take advantage of it.

"I'm not spying on you. I swear." He tried to smile. "Though I have to admit, I kind of like the idea of working where you are. Being a team again. But in a good way," he hurried to add.

"We're never going to be able to put all those memories behind us, so why should we try?" Nikki frowned as his words resurrected her shock from earlier that day. "Brock, someone lodged a complaint against you with the police, claiming you were harassing me."

"Oh." He took a step backward, nearly tripping over Gray, who had settled down a little distance from them. "Sorry, buddy. Who?"

"I can guess, but the thing is, I told them I didn't consider you a threat, to me or the Mission or anyone. But now the police in town know about you, and that complaint is on the record, even if I said it was false."

"Well, it was bound to happen eventually." He managed a shrug. "Thanks for sticking up for me."

"It was the truth. You don't need the hassle."

"Thanks, anyway. Can I—" He chuckled. "Can I take you to dinner tonight, to thank you? Before my Bible study, anyway."

"Brock... " The hopeful, puppy-dog look in his eyes made her laugh, just a little.

"I like doing nice things for you. You'll always be my lady," he added on a whisper.

"We can't go back to the way things were."

"I don't want to. What we did was wrong, even if so much of it felt right. I know that now. I know how much I hurt you, even when I thought I was taking care of you. But if we made something new and better... well..." He shrugged again. "You can't blame a guy for hoping, can you?"

"Yes." Nikki grinned when he took another step backward, stunned by her agreement. "I mean, yes about tonight."

"Great. Where?"

"I have no idea. Where do you want to go?"

"There's a coffee shop on Main. The sandwiches are good, and we'll get served fast."

Nikki almost said no, but that was silly, she knew. Why should she refuse just because she had gone to the Perk-and-Perch with Rich?

They had a nice time, to her surprise and gratification. By the time she walked home with Gray, Brock had driven to his boarding house and changed his clothes and walked to meet her, then they walked to the coffee shop. They continued their conversation from lunchtime, talking about the town and his job and the friends he was making who were friends of hers. They talked about the Mission. She told him about some of her friends, her new adopted family at Quarry Hall. They never mentioned Ringo or his henchmen. She considered, just for a moment, adding the few details Sophie had found out and passed on to her, but she had already warned him about Angelo and Marcus having fallen off the grid. There wasn't much to add. Besides, if the danger was more than a suspicion, Nikki reasoned that Brock would already have been warned by his contacts at the DEA who had an obligation to look after him.

They never mentioned the trial or his prison term or their lost child. Brock walked her home by 6:30, and then hurried down the street to the church for his Bible study group. He never touched her, not her arm or hand, and certainly never tried to kiss her.

She dreamed about Mercy Grace that night, and it was a dream full of sunshine and laughter, playing with her little girl in a green meadow scattered with wildflowers that seemed to stretch on forever.

*Thursday, April 17*

"Hey, pal." The rich, quiet voice sent a chill up Brock's back. He paused with one foot on the bottom step of the fire escape leading up to his floor at the boarding house.

The man stepped from the shadows of the poplars. Sharp cheekbones, wide-set, deep, dark eyes, skin the color of molasses, shaven scalp. Brock could hear Mandy's TV set in the house next door. If he shouted, she would probably call the police. The station was just a few blocks away.

"He doesn't recognize us," Angelo said, and his smile bared his teeth. The faint lilt in his voice brought back memories, rattling through Brock's mind.

Then a thickset man in faded jeans, baggy blue work shirt and greasy, iron-gray hair stepped out of the bushes. His face was flattened, like it had been hit with a shovel. Brock fought a shudder that was part nausea and part chill from the memories that face evoked.

"Angelo. Marcus. I really never thought I'd see either of you again."

He thought about the note Nikki had left for him, and how his contact at the DEA had laughed and told him he had nothing to worry about. The authorities believed Ringo's two henchmen had been killed in the smoldering battle over his territory, rather than falling off the grid.

Obviously, the Arc Foundation's connections and sources were right and the DEA was wrong. Brock wished he had been brave enough to bring up the concern in Bible study, to ask his new friends to pray about it.

"You hoped." Angelo rested a hand on the fire escape rail. "Been watching you a few days now, brains. You got a nice set-up here. Your finger on the pulse of the town, so to speak. Newspaper and the rescue mission. Sweet. What's the scam? How much did you take so far? Enough to share with your old friends?"

This was worse than the deepest, darkest fever dreams Brock had in the prison hospital, after Ringo had been captured. He had thought he would be free from reprisal when his former employer died. Brock had hoped without Ringo to give orders and do their thinking for them, Angelo and Marcus would fade from his life. He was wrong. The slim Jamaican and his ever-silent partner were out to survive, and they probably blamed him for their troubles.

"There's nothing to take." Brock took a deep breath and fought the urge to run up the stairs. They could and would follow. Even if he locked his door, they would batter it down—and batter him. Besides, how could he explain to Mandy the damage to her door without endangering her? The fewer people who knew Angelo and Marcus were around, the safer the whole town would be.

He had to make sure they didn't know Nikki was here. They blamed her for Ringo's downfall, even after they found out about Brock's deal with the DEA. Brock hoped Gray was as deadly a bodyguard as he looked.

"You were never my friends," he continued. "The police know about my past. So does my boss. Even if I wanted to run a scam, I couldn't. And I don't."

"Wrong answer," Angelo purred. He glanced at Marcus, who bared broken teeth in a grin that made Brock twitch. "Better figure out something. We know where your lady lives. That's how we knew to come look for you here. Knew the babe would run home someday."

"You'll never get near Nikki." Brock fought nausea at that slim hope dashed. He flashed on a vision of Gray shot dead and Nikki kidnapped again. She was starting to relax around him and forgive him now—would she ever forgive him if anything happened to her dog?

"Don't have to. Lots of folks to get to around her. Lots of your friends. You're one friendly guy, aren't you? Don't bother telling anybody, because you know what'll happen. Especially if you go to the police."

"No, I don't know." He contemplated lunging at them. The fuss of shooting him would bring people, who might then be in danger. But if he died, Nikki would be safe. They would have no reason to hurt her to control or punish him.

"Don't make us show you." Angelo frowned as a car pulled up in front of the house. In seconds, he and Marcus vanished into the afternoon shadows and bushes behind the house.

"Brock!" Joel Randolph waved as he stepped through the screen of poplars around the fire escape. "Good timing. I was hoping I'd catch you before you headed over to the Rec Center. I didn't manage to catch you at work. Our Bible study's been moved to Common Grounds."

"Thanks." Brock forced a smile. "Let me run upstairs and get my stuff and I'll be right down." He thumped up the fire escape stairs and wondered if he should just leave town, no word to anyone. That wouldn't do his record any good. He'd destroy his chances with Nikki, just when he was finally earning smiles from her. Besides, where could he go that Angelo and Marcus wouldn't eventually find him?

If he did lose them, who would stop them from returning to Tabor and hurting Nikki and her family to punish him?

He took a moment to make a call to his contact at the DEA and report that Angelo and Marcus had made contact. It irritated him more than he liked when he had to leave a message. When he was working with them to take down Ringo, they called him at all hours of the day and night, enough to be irritating and dangerous if the wrong person overheard or saw the numbers on his cell phone. Why weren't they constantly available now?

# Chapter Sixteen

Brock suspected the authorities considered him used up and worthless, with nothing more to give them. Other than the vague hope that they might need him to testify against anyone who survived the territory wars. The only ones he could rely on now were his new friends and God. He could pray, but did he have the right to put such worries on their shoulders?

He made a vague request for prayers about his past at the Bible study and wished he could confide in someone. Maybe Xander, their host? He was a lawyer, after all.

Brock put the possibility aside for later. He would wait to see if his contact at the DEA had anything for him, and he would share the information with his parole officer as well. It was always good to put things on record, just in case something went wrong and he needed proof that he wasn't part of the problem. This time, at least.

*Sunday, April 20th*

Nikki heard about the Randolphs' accident when she arrived at the church that morning. Her first impulse was to leave immediately and head down Sackley to the hospital, to sit with Max, Joe and Jeremy and offer whatever help they needed. Then she looked around the church gym, where nearly everyone stopped to get a cup of coffee, tea, or juice and a cookie between services and class sessions. It stuck her instantly that everyone within earshot was talking about the Randolphs, how their three children would manage, but nobody was doing anything. She had grown up in this church, and she knew most of the people were willing to step in and help, but they needed someone to take that leadership role or offer options of what to do.

She herded Danny and Davie to their Sunday school room and detoured to the church office to find out what was being done. Rita was at the front desk, and Nikki proposed her half-assembled idea. Ten minutes later, she stood at the central printer, waiting for the printouts of the sign-up sheets Rita had modified from the standard template.

"You have a good heart, Nikki," Rita said, stopping her for a brief hug before she ran back to the gym. "A servant's heart."

"Somebody else would have thought of it." Her face felt hot enough to melt her lipstick.

"You thought of it first." She winked and handed her a canister full of pencils to go with the sign-up sheets.

Nikki stayed in the gym, overseeing the sign-up sheets and explaining what she had gotten straight from Rita, to keep the stories about the Randolphs' situation from being too twisted out of shape. By the time the gym cleared out and everyone was either in the third service or in classes, she had filled up six sheets with volunteers to help run errands for the Randolphs or bring meals—more than two-thirds of the sign-ups were for that—or help with the upcoming production at Homespun Theater. Most of the people who volunteered there were Joel Randolph's students at Butler-Williams University, but that only made sense. She laughed when Pastor Glenn hurried in and put his name on the tech crew list. It was a common joke around the church that the senior minister preferred emulating Christ by being a carpenter.

She didn't stay for the third service, but ran home, changed her clothes, and got in her car to take the news to Max and her brothers at the hospital.

Seeing Brock standing in the hospital hallway with Dr. Morgan and Pastor Wally, looking serious and concerned, put a heavy, painful lump in her chest. She halted for a few seconds, unsure what she felt. Angry, considering him an intruder? Or grateful? What was he doing there, anyway?

"I'm in the Bible study Joel runs," Brock explained, when Nikki joined them, and before she could even ask. "I don't know the rest of his family at all, but... whatever needs doing..." He shrugged and blinked rapidly a few times.

It startled her to realize he hurt for Joel and his family. Nikki recognized some of that sharp, hot sensation in her gut was jealousy, maybe even fear. Brock had made a place for himself here in Tabor Heights, her home, her town, among her friends.

"I suggested that he help Jeremy and Max with the theater books, since he's so good at accounting," Dr. Morgan offered with a weak attempt at a smile.

"No. Keep me away from other people's money right now," he blurted. Real fear flickered in his eyes as he looked at Nikki, then down the hallway.

"Want to help me with organizing volunteers?" she offered before she quite realized the words were in her mouth. She waved the sign-up sheets and then explained what she had done, with Rita and Pastor Glenn's blessing.

"If that doesn't make Max start bawling, nothing will," Dr. Morgan said. He tipped his head toward a doorway. "Go on in. The crowd has gone down for right now. It's a good time to coordinate with her."

Nikki busied herself checking with Max what needed doing at the theater and print shop and around the house. Dani showed up a short time later, offering her organization skills.

Brock followed her when Nikki went looking for the hospital cafeteria, to get something for Max and her brothers to eat. He didn't say anything and she wasn't sure what to say. She realized they were both concentrating so hard on each other that they got lost after only three turns of the hallways, and ended up in what must have been the backside of the emergency room.

"Wait." Brock caught hold of Nikki's arm when she started to turn and go back the way they had come. He pointed at a cluster of men at the other end of the hall.

The sound of raised voices finally penetrated her swirling thoughts and all the mental lists she had been compiling. Most of those people wore uniforms. The gray of highway patrol, the dark blue with the light blue patch of the Tabor Heights police, another municipality's brown uniform, and a man wearing a light green jacket that advertised a construction company.

"You're trying to pin all this on me, and it ain't fair!" a man shouted, his voice tending toward a harsh shriek. He staggered out of an examination room and was visible just long enough for Nikki to see a bandage on his hand and the side of his face, before one of the highway patrol officers caught him by the shoulders and guided him back into the examination room. "It ain't my fault! You got no right firing me."

"Maybe you shouldn't be here," Brock said, his voice raised to drown out the cursing that followed. He turned to put himself between Nikki and the conflict that still churned despite the visible efforts to quiet the man.

She nodded and let him turn her around. The tactic was far too familiar. When they were on the road together, he had sent her out of restaurants or nightclubs or other situations that were just startling to prickle with uneasiness. Only later did she realize that Brock had an uncanny talent for sensing when profanity or violence or both were about to break out. He always sent her away before she witnessed anything unpleasant. Or dangerous.

Nikki made two turns before she realized Brock wasn't there. She backtracked to the same spot in the hall, just in time to see the knot of officers dispersing. There were no more shouts. She hoped the foul-mouthed man had been given a sedative with a big, long needle. That thought vanished when she saw the somber expression on Brock's face, worry crinkling his forehead and around his eyes and mouth.

"You need to warn Max," he said, and caught her arm to guide her back the way they had come.

"Why?" Nikki didn't tug her arm loose, although later she supposed she should have, just on principle.

"That's the truck driver who hit Joel and his wife." Brock sighed and slowed his steps. "He's blaming them for the accident and for getting fired from his job. His drinking and driving a company truck without permission, running a red light and going way over the speed limit had nothing to do with it, of course."

"What does that matter? Nobody believes him."

"I've run into his kind way too often. In legal and illegal situations," he added. "His kind makes preemptive strikes. The more in the wrong he is, the nastier and louder he gets. The sad thing is, he's a union man, and because he got fired as a result of the accident, the union will get involved. They have to. They'll stand behind him even if all the evidence puts the blame squarely on him."

"But he'll lose in the end, won't he?"

"Yeah, but until he loses, things are going to be pretty rotten for Joel and his family." Brock stopped them, back in the hall of the waiting room that had been given over to Max and her brothers. He exhaled loudly and looked as if the weight of the world rested on his shoulders. Something ached and melted inside her, seeing how Brock cared about the Randolph family. "I don't know—the Arc Foundation sure seems to have the connections. Do you know any lawyers who can jump in and try to head the guy off before he can follow through on all his threats?"

"What kind of threats?" Her mind raced and she reached into her pocket for her cell phone.

"Somebody told him Joel runs a theater, so he's ranting about rich people and artists running around, ruining people's lives. He's going to try to take everything Joel has built up since he got to Tabor. And it'll probably take everything Joel's got just to defend himself, whether the slime-dog wins or loses."

"Not if I have anything to do with it. Arc has a fantastic lawyer, right here in town." Nikki flipped open her cell phone, then looked around. "I suppose we can't make cell calls in here."

"This way. You're talking about Xander, right? Should have thought about him in the first place." Brock pointed down the hallway opposite the way they had gone before.

She could have laughed at how easily they had gotten lost, right from the start, but Nikki was too busy framing what she would say. She let him lead her outside and was grateful that he stood with her while she placed her calls, leaving messages at Common Grounds' Tabor Heights office, then on Xander's personal cell phone, then the general message center at Quarry Hall, then on Joan's cell phone. There was no reason to wait until the problem actually materialized before they called in the heavy artillery, after all — prayer as well as legal help.

~~~~~

*Okay, God, I understand now why I wasn't able to wrap things up and get out of here right away like I thought I should.* Brock walked down the long hallway of the hospital, which had become as familiar to him in the last ten hours as his rooms at Mandy Gordon's house. *Whatever I can do to help Joel and his family, I'll do. Just don't let my staying in town put more people in danger, okay?* He made a mental note to call Paul Hunter when he got home and ask him to send the word around their prayer chain, so people around the country would be praying for Joel and Emily.

"Pierson?" a man said, stepping out of the shadows of the parking lot, as Brock exited the hospital.

It had been dark when he got the news about the Randolphs' accident and he came to see what he could to do help, and it was dark now. He wondered if there was something symbolic in that, or if he was just tired enough to be loopy.

"That's me. What can I—" Brock hated the cold jolt of fear that shot through him when the light hit the man, revealing a Tabor Heights police uniform. Another man in uniform stepped into the light from the other side of the door.

For half a second, he considered confiding in them about Angelo and Marcus catching up with him. But why would the police believe him? Especially if they knew who he was.

"We heard what you did today," the second officer said. He rested his hands on his hips, in that stance that must have been taught in the police academy, emphasizing the gun on one hip, the nightstick on the other, and somehow made the handcuffs clipped behind it glisten in the reflected light.

"Uh... what did I do, exactly?" He supposed Angelo had done something, robbed someone, and left evidence to pin the guilt on Brock. It would be enough to get him in trouble, and if Brock didn't cooperate, the trouble would escalate.

"We're talking about you and Nikki heading that truck driver off at the pass." A hint of a smile touched the first officer's mouth.

"Oh. That." He managed a grin. "That was purely by accident. We didn't even realize he was trying to slide out of here until the security guard caught up with him."

After Nikki finished her phone calls — and Brock had been impressed by how business-like she was, how smoothly she handled what had to be an upsetting situation — they went back inside and nearly ran head-on into the truck driver scurrying down the same hallway to the doors. Nikki had stepped away from Brock, effectively blocking the hallway, and asked him
~~~~~

to stop and talk about the accident.

The man had reared back like a rattler preparing to strike and his face wrinkled with fury mixed with fear. Brock reached out, preparing to stop him from lashing out at Nikki, but the fear took over the man's face. He went pale and took a step back, staring at her. Brock turned, but whatever the man had seen on her face, it was gone now. Then a hospital security guard showed up.

It turned out the truck driver had been refusing to answer questions about the accident. He had tried to avoid breath and blood tests to document the changes in his blood alcohol level—which, as far as Brock was concerned, was proof enough the man knew he was legally drunk and to blame for everything. Now, he had added fleeing to the charges of obstructing an official investigation. The truck driver had started spitting and swearing as the security guard led him back into the hospital to face the officials.

"Yeah, well, you were in the right place at the right time." The first officer paused and narrowed his eyes at Brock. "This time, at least."

"Look, officer, I don't—"

"I'm Nikki's Uncle Mike, and this is her Uncle Todd. Did she ever mention us?"

"Yeah." Brock wondered if he should just go to his knees and plead for mercy. Nikki had most definitely talked about the police officers who pulled her out of the sinking car when she was an infant. "Look, the bottom line is, I love Nikki, and I would never do anything to hurt her."

"Why should we believe you?" Todd James said softly.

"You don't have any reason to." He wished he was close enough to the wall to lean back against it, maybe slide to the ground. Brock felt like he had spent five days without sleep. He suddenly ached all over, physically as well as emotionally. "But I'm a Christian now, and the law says I've paid my debt. I'm here to make a new life, to try to make up to Nikki for what happened... and prove I really do love her. The right way. And I came here today for Joel Randolph, because he's my friend."

"Yeah, that's what we heard from some other guys in the Bible study. Pastor Wally thinks you're an okay guy," Mike added, nodding. Some of the sternness around his mouth and eyes relaxed.

"The thing is, a guy with your past..." Todd shook his head. He actually looked like he regretted what he was saying, just a little bit. "Sometimes you can't shake it off, no matter what you do. Get me?"

"Way too much," Brock whispered. "If I thought my past was catching up with me, that it threatened Nikki, or anybody else here, I'd take off. You have to believe me."

"No, we don't." Mike shook his head. "But we'll give you a chance to make us believers. Just don't hurt our little girl again, whatever you do."

"Believe me, I took a bullet for Nikki once, and I'd do it again."

"Let's hope it doesn't come to that."


*Monday, April 21*

"I think you need to talk with Brock," Pastor Wally said as the early morning staff meeting wrapped up. He had been gone all day Friday and Saturday at a conference in Mansfield and spent most of this meeting reporting on things he had learned from churches with similar outreach efforts as the Mission. "He's having problems with his past." He gestured for Nikki to follow him to his office.

"Problems with his past?" Nikki echoed. Her thoughts churned through the implications as she followed him down the hall and into his office and sat down. There were so many possibilities, she drew a blank and shook her head at the elderly minister from across his scarred, cluttered desk. "What kind of problems?"

"That's as far as he'd go at our Bible study Thursday night. He asked for prayer and said there were some problems from his past catching up with him. He did say something about being afraid those problems would endanger others." The big man crossed his arms on his desk and leaned forward. "You know him better than anyone. I think this is something you should talk to him about, get him to open up. He hasn't been here that long, but I know a lot of people who would willingly help if they could."

"I know. Brock can be a great guy," she murmured. Had Angelo and Marcus showed up? Or was the DEA giving him a hard time because he wouldn't go into the Witness Protection program when they told him to?

"Talk to him? I know it's asking a lot, but it seems to me, you two are getting along much better."

"We are." It didn't bother her to admit that.

"Enough to worry Eleanor Thomas," he said with a chuckle.

"What?" That bit of news startled a chuckle from her.

"She seems to think you and Rich are picking up where you left off and heading toward the altar." Pastor Wally said it in all seriousness, but Nikki wanted to accuse him of teasing her. She prayed he was teasing her.

"I had coffee with Rich one night. I've done nothing to encourage him or his mother. I see Aurora more than Rich."

"I know. Eleanor's so happy you've practically adopted her granddaughter."

"That's going a little too far."

"You baby sit her at least twice a week, and you're always talking with Rich here. Though it looks to me like he's chasing you."

"He's too lazy to chase anyone." Nikki sighed. "Pastor Wally, you sure seem to know more about my life than I do."

"You get to be my age, you learn to save energy. I do a lot more listening and watching and thinking than I used to."

That was true. Nikki had noticed how everyone made an effort, at the Mission and at church, to save Pastor Wally as much effort as possible. He got out of breath simply walking down the hall. His bulk worked against him now, and that made her more sad than she liked to contemplate.

When she dropped by Homespun Theater later that morning to bring more food donations to the house, Nikki noticed several cars parked along the street with rental stickers or out-of-state licenses. She didn't think anything about it until she pulled into the private parking lot behind the house and two of them followed her. Gray leaped out of the Jeep as soon as she opened the door to get the cardboard box of casseroles and containers. While she pulled the house key Max had given her from her pocket, the big dog darted down the gravel drive, his fur ruffled and making him look even larger than usual, and effectively stopped the cars. By the time Nikki walked to the back door, six strangers stood at the end of the flagstone walkway between the scene shop and the house, stopped by Gray and watching her. She opened her mouth to ask what they wanted when one raised a camera. Then she knew.

"Look, I'm a friend of the family and I'm not going to tell you anything for your gossip rags, so you better leave before I call the police and report you for trespassing." She set the box down on the white plastic table on the porch and pointed at the big sign designating the back parking lot as private and forbidding trespassers.

"Who are you?" a sharp-featured woman called, holding out a micro-recorder.

# Chapter Seventeen

"I'm the niece of two police officers, with a lawyer in my back pocket, and friends who work for the FBI and CIA. Don't mess with me—and don't take any pictures, either," she added, raising a hand to block the shot of the one with the camera as he brought it up to his face.

Gray growled, low and hard enough to bounce off the siding of the building. He took one step closer to the paparazzi and reporters, and his growl went up several notches in volume. Nikki thought the gravel would start rattling and bouncing in the driveway in another minute. In a ragged clump, the intruders turned and fled. Nikki stood on the porch, waiting, until the footsteps faded and Gray finally turned away from his guard post and joined her.

"Oh, good monster," she whispered, and bent to wrap her arms around him and give him a brisk rub in appreciation. "Now what are we going to do about those nosey jerks hounding Max and her family, huh?"

She put the food away in the downstairs freezer, left a note for Max to tell her what new dishes had been added to the donations, locked up the house and left, all the while thinking about the problem. Two of the cars tried to follow her, but she lost them in late morning traffic and the one-way streets of Tabor Heights. Just to be safe, Nikki took the long way around before returning to the Mission. She certainly didn't need to lead the nosey media back there.

She called Joan to discuss the problem, which resulted in her sister calling Jenni Doran, a traveling reporter for *America's Voice*, a positive-focus, conservative magazine. Joan had made friends with Jenni a year or two ago, and promised Nikki that if anyone could think of a way to defuse the paparazzi situation for the Randolph family, it would be Jenni.

That afternoon, Jenni showed up at the Mission and explained that she had been sent to Tabor by her editor as soon as the news broke that Emily Keeler-Randolph, former Hollywood starlet, had been discovered living in Tabor Heights. She smirked when she said she "just happened" to be close enough to be the logical choice for the assignment. Nikki laughed with her, understanding the unspoken meaning—Jenni had learned that when it came to the Arc Foundation and its friends, there was no such thing as coincidence.

It wasn't a coincidence, either, when Nikki took Jenni over to the hospital to find Max and propose the plan she and Joan had come up with to protect the Randolph family, and she saw her friend stepping outside. It was the same doorway Nikki had gone to the day before to make the calls to stop the angry truck driver in his tracks. Max pulled out a cell phone and leaned back against the wall. She looked tired. Nikki called her name.

"Hey, Nikki." Max looked around. "Where's the bear?"

A muffled growling snort showed where Gray had come around Max from behind her. She looked over her shoulder and froze, staring into the big dog's eyes.

"She claims that means he likes you," Jenni said, sauntering around the corner of the building. She traded a grin with Nikki. "Personally, I don't buy it."

"Max, this is Jenni Doran. She's a reporter for *America's Voice*. She's here to help," Nikki hurried to say, when Max's eyes widened and a look that was clearly disappointment and maybe fear wiped away the weariness in her expression.

"The only way to defeat the Evil Empire is to steal their thunder," Jenni said, with a diffident shrug. She tucked a long strand of her straight, platinum hair behind her ear. "Nikki told her sister how the media is coming in like sharks in a feeding frenzy. Joan asked me to come and play spin doctor. You know how royally pissed some of those gossip rags will be, if you're giving exclusive stories to a goody-two-shoes publication like mine?"

Max only hesitated for a few heartbeats, then she mirrored Jenni's wide grin. "You're hired."

Nikki headed back to the Mission, feeling close to smug over the wrench she had helped to throw into the plans of the paparazzi. Hollywood and the media had ignored Emily Keeler-Randolph all these years, since she gave up her movie career. They had no right to gather around and write wild stories and intrude into her family's life during this time of crisis. Emily hadn't awakened yet from her coma. The last thing she needed was to wake up to find out all sorts of wild speculations and completely false stories were being written about her in supermarket tabloids and glossy entertainment magazines.

"We did good today, didn't we?" she murmured to Gray as she parked at the Mission and climbed out of the Jeep. "If only we could solve all our problems that easily," slipped out of her lips before she really thought about her words or even realized what she was thinking.

Her cheerful mood darkened and she nearly staggered with the sudden wave of exhaustion that swept over her. Brock returned to her thoughts, and the conversation she had with Pastor Wally that morning. What was she going to do about Brock? How much could she or should she do, how much concern should she feel or show, without giving him the wrong idea? And while she was on the subject of wrong ideas, what was she going to do about Rich and his mother and their expectations that she would settle down with Rich and be a mother to Aurora?

Nikki went over that conversation and those concerns several times as she finished up her day's work at the Mission. She couldn't do anything about Rich Thomas or his mother. He was impossible to avoid, and she had certainly tried, short of setting Gray on him every time he came around. Mrs. Thomas had her own version of reality and nothing could talk her out of it. If she thought Nikki was going to eventually marry her darling son, nothing short of Nikki's marriage to someone else could dissuade her.

Other than pestering her and wasting her time, what had Rich done in the last three weeks to show his interest? Nothing Nikki could think of. His hostility to Brock could be attributed to jealousy, but she doubted it. She had done nothing to encourage him. If anything, the time she spent with Brock should have discouraged him.

She certainly couldn't tell him to give up — that would challenge Rich to get more aggressive in pursuing her. He would probably be delighted she had noticed.

That still didn't solve the problem of Brock. What could be troubling him? Had he been wrong, and someone who had taken over Ringo's position and power was actually out to destroy him? She placed a call to Quarry Hall, then flipped her cell phone closed before the connection was made. This was a question she needed to think over and get in writing and send by encrypted e-mail, just in case someone was watching or listening. Brock had to have enemies on both sides of the law, because of his association with Ringo and what he had done to help bring down his former employer. If a mayor in a town like Tabor could turn crooked and threaten innocent children to silence their parents, as had happened while she was in high school, anything could happen. She had seen first-hand what kind of technology was available to spy on people and steal their financial security and identities, and what an illusion privacy really was. Just because they were supposed to be on the right side of the law didn't mean some authorities and agencies would hesitate to hurt innocent people in their pursuit of justice. Even if it meant throwing Brock to the wolves when they brought down the alleged "bad guys." Nobody wore black and white hats anymore, to identify what side they were on.

Before she went to bed, Nikki checked her e-mail for an answer to her query. Sophie confirmed Ringo Esteverde had been murdered in prison, a deliberate hit rather than an accident as a result of a fight. A few contacts in the DEA confirmed the fighting over his territory had settled and no one who mattered in the conflict seemed to care about Brock Pierson, who had only been his accountant, financial consultant, and go-between. Brock simply didn't have enough current or useful knowledge to be a worthwhile tool or a threat. Sophie's contacts also confirmed that Brock's conversion was real enough to get a reaction from fellow inmates and the probation review board. Some applauded the change in him, and others mocked. She confirmed Brock's involvement and requests for help from Open Doors Ministries. Everything was just as he had told Nikki.

However, Sophie added at the bottom of her report, a lot of records hadn't been accessed yet. She promised to have more in the morning.

Nikki imagined the elfin black woman staying up all night, surrounded by her beloved computers, manipulating four at a time, and dozing in her wheelchair while waiting for her search engines to come up with something. She could well believe Sophie would get all the available information by morning, just on willpower alone.

All that was left for Nikki to do was say her prayers and go to bed. She felt a little irritation at Brock that he hadn't come to her with his problem. Wouldn't some problem from his past involve her, too? Didn't he know she'd willingly help him? Or was he ashamed to admit his need and ask for help?

Maybe she had done too good a job discouraging him in his quest to win her back. That thought made her heart skip a few beats, painfully, and put a thickness in her throat and pressure at the back of her eyes, like she might cry.

### Tuesday, April 22

The next morning, Nikki took one look at the files and photos Sophie had dug up and sent her in the night, and had her answer. She saved them to a flash drive, got dressed, and headed downstairs, planning to go to the *Picayune* and wait until Brock showed up. Or should she go to his boarding house, since it was just across the street? He didn't have a computer there. Should she go up to her room and get her notebook to take with her?

"Nikki?" Doria called, as she thumped down the steps.

"No time, Mum. I have to go out right away."

"Nikki?" Brock appeared in the dining room doorway.

"What are you doing here?" She winced when her voice cracked.

"Mostly to say good-bye. And warn you."

"Angelo and Marcus." She held out the flash drive to him, as if that would explain everything. The misery on his face—sagging mouth, dark smears under his eyes—and the weary defeat in his voice all combined to squeeze her heart. Nikki wanted to fling her arms around him and beg him to tell her what was wrong, what she could do to help.

"What's going on, Nikki?" Dr. Holwood said, emerging from the kitchen. He had his suit coat tucked under one arm and his tie hung untied around his neck, all set to be worked on as he walked four blocks to his classroom building.

"Angelo and Marcus were Ringo's goons." She watched Brock as she spoke. "They're missing, presumed dead. But they aren't, are they?"

"They want in on whatever game they think I'm playing now. If I don't give them what they want, they'll go after you." Brock glanced from Nikki to her parents. "And everyone who matters to you. I can't go to the police, but you can. I'll leave town and hope they follow me, and you get Arc and the police to protect you. It should work out just fine."

"But—" She took a deep breath, fighting not to say, *But I'll never see you again.* Nikki thought a quick prayer for the right words, and for understanding of what was going through her mind and heart right that moment. "Brock, you can't run away."

"Try me."

"It'll mess up your parole. You did enough damage changing plans to stay here in Tabor."

"Worth it. For a while, at least." He tried to smile, but she knew him well enough to feel the pain he hid.

"I know Angelo and Marcus. Maybe not as well as I should, to predict their moves, but... Mum, Daddy, I'm betting they threatened Brock not to tell the police. Or me, for that matter."

"They still have no idea what Arc can do," Brock said.

"They have no idea what God can do," Dr. Holwood said.

"Walk me to work," Nikki said. "If we spend too much time in here, they'll think you're telling me, right?" She almost smiled when he nodded and swallowed hard. "I'll tell the police. I'll give them all the files Arc can send me on Angelo and Marcus. Who knows? Uncle Todd and Uncle Mike might come up with something to trap them. Like a sting."

"It's not a game," he whispered, but he didn't seem quite as white as he had a few moments ago.

"Daddy—"

"I'll send the prayer chain around. Not too many details, I assume," Dr. Holwood said with a nod for punctuation.

"Vague always works. God knows what we need better than we do," Doria said. "Gray, you move your lazy tail and take good care of Nikki and Brock, you hear me?" she said, waving her finger at the big dog in the doorway.

He thumped his tail against the polished wood floor, then leaped to his feet and skittered across the floor, claws clattering, and beat Nikki and Brock to the door.

They were silent all the way down Church to Trough. Instead of turning left to go to the Mission, Nikki turned right, heading toward Main. Brock nearly stumbled, but he kept in step with her.

"Buy me a donut for breakfast." She winked at him, earning a glare. "You did bring money when you left the house, didn't you?"

"Nikki..." He sighed, but a little more tension left him and his shoulders slumped. "I could swear you're enjoying this."

"I'm not. I've just learned that it's no good making ourselves sick worrying. It's being turned over to God, and we just have to trust, and be careful, and act like there's nothing wrong."

"Everything's wrong," he said, as they continued down the sidewalk. Rick's Bakery waited ahead of them, already perfuming the cool morning air with the scent of donuts frying and bread baking.

"Nothing can be wrong if Rick's is making date-nut cake. Smell that? It's a tradition around here."

"Date-nut?" He wrinkled up his nose for a moment, then took a tentative sniff. The rich aromas of spices and dried fruit filled the air, and Nikki could almost track his reaction to the aroma. "Smells good."

Gray stayed outside the door, propped open to let in the early morning freshness, when they went into the bakery. Nikki took her time picking out what she wanted, settling for a blueberry scone instead of a donut. She positioned herself so she could get a reflection in the glass fronts of the display cases of what lay outside the bakery. Vincent would be proud of her. She saw nothing and no one unexpected. The flash drive with the pictures and files on Angelo and Marcus lay heavy in her pocket. The next stop would be the police, by way of some subterfuge.

After arming themselves with little white paper bags holding their purchases, a carton of orange juice for Nikki and a cup of coffee for Brock, they went back outside.

"Let me walk you to work, instead," he said, as they stepped out onto the sidewalk. They could continue down Main to Span and turn right to walk the six blocks to the *Picayune's* new office, or they could turn left on Trough and take it to Coast to get to the Mission. "Looks kind of funny, you watching out for me." He swallowed hard. "I'm so sorry, Nikki. I promised I'd always take care of you, and I just seem to be making things worse."

"No, you're not. They're the ones choosing to do this, not you. Why should we make ourselves hostages to the evil people of the world? Sure, they're threatening to hurt innocent people if you don't play along with them, but they're still the ones who choose to cause the harm. You have to choose what's right. You can't force them to do wrong, any more than you can force them to do right."

"Wish I could."

"So do I... you're right, though. It wouldn't look right for me to walk you to work. Or for you to walk me to work. We're not—we're not that close anymore." She felt a hollow, dropping sensation inside at those words. Right now, looking into Brock's sorrowful eyes, knowing he ached for her sake, she didn't know what she felt for him anymore. Everything was so tangled.

"You're right." Brock took a deep breath, straightened his shoulders, and saluted her with his coffee cup. "You have a good day. I'll see you this afternoon when I come in to work on the books again?"

"Sure. It's going to be a busy day and I have a ton of work to do, like always."

Nikki stayed on the corner for a few seconds after they parted, watching Brock trudge down the street. She had the oddest feeling, just for a moment, that he had been about to kiss her. What would she have done if he had?

Why did she want him to? Weren't they through, forever and ever?

Why did the thought make her feel so heavy and weepy inside?

~~~~~

Nikki didn't tell anyone at the Mission what had happened. She needed time to think and plan. There was a good chance Angelo and Marcus would be watching her, too. They might have access to enough technology to listen in on conversations. Maybe they still had the connections to hack into her cell phone?

Correction: they might have the technology, but the Arc Foundation had Sophie and Joan and their superior tech skills to keep all their gear secure. Still, that was no excuse to get complacent. She had to get the flash drive with the information to the police before those two did try to spy on her, and realized just how protected she was. Defensive measures always signaled there was something worth defending, after all.

Then she thought of her computer and the rest of her equipment, sitting in her room at home. How safe would it be, if they decided to break in and look for evidence of what she knew? Brock had always kept her shielded from the seamier side of Ringo's business, but she had picked up enough to know either of those two henchmen could get into the Holwoods' home without being seen if they wanted.

Her first step was to call Quarry Hall and leave a message for Vincent, using the code words for when phone lines might be compromised. In what she hoped was an innocent message, Nikki reminded Vincent that he had promised to do a security check on her parents' home, to make sure that parents who had lost custody of their children couldn't break in and kidnap those children from their foster home. If that didn't bring Vincent up from Quarry Hall with a bag of gadgets and advice, nothing would. And, hopefully, if anyone was listening in through illegal wiretaps, they would be discouraged from
~~~~~

invading her parents' home without ever suspecting that she suspected them.

Such roundabout thinking made Nikki tired. She wondered how Joan and Vincent and the other, more experienced daughters of Quarry Hall could think that way all the time.

She ran home at lunchtime to get her computer, and mentioned to a few people on the way out and coming back in that she had to get started on her reports and needed it. She needed more to protect her Internet connection to Quarry Hall and her files.

Pastor Wally volunteered to take the flash drive to the police when she explained the situation to him. He seemed delighted to have an excuse to take a walk in the warm spring afternoon sunshine and balmy breezes, as well as escape the pressures of the Mission for a short time. She was glad to let him go. Who would ever expect an aging, heavy-set, genially smiling man of playing around at a little cloak and dagger?

~~~~~

The Tuesday Bible study group met at the Tabor Heights office of Common Grounds legal clinic. Brock showed up a little earlier than usual that night, intending to ask Xander Finley for some general legal advice. He wasn't quite sure yet what or how much to tell the man about his situation, but the young lawyer had been friendly from the very beginning. Part of that was because Mandy Gordon was his landlady and he had joked about her threatening to evict his office if he wasn't nice to her "new boy."

Brock needed advice, and support. He had sent a message to his contact at the DEA as soon as Angelo and Marcus approached him, but that had done him little good. When someone deigned to call him back, they essentially accused him of mistaken identity and exaggeration. Brock could read between the lines. As far as the DEA was concerned, Ringo's two henchmen were out of commission, either dead or edged out by the bigger, stronger players struggling to take over the territory their boss once held. Essentially, they felt Brock was in no danger and implied that he was crying wolf and had lied to them to get him out of whatever trouble he was making for himself in Tabor Heights.
~~~~~

# Chapter Eighteen

Pastor Wally and Xander were the only ones in the office when Brock walked in, and the three settled down in the conference room to wait for the other six men who were expected that night. Their numbers were down because almost half their group, starting with Daniel Morgan, was busy helping with the production of *Taming of the Shrew* at Homespun Theater.

"It's always this way at production time," Pastor Wally explained with a chuckle. "It wouldn't matter what night we changed our Bible study to, because nearly every night is either rehearsal or production, from now on." His smile faded, with a touch of weariness. "We're grateful for what you did for Joel and his family."

"I didn't do anything," Brock protested.

"Yeah, you did," Xander said, settling down at the conference table across from him with a glossy black mug big enough to take two hands. "You figured out that driver was going to blame Joel for the accident. Once Nikki got me involved, I did a little preemptive strike on my own." He tipped back the mug and took a long drink.

"Meaning?" He was able to relax a little, seeing the slightly vicious glee in the lawyer's eyes.

"The union would have supported their man, just because he was fired as a result of the accident. However, with the help of the research geniuses at the Arc Foundation, I was able to dig into Mr. Craig Schwarz's past and found out that not only is he not Craig Schwarz, but he has had two other false identities in the past six years. He lost his license and his job from drunk driving and accidents three times, along with enough close calls and complaints against all his identities to put him in jail for a long time. Once all the legal tangles get straightened out, of course."

"So nobody is going to file any claims against Joel." Brock matched Pastor Wally's and Xander's grins. "I'm glad."

"They certainly don't need to even worry about such a situation," Pastor Wally rumbled, nodding sagely. "And we were hoping you'd show up early tonight, because we want to help you with your problems."

"My problems?" His relaxed, warm feelings swirled away like dirty water down the bathtub drain. He felt even colder when Pastor Wally explained what he knew about the situation with Angelo and Marcus, thanks to Nikki using him as a courier to get the information to Chief

Cooper at the police department. "I didn't want anybody involved—you could get hurt."

"Safety in numbers."

"A smart man takes advantage of all the defense and support he can get," Xander added. "I haven't known you that long, but you strike me as pretty smart."

"Not smart enough to avoid the whole mess in the first place," Brock shot back.

"Hmm, maybe." Pastor Wally reached over and clapped him on the shoulder. "Xander here will be your legal counsel, and I'll put in a good word for you with Chief Cooper." He chuckled. "I suspect you've already had a visit from Mike Nichols and Todd James."

"Oh, yeah. Adopted uncles are worse than big brothers."

"Nikki's special to them. Saving an innocent life creates a bond... well, we recommend confiding in Chief Cooper. The more watching eyes we have, the safer you'll be—and the people you care about."

Brock mentally kicked himself for not realizing that. Just because the DEA thought he was imagining things and wouldn't send help didn't mean he had to go it all on his own. And he liked the idea, the possibility that he wouldn't have to flee Tabor Heights to protect Nikki.

By the time the rest of the men in the Bible study arrived, they had a barebones plan put together. Xander would approach Chief Cooper and enlist him for his advice, and learn how he felt about Brock essentially playing decoy. The plan was simple enough: lure Angelo and Marcus out into the open, get them to make mistakes and let the authorities deal with them before anyone was hurt. Xander also promised he would pass on the Arc Foundation's research to friends elsewhere in the DEA and get them to take Brock's allegations seriously.

The three of them agreed not to tell the rest of the Bible study group the details, but they asked for special prayer for Brock. All the men there knew about his past, his connection to the drug industry, and his former relationship with Nikki. They could probably guess enough details. It was enough for Brock to look at their faces and see concern and no condemnation.

He walked home in the quiet and darkness, amused and awed by the sense of protection and support closing around him. Brock wasn't used to people going out of their way to help just because it was the right thing to do. He wasn't used to good people believing him with little evidence except their own hearts and their faith.

A faint rumble of an engine and a momentary flash of headlights coming from behind him jolted Brock back to alertness just as he turned the corner onto Church Street. He flinched and nearly turned to face whoever came up behind him, but the lights were gone. He supposed it was just someone turning from one street to another. Still, the confident, safe feeling fled. How easy would it have been for Angelo and Marcus to come up behind him while his thoughts were elsewhere, and attack? Maybe they realized he was useless, or maybe they suspected that he had ignored their warnings and gotten the authorities involved. Despite their brutality and arrogance, they were smart, and smart men in their line of work would cut their losses, eliminate witnesses, and get out of town.

"Please, God, whatever happens to me, protect Nikki," he whispered, and then picked up his pace. His boarding house was only a few driveways away. Brock had no idea if it was real or his imagination, but the hairs on the back of his neck prickled. Someone was watching him. Friend or foe, someone who knew him or someone who was just bored and sleepless and looking out onto the quiet residential street? He paused at the end of the driveway and glanced down the street at the Holwoods' house. He prayed, with all his strength and faith, that he hadn't brought trouble to Nikki's life again.

He had just started to relax back to the hopeful, tired looseness he enjoyed after the Bible study when he reached his room on the third floor. Brock unlocked the door and stepped inside, and felt another presence in the room before he reached for the light switch.

"Nikki sent me," the smooth baritone voice said. A hand reached out of the darkness to shut the door. Then the light came on.

The man who leaned against the wall, his hand still resting against the door, was tall, black, with a shaved head and almost elegantly casual in his neat navy shirt and creased navy pants. He tipped his head slightly to one side and studied Brock for a few moments. Then a slight smile warmed his expression and took away the suffocating sensation of approaching death that had enfolded Brock from the moment he sensed the intruder's presence.

It didn't, however, remove the certainty that if he wanted to, he could strike and kill Brock in utter silence, and then vanish into the night without anyone knowing anything had happened.

"Why?" Brock asked, finally prying sound from his vocal cords.

"Actually, she didn't. Not consciously anyway." He nodded, looking Brock up and down again, then stepped away from the door, aiming for the chair that had been pulled out from the two-seater table. "I figured that might catch your attention and keep you from running for your life before we could talk."

"Just talk?" Brock chose to lean against the counter of his tiny efficiency kitchen. He was pleased his voice didn't shake, though he feared sweat stains grew on his shirt, revealing the thundering fear racing through his body.

"I'm Vincent, head of security for the Arc Foundation. Nikki told me about your visitors. I came up to install some gizmos to help protect her and her folks, keep watch on things, let the local gendarmes know if there were intruders. And she agreed you could use the same kind of help."

"Uh huh." He wasn't sure why, but he sensed something about that explanation amused Vincent. Or maybe he just felt better knowing someone so thickly cloaked in efficient threat and danger was there to watch out for Nikki. "What do I need to do?"

Half an hour later, he and Vincent had installed sensors on his doors and windows and he had caught the trick of the small, deceptively simple remote control. As long as he carried it with him, he could go in and out of his rooms without needing to re-set anything or tap a code in. The sensors were to alert him if anyone entered his rooms without his permission. Brock was most impressed by the set-up when Vincent informed him that he had already talked to Mandy Gordon and had her permission to make his installations in Brock's rooms.

"Somehow, I don't see you and Mandy moving in the same circles," Brock admitted.

"There were some tense moments this past winter, and I met her when I was putting security equipment in at Common Grounds and at Hannah Blake's place," Vincent said, his smile getting a little wider. "Mandy's a good woman, and smart. She has a right to know what we're doing to her property, you know."

"Yeah. You're right." He inhaled deeply, feeling as if a heavy weight had just slid off his back. Now he was exhausted, not just pleasantly tired. "Thanks. For everything."

"Glad to do it. I know her story, and it seems to me the last thing Nikki needs is to worry about you. Or be hurt if you get hurt."

"You think she would?"

"Most definitely." Vincent thumped him on the back. "I think you'll do, Pierson."

*Wednesday, April 23*

Tuesday night, Rich had asked Nikki to watch Aurora overnight, while he went to help a friend who was having car trouble. He didn't know how late they would be working, and he didn't want to disturb Aurora by waking her up to take her home. It sounded reasonable enough and Nikki didn't mind, even though as Pastor Wally had said, she was babysitting the little girl at least twice a week now, and Rich seemed to expect her to always be available.

He didn't show up for work on time the next morning. All the things she had thought about him in the last week, as well as the warnings from concerned friends, all crashed down on her. Nikki tried to push those thoughts from her mind so she could concentrate on her reports, even as she kept an ear tuned to listen for his voice, so she could give him Aurora's backpack. And maybe tell him she wasn't available for babysitting in the future. As the morning wore on and he didn't appear, spouting excuses or blaming someone for getting in his way, she grew uneasy.

He came in just before lunchtime. She wouldn't have known if Joe Horse hadn't told her when she stopped in the kitchen to check some figures the old cook had given her. Rich didn't poke his head into the doorway of the office where she was working, and she didn't hear him calling to the children as they went past him on their way to the gym or the bathroom or to another classroom for story time or craft time.

She ran into him in the hall on her way back to her office. Her irritation faded when she saw the strips of tape and the three-inch long strip of gauze on his forehead.

"Are you all right?"

"Hit the steering wheel," Rich muttered. He reached up like he would rip the tape off, then winced and turned to walk away without the gusher of questions or comments or complaints that seemed to be his standard practice. Maybe, Nikki mused, he didn't say anything because he knew she had figured out his tactic was to avoid going back to work.

"What steering wheel? On your car? Were you in an accident?" Nikki followed him down the hall, abandoning her looming report deadline for a moment.

"Some jerk plowed into me at 4a.m. It's a good thing I was nearly half-asleep."

"Is your car—"

"Totaled. But it was a rust bucket anyway. Insurance ought to get me a new one." He grinned, but it couldn't take away the paleness of his cheeks or soften the dark smears under his eyes. "I should have wrecked the junker a few years ago and got myself a new one the easy way, huh?"

"That's not..." Nikki sighed and scolded herself not to lecture him. Not when he had been in an accident. Still, this proof of his entitlement attitude irritated her.

Rich swayed his way down the hall in a modified, slowed version of his usual saunter.

Nikki was still wondering about the accident when Brock showed up to work on the Mission's books again that evening. He had the computer software figured out and had promised to teach Claire how to use it. Nikki wanted to sit in, just to see if it was as tricky as he said. She had mentioned the software to Sophie, who said that company was too new to have a track record. Then she asked Sophie to evaluate it so she could pass the word along to others, so no one would get trapped and messed up like the

Mission had been. She mentioned Rich's accident, and commented on how much more he got done that day, despite his late arrival.

"He wasn't half asleep," Brock said.

"He wasn't?" Claire snorted and shook her head. "Seems like Rich goes through life half asleep most of the time."

"Because he was drunk. He also didn't mention he was going the wrong way down a one-way street. The guy who he claimed plowed into him wasn't even in his car, which was legally parked in front of his own house."

"How do you know?" Nikki asked.

"I work at the *Picayune*, remember? Curt was grumbling about it when he came back from getting the news for the police blotter. He had a few more stories about good old Rich's driving record, too." Brock snagged another rolling chair by its padded arm and dragged it over in front of the computer. "Are we going to work on this mess, or do you want to gossip all night?" He grinned to take the sting from his words.

"Oh, gossip is such an ugly word," Claire said. "I prefer more theologically correct language. Like 'sharing.' Or 'fellowshipping.' You know, so sweet and religious-sounding."

"You mean 'fellowship' instead of 'pigging out'?" Nikki said with a snort of laughter. "I've heard it all, believe me."

"Either way, the truth's pretty far away from the story Rich told you."

"If he was drunk, how would he know the truth anyway?"

Brock nodded, his smile flat. They shared a quiet moment, there in the somewhat stuffy office with Claire sitting between them, studying the first computer screen he had opened up. His gaze asked if Nikki was all right; she responded with a tiny nod and a raised eyebrow meaning "And you?" He nodded and gave a tiny shrug.

*Sunday, April 27*

Sunday morning, Pastor Glenn waylaid Nikki on the way into the sanctuary and asked her to meet him in his office. Since Tabor Christian had started the Mission, she assumed the senior minister wanted to know how her evaluation was coming along. Nikki imagined Pastor Glenn hadn't heard enough about the Arc Foundation and wanted to know exactly what they could do for the Mission. She smiled, anticipating his pleasure in all the possible improvements and expansion in both facilities and outreach.

"Thanks," Pastor Glenn said, coming in with Rita. "I'm glad your family always shows up early, Nikki. I just haven't been able to get hold of you the last few days, what with everything going on with the

Randolphs' accident, and this is something we need to talk about."

"What is?" Nikki smoothed her skirt over her knees and gave Rita a questioning little frown. The woman just shook her auburn head and gave Nikki that patented unruffled minister's wife smile.

It reminded Nikki of the month the Holwoods were out of town taking care of Doria's sick mother and she had stayed with the pastor and his wife, while the other foster children had been split up among other foster families in the church. Nikki had been fourteen. Rita had worn that same concerned, determined-to-be-calm-and-supportive look when she told Nikki some people had arrived who believed they might be her relatives. They had an infant girl kidnapped about the same time Nikki had appeared in Tabor. It had been a false alarm and Nikki had been grateful, because the people she met rubbed her the wrong way.

"We're having baptisms at the end of the service," Pastor Glenn began. "Several people are joining the church. We thought you should be warned that Brock is joining."

"Oh." She gripped the arms of the chair and waited for some reaction. Maybe she just felt numb. Maybe she felt it was a little letdown after expecting something earth-shaking. "Thanks. I probably would be surprised. I mean, he could have told me..." Her face heated a little. She and Brock hadn't really had the opportunity for personal discussions the last few days. They had been busy with Mission business or comparing notes on incidents when they thought Angelo and Marcus had been spying on them, anything unusual in the neighborhood, and what the police had passed on to Nikki through Pastor Wally.

"I want to assure you, Nikki, I am convinced Brock is genuine about his salvation and about joining this community and becoming an active member." Pastor Glenn folded his hands a little tighter on his desk pad and glanced down at his fingers a moment. "I'm also convinced, just from the things he doesn't say, that Brock is here to win you back."

"He talks about you at every meeting we have," Rita continued. "He carries such guilt over what he did to you, how he convinced you to backslide, how he put you in danger. He will never forgive himself for Mercy Grace's death." She sighed, ending in a chuckle and a tight little, frustrated smile. "Sometimes I think he's disappointed his former employer is dead, that he'd like to take some of his anger out on the man."

"Ringo was driving the car. The accident killed our baby," Nikki murmured. She took a deep breath, trying to find something to say. "Is that all you wanted to talk to me about?" They nodded. She took another deep breath and stood. "Thanks. I really appreciate it. I mean, I wouldn't have screamed or run out of the sanctuary crying or anything but... thanks."

"Nikki?" Pastor Glenn began to rise from his chair, then paused.

"I'm okay. I just have a lot of other things on my mind. It's a surprise, but it's a... it's a good surprise." She backed toward the door. "I don't hate Brock. I don't even think I'm angry at him anymore."

"Apathy is worse than hating someone," Rita said, turning to watch her.

"It's not apathy." Nikki almost laughed. It caught in her throat, choking her. "I'm just so busy with other things, more important things, I don't know what I feel. Um... thanks." She twisted the doorknob, half-expecting to find it locked. That was the way it went in her nightmares. But it opened and she tugged the door open just wide enough to slide out and shut it again quickly.

Was that what this was? A nightmare? If Brock joined the church she had grown up in, that meant he planned on staying. She would see him every time she came home to visit.

She almost stopped short, in the hall leading from the offices to the sanctuary. Actually, that didn't sound so bad. She almost liked the idea.

Why did Pastor Glenn and Rita expect her to be angry or upset? What had Brock told them about their former relationship? Despite how well they were getting along, did he think she hated him, and was only being nice because he was in trouble now?

As if thinking of him had conjured him, Brock stepped into the church through the door from the side parking lot. He rocked back on his heels when he saw her, half-smiling, and the closing door hit his back.

"Can we talk?" Nikki didn't wait for his response, but pushed the door open again and stepped outside. Brock followed.

"Pastor told you, huh?" He jammed his hands into his pockets and managed a half-grin. "I'm sorry —"

"Would you stop feeling guilty? Brock, you didn't kidnap me. You didn't brainwash me. I went with you because I thought I was in love with you. I chose to stay with you. It took a lot to make me leave you. I didn't want to choose between my baby and her father. What we did, we did together. It was wrong, so we were wrong together. Stop punishing yourself, okay?"

# Chapter Nineteen

Nikki jolted to a stop and nearly laughed, feeling a little breathless at the spill of words. Belatedly, she looked around to check for witnesses. With the way things were going lately, she wouldn't have been surprised if the worst gossips in the entire church had been five feet away, eagerly gobbling up every word she said. By a minor miracle, she and Brock were totally alone.

"I know, but you stopped loving me, and that's completely my fault." He let out a rattling breath, as if he fought sobs. Nikki understood that feeling all too well. "I keep hoping somehow..."

"Hoping what?" She thought she knew. Part of her wanted to hear it, and part of her prayed he would keep his mouth shut.

"I want you to love me again."

"The love we had was wrong. It's not real love if it violates what's right. Love doesn't rejoice in wrong. It doesn't lie, it doesn't hurt—"

"I know. I just about have that chapter of Corinthians memorized!" He grinned, but that brightness in his eyes wasn't humor. "What if we found the right kind of love now? What if God blessed us getting back together?" He held out both his hands, as if he expected her to give her hands to him. Maybe make a pledge to try. Maybe let him hold her?

Nikki couldn't breathe for a moment. Part of her wanted to feel Brock's arms around her again, to kiss him, to feel that wonderful, tickling, electric thrill race up her spine. She had always felt safe in his arms, even when she overheard things and imagined things that brought on nightmares. Brock had kept her safe and sheltered, and innocent in so many ways, even as she slept in his arms without the blessing of marriage.

In a sense, because she had given her virginity to him already, because they had conceived a child, weren't they already married?

"I'm sorry. There's just too much going on," she whispered, and turned, banging her hand on the door handle before she could get it open.

How many times had Joan and Elizabeth, and even Vincent, gently scolded her about her tendency to run away from hard situations? Nikki didn't care right now. She couldn't think straight with melting memories filling her mind and Brock watching her with that pleading hunger in his gaze. How many nights, especially after she had run away from him, had she awakened in tears from dreams of what might have been? Nikki didn't know if she could go through that sweet, painful longing again. She had lived in daydreams of Brock coming to find her, apologizing, carrying her off to a little cottage with a white picket fence and a church wedding. Those dreams were gone, torn from her as surely as Mercy Grace had been torn from her womb.

Could they be given back? Anything was possible if she trusted in God, but did she dare even ask?

*Monday, April 28*

Monday morning, Nikki saw the flashing lights from the police cruisers long before the Mission was in sight. She shifted her computer case strap from her shoulder to across her chest, so the weight of it hung down her back, and ran. Gray stayed at her side. She lost her breath almost immediately and her stride faltered as images of Brock lying in a pool of blood in front of the building filled her mind.

That was ridiculous. If Angelo and Marcus killed him, they would have caught up with him at the Gordons' house, or brought his body to her house or ambushed him as he walked through town to the *Picayune's* office.

She didn't smell any smoke. There weren't any fire trucks, anyway. She hadn't heard any sirens as she got ready for the day or had her devotions or started her walk. What had happened?

Mike Nichols stood in front of the main door, stringing the bright yellow barrier tape across the shattered glass panes. Workers and parents gathered on the lawn, watching, some holding the children back from the glass spattered down the sidewalk.

"That doesn't make sense," Nikki said, as she came to a stop a few feet behind him. The officer gave her a frown of question as he finished fastening the tape to the brick enclosing the doorway. "The glass is thrown outside — if they broke in, the glass should be inside the building."

"There's glass all over my office," Pastor Wally said from inside the darkened lobby. He stood against the wall, gazing at the snowdrifts of papers and streaks of spilled tempera paints and the footprints all through the mess.

"What's missing?" Mike asked.

"Hard to tell in this mess." He shook his head, and Nikki thought he had never looked so tired before, in all the years she had known him. He looked his age, and that scared her.

"The first thing we check is money and drugs. Any prescription medicines you keep for the kids in daycare, or the seniors?"

"The nurse's office is still locked, and it doesn't have any windows." Pastor Wally thought a moment. "Parents are supposed to pay fees this week, so we didn't have any money in the office for waiting bank deposits."

"What about the pop machine?" Nikki offered.

She and Mike picked their way around the edges of the mess. Photos had already been taken, and samples from the footprints, but Mike admitted he had little hope for workable evidence.

The pop machine in the senior center room was untouched. The cash boxes from the cafeteria and the senior center administration room were both missing, however. Pastor Wally estimated the thief or thieves had gotten twenty dollars, maximum.

"Still, it's the principle of the thing," Nikki said to no one in particular as they got to work, organizing to clean up the mess.

Rich was in a foul mood over the mess, though everyone who could be spared pitched in to help clean up. They kept the children away, both because of the glass and because some burst into tears at the sight of the vandalism.

"Let's hope this stops them from becoming vandals and crooks when they grow up," Claire said, as she and Nikki mopped the lobby floor for the third time. The dust from the spilled tempera paints got into everything, clung to every surface no matter how slick. They had swept twice, then used the dust mop, then the shop vacuum. Despite that, paint residue remained. The people washing the walls found rainbow streaks everywhere once the water touched it.

"Yeah, how about running the crooks out of town?" Rich grumbled. He glared at Nikki. "Why don't you tell that creep, Brock, to stop drooling over you and go back to jail where he belongs?"

"This isn't Brock's fault," she said, startled at the fire in Rich's eye and the bitterness in his voice. She hadn't meant to defend Brock at all, but she knew he was innocent.

"Prove it."

"He's never done anything like this before, why should he start now? Besides, he's a Christian now."

"Once a crook, always a crook." He jammed the mop into his bucket and rolled it down the hall. Nikki and Claire just looked at each other for a few seconds until the rattling of the wheels on the tile had faded away.

"Once a lech, always a lech?" Claire murmured.

"What do you know about him that I don't?"

"Oh, he seemed to think I'd be desperate for male company, since I'm 'tied down' to take care of my handicapped brother. As if Tommy wants or needs help from anybody. I accepted one date because he really does have a nice smile, and he's intelligent. Or at least he *seemed* to be. One date. Never again."

"He made a move on you?"

"He *imagined* he was subtle and romantic. Let's leave it at that." She rolled her eyes in disgust. "It really makes me wonder about Aurora's mother. Was she desperate, or has he lost his Romeo charm? He always hits on the new girls, whenever anybody joins the staff. He was hassling Dani, just before you came home." Claire looked around the lobby and leaned closer, her voice dropping to a whisper. "The way he hangs around you all the time, people think something is going on."

"So I've heard."

"Anybody who was really listening probably thinks you just had a lovers' quarrel. Or maybe you're trying to make him jealous by sticking up for Brock. Who is a wonderful guy, by the way. I can't understand why you don't let him take you out more often."

"I let Brock take me completely out of town," Nikki murmured.

Claire stepped back, eyes widening. Obviously, Nikki realized, her new friend hadn't heard that particular part of her story yet. It made her wonder just what stories were going around town, about her and Brock and Rich, how much of it was truth and how much was idle speculation.

Nikki sighed and closed her eyes for a moment. She didn't look forward to making a report to the Arc Foundation about the break-in. The Board would insist on focusing on security before any other program, and rightly so, but with her hands sticky with spilled paint and stinging from paper cuts, Nikki wanted to replace those lost supplies first. She much preferred telling Arc about these new problems, compared to facing Rich. If people besides his mother thought something was going on, she had to put a stop to it. Did he think he owned her, just because they dated in high school and she wasn't attached to anyone else right now?

~~~~~

"Angelo," Brock said, when he arrived to work with Claire that evening and found the glaziers still repairing the shattered window in Pastor Wally's office. Nikki was helping Claire catch up on all her delayed office work, and she told Brock what had happened while Claire was in Pastor Wally's office, answering some questions from the glaziers.

"Milk money isn't their style," she protested.

"No, but what if it's just to make a point? Or maybe find out how much I really can get my hands on? If they'll attack the Mission, what's to stop them from burning down our church? They get what they want, or people suffer."

"Rich thinks you did it."

"In a way, I did. Nikki, you could leave town. Say you're done with your work. Maybe take your folks on a vacation."

"Running away doesn't solve problems. It just delays them." She took a deep breath and looked away, unable to face the concern in his gaze. Nikki dropped to her knees to hug Gray, who had patiently endured the
~~~~~

mess and little children yanking on his fur all day, and little bodies climbing all over him. "The armor of God never mentions anything for your back, you know."

"Huh?"

"Read Ephesians. The helmet of salvation, the breastplate of truth. It's all for your front, not your back. God commands us to stand firm and face the enemy. Not attack, but just resist. Running makes us vulnerable."

"When did you get so tough?" he murmured, and bent down to stroke a strand of hair back behind her ear.

Nikki shivered, welcoming the warm thrill at his gentle touch. She wanted more, but this was not the time or place.

"I've always been tough. I just got... lazy, I guess."

*Tuesday, April 29th*

Rich showed up half an hour after Nikki got home and swung his wriggling little girl into her arms the moment she opened the door. Behind her, Dani and Lisa watched, curious. The three had plans to go to opening night of *Taming of the Shrew* and then go to Stay-A-While for dessert. No one else was home. That was the first thought in Nikki's mind. She bit her tongue, when she wanted to snap at him that he should have asked her if she had plans, instead of just assuming she was available. She took a deep breath as she swung Aurora back into her father's arms before he could withdraw them.

"What's going on?" she asked, and glanced over her shoulder at her friends. If Rich had been two minutes later, nobody would have been home. She was glad Aurora only giggled at the exchange. Rich, however, glared at her. As if she had broken a promise she made to him.

"I need you to watch Rory for me." He tried to hand the child to her again, but Nikki crossed her arms. "Come on, Nikki, I thought we had an agreement."

"You should have told me about this agreement, which requires two people to agree. I have plans for tonight." She jerked her thumb over her shoulder, and Dani and Lisa dutifully stepped up to the door. Dani gave Rich an innocent, wide-eyed look of inquiry. Lisa wasn't such a good actor, and settled for refusing to look at either Nikki or Rich.

"You can cancel for me, can't you?" His tone turned soft, warm and husky, but Nikki heard the whine under it all. She wondered if he had used it before, and she just never listened closely enough to hear it.

"No, I can't. We have plans, we have tickets, and I'm not changing things at the last minute."

"Why are you doing this to me?" The whine got stronger.

"Why couldn't you be bothered to *ask*? The fact that you just assumed..." Nikki wanted to slam the door on him. They sounded like a stereotyped bad marriage, and she hated the implications.

"Come on, I thought we had something special." He grinned and reached out to try to stroke down her arm. His grin went flat when she sidestepped out of his reach. Aurora's wriggles cancelled a second attempt. "Don't go ruining it."

"We have nothing but friendship. Which you presume on too much."

Nikki felt like she had fallen into a movie about her past, individual scenes all spliced together. Times Rich had guilt-tripped her into complying with his plans, going to movies and games that bored her silly, just to make him happy, because she mistakenly believed they were meant to be together. Hadn't Brock used a line similar to Rich's "something special" when she balked the first time he tried to make love to her? Was she ever going to get free of men trying to get her to do what they wanted, with no regard for what she wanted, or what was right?

"Who's going to watch Rory if you won't help out?" he demanded, finally putting the child down on the porch on her own two feet.

"What's your mother doing tonight?"

"How should I know?"

"Ask her. For heaven's sake, Rich, who watched Aurora before I came along?"

He went white. Aurora whimpered and backed away from him. Nikki almost bent to pick her up and comfort her, but if that happened, she would be stuck. Before she stood up again, Rich would be down the steps and running for his rental car.

"Aurora is your responsibility, Rich. It's about time you grew up and faced it." Nikki beckoned for her friends. "Come on, we're going to be late." Dani and Lisa kept silent, ignoring Rich as they trooped out of the house and down the steps. She pulled the front door closed and made sure it locked.

"What about your folks?" he said, tone sullen. He caught up Aurora around the waist, settled her on his hip, and followed Nikki down the steps.

"Out for the evening."

"Come on, I thought you loved Rory."

"I do, but she's your responsibility. Fatherhood means sacrifices."

"Tell me about it!" He stomped across the lawn to his rental car. Nikki thought for a moment he would throw Aurora through the open window into the back seat. "I thought you'd love having Rory around, since you lost your own kid. I thought we were helping each other out."

"Playing with your daughter doesn't give me back my own!" Nikki clenched her fists and took deep breaths, and wished she hadn't let Gray go with Brandy for the evening with her grandparents. Maybe it was weak to depend on her bodyguard companion to drive people away, but she really wanted Gray to growl and bare his teeth at Rich and send him running before she started crying.

"Spoiled brat, that's what you are. Rory is just a toy to you, isn't she? Just like her mother. I thought Sue was selfish." He glared at Rory and halted himself in time. He yanked the back door open and tossed her into her car seat.

Nikki sensed the profanity waiting to spill from his lips. The boy he had been in high school had acted like he didn't know such words. She wondered now if he had ever truly been, inside, the boy he appeared to be on the outside.

"Selfish?" Nikki knew she was about to make a scene, and it was all she could do to keep from launching herself at him. "I left my daughter's father to protect her. I worked my fingers off, to support myself. I didn't expect everyone else to bail me out of my mistakes."

"Yeah, Saint Nikki." He slammed the door and flung himself into the driver's seat. "Thanks for nothing!" he shouted, punctuated by slamming his own door.

"You're welcome!"

Silence seemed to pulse up and down the street, muffling even the rumble of the engine and bad muffler of the rental car as Rich sped away, tires squealing. Nikki closed her eyes and counted her breaths until her racing heart finally slowed to normal.

"Think he finally got the message?" Dani said with a nasal, nagging tone. It prompted a few sputtered chuckles from Lisa.

After all that, Nikki was surprised to enjoy the opening night's performance of *Taming of the Shrew*. She didn't even mind when she read Brock's name in the program, giving him credit for helping with the set and lighting and being in one of the tech crew teams.

Her twisted, uneven relationship with Rich had been bothering her, but she couldn't decipher the root cause or what to do. Maybe he was right, and her empty arms had drawn her to Aurora. But the opposite was true, and the little girl's presence added to her pain. The bottom line was that Rich was a taker, a user. The world revolved around him, and anyone who rebelled against his wishes was in the wrong. She shuddered at the realization that when Rich said he wanted to pick up their relationship where they had left off, it meant he wanted to go back to where Nikki adored him and would do whatever he asked.

Had she really been so gullible and so foolish that she believed giving and giving and giving without ever receiving was healthy?

Nikki watched Dr. Morgan as a flamboyant Petruchio stomp around the stage, bantering and arguing with Katarina, and thought about Rich and Brock and her relationship with them. Brock's idea of love, even when it was outside of God's will, was far healthier and closer to the real thing than Rich's version. So what if he had manipulated her and guided her perceptions, just like Petruchio manipulated Katarina and tricked her into becoming his playmate? Brock had been good to her. He was a far better man than Rich Thomas had ever been, even before he got right with God.

That settled, Nikki let herself relax and enjoy the rest of the play, and laughed with the rest of the audience at all the appropriate places. She and Dani and Lisa stayed behind after the audience left, to congratulate Max on a grand opening night. They were invited to come into the house and share the remains of the opening night feast Max's Aunt Rose had prepared. It was easy to sit in the cluttered living room and laugh with the cast and crew as they went over every glitch and emergency, to meet Brock's gaze from time to time, watch him laughing and talking with his new friends, and to be glad for him.

*Please, Lord, fix things for him?* Nikki wasn't exactly sure what was encompassed by her prayer, but she honestly wanted everything to work out for Brock—for the problem with Angelo and Marcus to be settled, for him to become part of Tabor and have friends and make a good life for himself. Anything else that came with it, she would just have to trust God to know what was best.

# Chapter Twenty

*Wednesday, April 30*

Nikki expected some sort of reprisal the next day, but Rich seemed to prefer to avoid her as they went about their various duties at the Mission, rather than nag her until she apologized. That wasn't so bad. The scene in front of her friends also meant Rich couldn't pretend it hadn't happened—a trick he had used a few times in high school.

Brock took off from work early that day to work with Claire, because she couldn't stay late that evening. Her brother, Tommy, had a comedy gig and Claire was the only one available to drive him downtown. Nikki appreciated Brock making the effort; Mr. Coffelt was a generous boss, but it was still a stretch for a new employee to take off early. She sat in with the two of them as they navigated their way through the system, now that Brock had it mostly untangled. Claire had been full of questions about the foundation all day and continued asking during the lulls while they waited for the computer to process the latest batch of data they were inputting. Brock asked questions too, which surprised Nikki. She had just assumed Brock knew about the Arc Foundation because of their involvement when Ringo was caught and put in prison.

"How does somebody get involved with Arc?" Brock asked, as they waited for a long stream of printouts to finish. "It sounds like you get recruited instead of applying."

"Basically." Nikki smiled, remembering her surprise when Joan suggested she come to live at Quarry Hall and work for the foundation.

"Do they recruit everybody they rescue?"

"Not all the time, but it seems..." She remembered the stories of some of her adopted sisters, the trouble they had been in, the danger they had escaped. How some had decided to dedicate their lives to serving God and others, and the foundation had found them. How others had come to Arc for help and new lives, and had been asked to join. "It seems like one way or another, you have to come through the fire. There are people at all levels, working for them. The people who take care of the little details and run rescue missions, the administrators who are there for phone calls in the middle of the night, the people who run legal clinics like Xander Finley."

"And then there are the ones who live on the road, like you," Claire said. "How do you get that job? I don't know if I envy you or feel sorry for you."

"Me, neither." Nikki felt Brock watching her, intense, as if he held his breath, waiting for her answer. "Those of us who travel are Arc's eyes and ears. We seem to find problems to solve no matter where we go. But I've only had a few assignments, all working as courier. This is my first big, post-graduation assignment, I guess you could say."

"Could you use somebody who knows money?" Brock offered. His voice sounded almost casual. Almost. His smile went flat, and he didn't meet her gaze but busied himself with papers that didn't need straightening. "I mean, if I could find a dozen ways a month for Ringo to hide his profits legally, I can unearth the same tricks other people are using. I know how to raise funds, how to direct money where it will work the best, make the most impact. You see a lot of that, even doing the things I was doing."

"I'll ask. We always have more needs than workers and resources." She caught her breath at the sudden flash of relief—maybe hope?—in Brock's eyes. Had he been afraid she would refuse? Maybe he thought he didn't qualify?

If anyone qualified, Nikki thought Brock had. He had gone through his own fire, hadn't he? Prison had taught him things he needed to learn about himself. He had put his life on the line to protect her from Ringo, hadn't he? He was involved in a Bible study here in Tabor, making friends, getting settled, trying to make something worthwhile out of his life. Even if it was to prove to her that he was truly changed, it counted, didn't it? His losses had been a refining fire. Just like her pain and shame and losses in the last few years.

~~~~~

"Nikki?" Doria called up the stairs that evening.

"Something wrong, Mum?" Nikki didn't like that odd, questioning tone in her mother's voice. She hurried to finish her e-mail message to Quarry Hall, reporting on the progress at both the Mission and what little the police had told her about watching for Angelo and Marcus. Pastor Wally had told her what Xander had done, calling on some friends in the DEA who were more likely to believe Brock's story. Nothing was definite yet, but chances were good that the DEA would send someone to Tabor to see if they could pick up the two fugitives' trail. She didn't like the idea. If the agents were spotted, who would Angelo and Marcus blame other than Brock?

"You have a visitor," was all the woman would say.

"Down in a minute." She signed off, leaving a discussion of her problems with Rich for a phone call with either Elizabeth or Joan. Maybe she should talk to Brooklyn. The brusque, wry woman was always a good
~~~~~

sounding board.

Mrs. Thomas sat in the living room, perched on the edge of the couch with her purse clasped tightly in her hands. Doria was nowhere in sight. Nikki faintly heard protests coming from the three children, who were outside, playing with Gray. Either her companion had reached the point of "enough" and was escaping, or Doria had gone out to separate combatants. The battles and allies changed daily.

"Hi, Mrs. Thomas. Something I can help you with?" Nikki debated sitting down on the other side of the room, or standing. She chose to stand, rationalizing she might need to run out of the room before she said something stupid. Rich had never gone whining to his mother about his relationship with Nikki before, but there was always a first time.

"I don't understand you, Nicole. First, you come to town and chase Richie, and now you're slapping him away because of Aurora. That mistake in college was five years ago. Can't you forgive him?"

"Forgive—Mrs. Thomas, is this about my argument with Rich the other night? Because if it is, he didn't tell you what happened."

"He wanted you to have some time alone with Aurora. If you two are getting married, you ought to get to know your daughter ahead of time, to avoid any transition problems."

"I'm not marrying anyone. The only person in town who thinks I want to marry Rich is you." Nikki caught her breath. "Or did he tell you that?"

"Richie's always loved you," the woman said, vertical lines of confusion appearing in her forehead. "Can't you forgive him for slipping so many years ago?"

"Who am I to forgive anyone? I don't care about Rich's past. His choices and his mistakes have nothing to do with me."

"Then why did you lecture him, in front of the entire neighborhood, about betraying you with that Sue creature?"

"I didn't—he yelled at me. He showed up here with no warning, expecting me to drop everything to sit Aurora. My friends were here— two friends, not the entire neighborhood—and we were on our way out the door. We had tickets for the play. I couldn't change my plans, and I wasn't about to. Did you watch Aurora that night?"

"Well, yes. I didn't have anything else to do." A few lines smoothed out of her forehead. "You mean to tell me Richie didn't bother asking, he just showed up?"

"That's exactly what I'm telling you." Nikki settled down on the hassock several feet from the couch. "I think we should straighten out a few things. First, I like Aurora, but I have no intention of being her mother. I'm home for a short while. I'm on an assignment for the foundation where I work, and in a few weeks I'll be leaving for my next assignment. I have no intention of starting a relationship with anyone. If Rich thinks I'm going to marry him and be a mother to his daughter, it's all in his head and he never bothered telling me. Just like he didn't bother telling me he expected me to take care of Aurora the other night. Just like he didn't bother telling me that he thinks we have an 'agreement' of some kind. About what?"

"That boy." Mrs. Thomas sighed. She closed her eyes and rubbed them, and a few lines left her forehead. "Just when I think he's finally straightening out. I was so glad when you came back to town. He was such a good boy when you were dating, and then he went away to college and he hurt you and you rejected him—"

"Rich rejected me. He swore at me when I caught him having sex in his dorm room. He never apologized, and he ignored me when he came home on breaks from college."

"Yes... that's probably the way it did happen." A wry chuckle escaped her. "But that's not how he sees it. Oh, Nikki, can't you find it in your heart to give him another chance? Richie is planning for the future again. He's going to go back to school and get his degree and be a coach. He wants to marry you and get a nice house and make a real home and family for Aurora. He has such ideas for changes, for wonderful things to do at the Mission if they'd only give him a chance. All because of you."

"It's not my job to reform your son," she said on a sigh.

"But—" She closed her eyes again, and then slowly nodded. "Won't you give him a chance?"

"He has to *ask* me to give him a chance. Rich... assumes a lot of things. He decides he's going to do something, or he wants something, and thinks everybody will cooperate."

"If he asks?"

"He won't ask."

"Well, I'll certainly straighten out that son of mine, I can promise you." Mrs. Thomas struggled to her feet. "Nicole, I truly would love to have you as my daughter-in-law. You've always been a good girl. Sensible. Kind-hearted. Aurora just loves you."

"I love her, too." Nikki bit her lip against saying "but she can't ever replace my daughter." That wasn't something she wanted to get into with Mrs. Thomas. Not here, not now.

*Friday, May 2*

"Hey."

Rich found Nikki working in the main art supply room to rearrange things. During her inventory of the two rooms, she had found items that had been replaced twice because no one could locate them when they were needed; little things like blunt-nose scissors and boxes of crayons, rolls of tape, bottles of tempera paints, cups to mix paint in, extra brushes, glue pots. The Mission had more than most of the people working there knew, and Nikki had made it her responsibility to arrange things so they could be found and used. She had also hoped that working in the art supply room would make her hard to find for a day or two. After the visit from Mrs. Thomas, she wanted to be alone, in silence, just to think.

Nikki paused to brace herself before lifting her gaze from the storage rack she had bought with Arc Foundation money, to store and keep separate all the colors of construction paper, colored index stock, tissue paper and other materials for art projects that could lay flat. It had taken her twenty minutes to assemble the contraption and two hours to gather all the papers together from the many shelves and boxes where they were scattered, and sort them into some kind of order.

"Hi," she finally said, and decided not to attempt even a friendly smile. After several days of silence from him, even walking away when they met in the hall, she didn't imagine this encounter with Rich would be pleasant. She hoped he wasn't going to tell her another of his ideas for a sports program when the Mission had more money — with him in charge of it, of course.

"So, Mom says you two talked." He jammed his hands into the pockets of his coverall and leaned back to glance down the hallway. Nikki heard no footsteps. Rich took another step into the doorway and lounged with his spine against the frame. "Guess we've got some problems, huh?"

"You have problems, and if you insist on believing something that isn't true and try to coerce me into playing along, and then tell warped versions of what happened to make me look like the bad guy, I guess then it becomes my problem."

"Ouch." He managed a grin. "Sorry. Really. I guess I'm just not that good at talking, huh?" He shrugged. "I guess I thought you just understood how I felt about you, Nikki."

"And I thought I made it clear that I wasn't interested in a relationship, especially since I'll be assigned somewhere else once this assessment is done." It took all her self-control not to add that all the money in the world couldn't persuade her to join her life with his. Not even to fill her empty arms with Aurora.

"Yeah, but don't you want to come home to stay? To get back together with me?"

"When did I ever tell you that?" She didn't know whether to laugh or scream when Rich opened his mouth, obviously to answer her, then stopped, his eyes narrowing in thought. Maybe this time she was finally getting through to him that she hadn't come home to Tabor to restart their high school relationship?

"I thought you understood," he repeated.

"I was hoping your mother misunderstood." She got up off her knees and dusted them off, groaning a little when her back refused to straighten immediately. "One project out of the way. Ninety-nine more to go."

"Huh?"

"Nothing." She flinched when it occurred to her that not only would Brock understand, but he would have been there to help her to her feet the moment she moved.

"Yeah. Well. I guess I talk to Mom more than anybody else. Maybe when I told her I hoped we could get back together, she thought I was saying... I don't know what Mom thought I was saying. Most of the time, I swear she doesn't hear a word I say. All mothers are like that, I guess."

"Not mine." Nikki paused in reaching up to bring down one of three boxes of new, untouched tempera paints she had found buried in three different places in the storeroom. She had bought a rack for those, too, to keep them organized and visible and to dispense them. After figuring out the paper rack, she hoped the paint bottle rack would be easier to assemble.

"Yeah, your folks are perfect."

Instead of bitterness or sarcasm, Nikki could have sworn she heard wistfulness in his tone. That was new.

"The thing is," he continued, "I really do want to fix things between us. I don't know, maybe I was wrong to think you felt the same about me. Why can't we go back to the way things were in high school?"

"We aren't the same people we were in high school."

"I hope we're both smarter. Here, let me help with that." He finally stepped fully into the room and crossed it in five long strides, to take the box from her hands as she slid it off the top shelf.

For a few moments, a peaceful cooperation flowed between them as Nikki showed him the boxes she wanted brought down and Rich helped her put the rack together. He did have a knack for assembling things, and she was grateful for his help.

"You know, Nikki, maybe I've been a little jealous. I mean, that Brock guy is always hanging around here—yeah, I know, Pastor Glenn asked him to help fix the bookkeeping problems. I can understand why he was asking all those questions, trying to figure out how things are done around here. And you were right. You've been asking a lot of questions, too, and making people think about how they've been doing things. But you sure don't make people feel like they're being spied on, like he does. You belong here and he doesn't."

"Brock is going to live here. When my job is done, I'm going on to my next assignment."

"I wish you didn't have to. I wish you could just stay here forever. I don't know, maybe you could take over the Mission. Pastor Wally is an old guy. He can't live forever. You could stay and train to take over when he's gone."

"Claire should be the director, then. She's put her heart and soul into this place." Nikki couldn't help smiling at the picture Rich had painted in her mind. It would be nice, she admitted, to stay here and invest herself into the town she loved.

"Yeah, I guess so." He sighed and yanked open the last carton of paints. Silence for a few moments, as he unloaded the box and she finished sorting out the bottles of powders so they could be put in the dispenser rack.

"So... does your mother understand that I'm not here to get married, and that I'm leaving town, and that I did not scream and lecture you in front of the whole neighborhood?" Nikki asked after a few minutes. She put a teasing tone in her voice and watched Rich carefully for his reaction.

"Oh, yeah, she understands." He colored a little, but he met her grin with his own.

*Do you understand?* she wanted to ask. *Has it finally sunk through your thick skull that I'm not the same silly girl who let you wrap her around your little finger? That I have important work to do, and no matter how empty my arms feel, I'm not going to marry you and adopt Aurora just to fill them?*

Nikki kept her silence. She knew better than to pursue the subject. Rich had apologized, and that showed a large growth in his character she had thought would never happen. She said a tiny silent prayer of gratitude for that.

"Mom said if I didn't apologize for imposing on you, that I'm a bigger jerk than I was in college," Rich mumbled a few minutes later, when they broke down the boxes to go into the trash. He paused. Nikki carefully didn't look at him. He sighed. "So, I'm sorry. I didn't think you'd get so mad."

"I forgive you. And you know something? If you think ahead and *ask* people, instead of assuming they're glad to change their plans to help you, they *might* change their plans to help you."

"Yeah?" He grinned.

"Most of the time."

"Uh huh. So, want to hit a movie tonight? Mom's watching Aurora. I mean, if you don't have any other plans."

"Sorry. I have reports to finish. The Mission won't get their money until the foundation makes a decision, and the Board can't make their decision without my report."

"Any chance of telling them to make you the boss, so we can run things the right way?"

"That's up to the Board." She held a fake, thin smile on her face and was relieved when he picked up an armful of boxes and hauled them away to the trash.

Talking with Rich made her tired. It was like battering her head against a brick wall. Did he have any idea how he sounded? Did he actually think that if she were put in charge of the Mission that she would give him any power and authority? And just what did he mean by "run things the right way"? Did he think Pastor Wally and Claire weren't running things the right way?

Maybe the only way to get through to Rich was to bang his head against that brick wall, instead of her own.

A moment later, she nearly laughed, when she wished she could talk to Brock tonight and get some advice from him on handling Rich. He had joined some committee to deal with repairs and maintenance at the church, which met the first Friday of every month. And just what kind of a message would she be sending him, if she went to him for help?

Still, it gave her a warm, peaceful feeling to know that she could go to Brock for help, for advice, and he would give it without hesitation.

# Chapter Twenty-One

That night just after 10:30, Nikki closed her latest report to Quarry Hall, attached it to an email, and hit the send button. Despite being aching tired from all the work she did that day, she was wide awake. At the back of her mind, she had been thinking about talking to Brock, the entire time she worked. Would he be on his way back from his meeting by now? Would it be wrong to go outside and sit on the front porch, and watch for him to come down the street to his boarding house?

Nikki flinched as a siren wailed through the warm night air. The windows at either end of her attic room were open to let the gentle perfume and coolness flow through, and the sound seemed to collect against the peaks in the attic ceiling and reverberate.

"Please, Lord, watch over whoever that is," Nikki murmured.

Gray whimpered and raised his head from his spot at the foot of her bed. He got up and slid off the bed and paced to the front window, then crossed the room to the back window, then went to the front again. His ears perked forward as he listened to the wail. Nikki closed her eyes and listened, trying to track the sound. It seemed to race up Trough Street, heading toward the fairgrounds. Rescue truck, or police car? On a Friday night, with the warmer weather encouraging late night, outdoors activities, either explanation was possible, even in quiet, small-town Tabor. The end of the school year at the university made the students more studious, but that didn't seem to cut down on their tendencies for stupid tricks. Two summers ago, students on a weekend beer binge had stolen one of the sandstone lions from in front of the little history museum on Span Street. They were only going to move it as a prank and put it on top of one of the towers in the Butler-Williams conservatory. They dropped it, breaking the lion in three pieces and breaking the foot of one of the conspirators—which was how all five of them were eventually caught. Nikki wondered if someone had tried an even more idiotic trick this time, and got hurt worse.

"I don't want to leave, but what's there for me to do if I stay here?" she asked Gray. The big dog just whined. Nikki clicked the exit button and closed her Internet connection. A few seconds later, her computer beeped and she shut it down completely.

Her last report had gone through. She had done everything she could think of to investigate the Mission: its financial status and fundraising activities; the services it provided to the town and surrounding communities; the services it could provide with better funding; its needs in terms of new equipment to replace old equipment—or just plain equipment, period, that the Mission never had to begin with; the rooms that were unused because of needed repairs or lack of equipment and supplies; the increased numbers in the community who could be served with the expansion of facilities and staff. Just as important as all the data she had gathered were the feelings of the people in the surrounding streets and neighborhoods. Did they like what the Mission was doing? Did they resent the traffic going through the former elementary school? Would they mind if the Mission expanded—say to the houses across the street?

Nikki recommended funding and additions to the staff. She tried to be honest in assessing the abilities and training and handicaps of the staff currently working for the Mission. It hurt to admit Pastor Wally's precarious health and advancing years. Claire was a wonderful administrator, but she was very clear on her desire to stay in her position as administrator and leave the public relations and leadership role to someone with those gifts. Pastor Wally would have to train a replacement someday, and she didn't like the idea that "someday" could be in the next few years. Nikki found it hard to imagine anyone taking his place, doing the work he did, carrying so many responsibilities with such seeming ease and so much caring.

At the end of her report, Nikki added one on herself; her assessment of her performance and the thoughts and feelings she had about both the assignment and herself. It was important to be honest and open with both the foundation and herself, so she could perform at peak ability and efficiency and proficiency. Nikki admitted how much she dreaded the thought of leaving. She included her changed relationships with both Rich Thomas and Brock Pierson, and how she could see growth and changes in herself by the way she reacted to and interacted with both men.

The siren stopped as Nikki put her computer back in its case. She flinched again, trying to judge by the duration of the sound how far the vehicle had traveled. Where was the emergency? Who had been hurt? Or was it someone getting caught breaking the law? She couldn't be sure, because she had been so caught up in her own thoughts and hadn't really paid attention.

Another siren started up. Nikki concentrated on it, trying to tell through the echoes in her room where the sound came from.

Definitely the fire station on the corner where Span crossed Horizon. The sound of the siren traveled up Span Street. Nikki counted softly and slowly, and this time she could hear how the sound changed slightly as it passed Church and continued toward the fairgrounds, following the previous siren. It sounded like it was heading toward Sackley now. And stopped.

Where?

Her cell phone rang. She jumped, the sound jangling up and down her nerves, loud enough to deafen her. Nikki cracked a grin, ashamed of her edginess, and dug the cell phone out of her purse, under her bed, half-buried under the decorative pillows she took off it when she settled down to write up her report. How could any sound penetrate all those layers? Yet it did, loudly enough to scare her out of her wits.

"This is Nikki," she said, even as her heart skipped a few beats.

An emergency with another Arc Foundation sister? Someone who needed help, and she was closest? She didn't recognize the number. Who had she given her phone number to, here in town?

"Nikki, it's Brock." He paused and she heard tense male voices in the background, and the hiss and metallic echo of voices on a police radio. "I'm at the Mission. You'd better get here. There's a —"

Sounds muffled, and Nikki guessed he had put his hand over the speaker. Who was he talking to?

"Nikki, it's Uncle Todd." Officer James used his "official" voice.

"What happened?" She was amazed she didn't shout.

"There's been a break-in." He paused as a siren started up, piercingly loud through the phone.

The siren in the distance returned. Nikki shivered, feeling the ice dig deep into her stomach. Now she knew where the squad car and rescue vehicle had gone.

"What else?" she demanded. "Is Brock all right?"

"Yeah, he's fine. But Pastor Wally's — Just get here, okay?"

Nikki ran, in her ballet-style slippers, with Gray at her side and not a word called to the rest of the household as she flew down the stairs and out the front door. She was halfway up the block before she wondered if she had pulled the door shut behind herself.

From three blocks away, she saw the flashing lights, splotches of red, blue and white. She heard the siren of the rescue truck fade into the distance as it headed for Sackley Road and the hospital. She kept running.

Two squad cars sat on the lawn in front of the Mission, pulled up before the front door, where streamers of yellow tape blocked the doorway that had just been repaired. Nikki saw flashes of light on the trees and houses behind the old school building and guessed more cars were in the parking lot, maybe even pulled up onto the playground. She saw the tail ends of two more cars at either end of the long main hallway of the old school building.

Blocking all the doors? Did they think someone was hiding in the building?

A figure moved out of the mass of shadows outlined in flashing lights, and resolved into Mike Nichols coming down the sidewalk to meet her. Nikki could barely make her trembling legs slow so she didn't run right past him. He caught her by the arm, as if he really did expect her to keep moving.

"What happened?" she demanded, and nearly broke out in coughing gasps.

"Somebody was ransacking the office. Pastor Wally caught them or interrupted them. There was a fight. He got thrown through the front door." He held tight to her arm when her legs tried to fold.

"How is he?"

Mike just shook his head and refused to speak. Nikki didn't need to push for an answer. They stepped between the two cars blocking the front door. There was glass all over the front walk and steps, and smears of blood, and scattered bits of debris from the materials the emergency crew used on Pastor Wally as they prepped him for transport. The empty frame of the glass door hung crooked, and Nikki could imagine the old man's bulk knocking it askew as he fell through.

"Brock?" she asked, remembering with a shock that made her feel cold. "Where—"

"Over here." Brock stepped out of the shadowy knot of people gathered around to one side of the car. He wore that crooked smile that she knew by now hid a lot of pain, and Todd accompanied him.

"Are you—" Nikki gasped when he stepped into the pool of light from the front door and she saw smears of blood on his sleeves and chest. "Are you all right?"

"Fine. It's not mine." He glanced down at himself and swallowed hard. Despite the shadows, he was visibly paler when he raised his head again. "I'm sorry, Nikki. I know how much you love him. He was already—I heard the crash and by the time I got here, he was alone."

"You were out walking?" She knew she was building excuses for him, but she couldn't help herself.

Why should she build excuses for him? Did she think he had attacked Pastor Wally? Nikki recoiled from that thought. No. Brock had changed. He was a good man. He liked Pastor Wally. He wanted to stay in Tabor.

Didn't he?

"No. I was supposed to meet him up here. I haven't had a chance to show him how to use his new Bible software he picked up last week. We were talking about it at our meeting. I agreed to meet him here."

"Why didn't you just drive over with him?" Mike asked.

Nikki glared at him. She knew right away such a conversation could be documented, even to what time Brock and Pastor Wally had left the meeting at their church. They had plenty of witnesses. If she knew Pastor Wally, he had been asking advice from half the men there that night.

"He had to take Mitch Snyder and his grandfather home, first." Brock started to rake his fingers through his hair in that distracted way Nikki used to love. He winced and slowly lowered his hand and stared at the drying blood glistening stickily on his fingers. "Can I—" He swallowed hard, audibly. "Can I go inside and wash this off, please?" he asked in a much softer voice.

"I don't know."

"Look, I know I'm a suspect, both because of the blood and because of my past. You can take my shirt for evidence and escort me the whole time, all right?" His flash of anger and energy died as quickly as it had come.

"Sure. That'll work." Mike gave Nikki an apologetic glance as he led Brock around the main puddle of broken glass and under the crime scene tape and into the building.

By the time Pastor Glenn and Rita, Claire, and half the trustees and deacons arrived, Nikki had learned everything the police could tell her, what they had determined by the trail of lights and unlocked doors and debris. Pastor Wally had parked in the back of the building in his usual spot and came in through the gymnasium entrance. He went into his office through the side door, not the main office door—his office had two doors. Whoever had been ransacking the office made enough noise to draw him out. A scuffle had ensued. The debris from the mess in the office didn't indicate how many people had been involved, but Pastor Wally had most likely been trying to get to the fire alarm. It was the agreed on response if there was any ruckus in the building, from actual smoke to one of the seniors having a heart attack, to a security crisis. Whoever he had been fighting either pushed or tripped him, and he went through the door.

He was cut all over his face and chest, having rolled through the glass. The impact of his fall and the blow to the side of his head had rendered him unconscious. When Brock found him, the big man wasn't breathing. Giving CPR had gotten blood all over Brock. He had pulled the fire alarm and had still been administering CPR when the police arrived.

"The medics think he might have had a heart attack in the struggle," Todd admitted. "Pierson may have saved his life. Good thing he was here."

"Yeah," Nikki whispered.

Then Pastor Glenn and the others arrived. She was glad to withdraw to the sidelines, sit on the front bumper of a squad car, and just watch. She felt numb inside. Things like this weren't supposed to happen in Tabor. Sure, they had endured the creeping terror of the White Rose Killer when he had been stalking his victims, but that was an isolated incident, big and sick and hitting people she never knew. Pastor Wally wasn't supposed to be hurt by anyone. Everybody loved him, didn't they?

"How you doing?" Brock asked, coming up through the shadows

behind her. "Sorry," he said with a stiff approximation of a smile when she leaped to her feet, startled by him. He wore a faded Tabor Christian Church t-shirt, and she shuddered at the knowledge that his shirt had been taken by the police as evidence. What did they need evidence for, when they knew the blood came from Pastor Wally?

"I don't know. How are you doing?"

"Nikki, I didn't—"

"It had to be Angelo and Marcus. They didn't find anything before, so they came back."

"Yeah. Had to be them."

"Brock..." She choked on the need to burst into tears, when she saw the relief on his face. "I know you would never do this. I know you're different now."

"Thanks," he whispered, voice husky with tears she knew he would never allow to escape. "I know it's stupid to be thinking about myself at a time like this, but—"

"It's okay." Nikki hugged him, something she had vowed she would never do again. But he was so miserable; so visibly afraid she would blame him, so relieved she thought of someone else as the culprit.

Brock slid his arms around her, tentatively, tension vibrating through him as if he expected her to punch him for taking the liberty. When she didn't flinch away, he let his arms tighten. She felt the shaking in his entire body, smelled his sweat, with adrenaline from fear and anger. Brock tucked his chin into the curve of her neck and shoulder, just like he used to do. Nikki's heart jolted, welcoming the touch. They settled into the old familiar stance, comfortable and warm and pleasant, from far happier times.

Was this so wrong, giving comfort? Nikki knew she needed the contact. She needed someone to hold her, someone to make her feel warm and protected, even if she was the one actually giving the comfort for a change.

All too soon, Brock had to give his statement to the police. Nikki held his hand and didn't care that Pastor Glenn and Rita were there, and it seemed like half the church elders watched.


*Saturday, May 3*

Rich came into the office where Nikki and Claire were still cleaning up the mess the next morning. He hovered in the doorway, watching them, fists jammed into his pockets and his shoulders hunched. He never quite looked directly at them, but seemed to be watching from under his eyebrows, his head bowed.

Nikki didn't have the heart to scold him to help instead of just hanging around. No one at the Mission could seem to get going that day. Everyone walked slowly, talked softly, and avoided most conversations simply because there was no answer to the one question most important to them all: when would Pastor Wally regain consciousness? Even the children were subdued, walking when they should have been running and laughing, talking instead of shouting. There were more fights over silly things, but even those didn't last as long as usual, as if the children didn't have the energy to squabble. Nikki understood exactly how they felt. If she didn't have Katie Green and Andy Paul's wedding to attend that afternoon, she would have called it a day, gone home, and curled up on her bed.

"Um, Nikki?" Rich finally got up the nerve to speak. He shuffled across the tile floor, which had been covered in broken glass from a vase of carnations and baby's breath Claire had brought in.

"Something wrong?" Nikki almost slapped herself for asking. Of course something was wrong. Everything was wrong.

"Some guy just called. He said he was walking by last night before the—the fight. He said your friend Brock is lying." Rich backed up a step when both Nikki and Claire stood up straight and grew too quiet. "He said he saw Brock punch Pastor Wally and push him through the door and kick him around before he passed out."

"Did he say who he was?" Claire asked, when Nikki couldn't get her mouth under control enough to speak. Rich just shook his head.

"Thanks," Nikki said. She reached for the phone to call the police. They had left instructions to call them if the Mission staff found anything unusual, no matter how small and insignificant and unrelated to the attack and robbery. Then Nikki remembered the phone was broken, the cord ripped out of the wall and the receiver shattered. She imagined Pastor Wally had been going for the phone when his attacker went after him. "Which phone did the call come in on?"

Rich led her in silence down the hall to the room that had been the nurse's station when the building was still an elementary school. Someone had brought a phone from home and plugged it in, so they wouldn't have to use the payphone in the gymnasium hallway. Nikki punched in the code to get the number of the last incoming call, but it didn't work. That meant whoever had called with the unfriendly tip about Brock had chosen to hide his identity and block caller identification.

She used her cell phone and called the police station. Mike came and got Rich's statement.

"Look, Nikki," Rich said, when the officer had dismissed him and he had already shuffled to the door to leave. "I'm really sorry. I know you think this guy has changed, but—well, if there were witnesses who say he did it, what can you do?"

"The word of one witness who won't identify himself won't hold up in court," Mike said a little too sharply.

Rich glared at him, then hunched his shoulders and continued shuffling out the door. Mike waited a few seconds, then tipped his head toward Pastor Wally's office. No one had gone in there all day. When Nikki followed him inside, he went to the other door out into the hall, opened it and looked up and down the hallway, then shut both doors.

"You worried about this witness?" he asked, his voice pitched low.

"He's lying, whoever he is. I know Brock didn't do it. He's not the kind of guy to attack someone he likes. Not even for money." She took a deep breath and forced herself to look her adopted uncle in the eye. "I ought to know, since I lived with the guy for two years."

"Yeah, there is that." He studied the tops of his shoes for a moment or two. "Would you get mad at us if we considered him a suspect?"

"I'd be... disappointed, but I know that's standard procedure. It just bothers me that you take the word of some anonymous creep over mine."

"Anonymous creep. I like that." A smile caught just one side of his mouth, and he continued studying his shoes. "Would you be mad if we slipped up a little and a nasty rumor started that Brock is our number one suspect?"

"You guys don't slip up."

"We do if we want to catch the real burglar. Until Pastor Wally wakes up and can tell us who did it, we don't have a single clue. But, the fact that somebody wants us to think Brock did it might be a good lead. They might help us trap them, if they think they can frame him and we're going to fall for it."

"Uncle Mike—" Nikki didn't know if the twisting sensation inside was anger or nausea or a baseless hope. Something about what he was saying didn't sound right.

# Chapter Twenty-Two

"Todd and I have been taking turns following Brock around in an unmarked car, or on foot when he's walking around town. So we can catch those two DEA fugitives, not because Rich Thomas says he's a crook."

"Rich did file that complaint about Brock? I should have known. I'm going to—" Nikki bit her lip to keep from saying "kill him." It was too close to what had nearly happened already.

"Anyway." He rested both hands on her shoulders and squeezed, making her look him in the eye as he spoke. "I'm a witness that Brock went straight home from that meeting, and then straight here. I saw him go down to his knees out on the front steps, but I wasn't close enough to see what he was doing. Then he ran inside and the alarm went off. By the time he came outside and started working on Pastor Wally again, I was close enough to see what was going on, and I called it in on my radio."

"Thanks," she whispered. Nikki blinked hard, fighting tears.

"You really care about this guy, don't you?"

"Yeah, I guess I still do."

"Well, you can count on us to catch those two characters who threatened him and clear his name and catch whoever really did hurt Pastor Wally. Just... trust us for a little while, okay?"

"That means don't tell anybody what you just told me. Okay, I can handle that."

"Even when the ugly rumors start spreading?"

"Just make sure the truth spreads just as far when this is settled."

"You got it, kiddo." He lifted one big, calloused hand and gently wiped away the single tear resting on the tips of her lashes.

~~~~~

Nikki called Quarry Hall as soon as she got home from the wedding that afternoon. She had called last night, knowing someone would be on duty in the communications room, as well as in the War Room, as they referred to the room set aside for heavy duty praying. With this new development with the police and someone trying to frame Brock for the attack, she needed to talk with someone totally separated from the situation, yet who cared. It helped her to know there were dozens of people praying.

Sue-Ma was on phone duty. She listened as Nikki made her report, then read back the notes she had made to ensure she had got all the details
~~~~~

right. Then she put Nikki on hold. The seconds ticked by and Nikki felt the imaginary spring inside her gut twisting a little tighter. Soon, it would break. Could she take it? She had been warned things like this would happen when she signed on to work with the Arc Foundation. Joan had only been half-joking when she said that taking an active ministry role was equal to painting a target on herself and begging Satan to attack.

She couldn't make herself believe any of this was directed at her. Was Satan so petty he would attack Tabor, the Mission, Brock, just to get at her?

"Nikki?" a new, soft, warm voice said as the phone link opened again.

"Aunt Elizabeth?" Nikki sat down hard on her bed, and nearly missed the edge. Gray whined and came over to sit against her legs, resting his head on her knees. Talking to Joan's stepmother had helped her through so many hard times at the beginning of her training at Quarry Hall.

"Your name has been coming up in so many prayers, dear. People who didn't even know where you were assigned have been calling, saying they felt the need to pray for you. This is an important time in your spiritual journey, as well as in the development of the Mission."

"Why me? Why Tabor? What could be so important?"

"Everything is important," Elizabeth Carter said with a chuckle that made the spring inside Nikki start to unwind. "Remember the poem about the horseshoe nail? We only see the limited view and circumstances around us. God sees the long view. Satan may be trying to keep us from linking with the Mission because there is someone very important to the future who needs to be helped there, and nowhere else. We won't know until Eternity, will we?"

"No," Nikki whispered.

"So much of this is tangled around your feelings for Brock. Tell me, do you think he's guilty of this latest attack?"

"No." She swallowed hard, hating the way her voice wavered. "No, even before I got the proof, I knew he wasn't guilty. He was just so torn up over it. The most important thing in the world to him was convincing me he was innocent."

"How do you feel about Brock now, after all this time seeing him, working with him?"

"Feel?"

"He is changed. Is it real, or only appearance? Is he doing all this to win you back, or is this a new life?"

"I want to believe this is a new life..." Nikki shivered, even as a chuckle escaped her. "And part of me is just greedy enough to want him to do it to win me back."

"When you leave Tabor, will he stay there and continue on the way he has begun? Or will he leave, follow you to your next assignment, and start over?"

"No." She smiled and felt a little warmer, a little less tense and ready to crack. "Brock will stay here. He likes Tabor. He doesn't need me here to make it feel like home."

That surprised her, but she knew it was true.

"Do you still love him?"

"I don't know. I know I like being with him. This is... in some ways, the time we spend working together is better than the good times when we were living together. We're getting something worthwhile done. We think alike. I can learn things from him and he asks me to teach him things from the Bible. That's a big change, because it always felt like he was the wise, experienced one teaching the ignorant little girl about the world. We're partners, I guess."

"Do you still love him? Not the mushy, high-flying romance, but the deep-rooted, lasting, trusting, supporting, Corinthians kind of love?"

"Yes. That kind of love. It's not stupid love, or wrong love anymore. But—sometimes I wish we could be romantic again and other times I'm scared to death he'll look at me that particular way again. Am I crazy?"

"You're human, dear." Elizabeth chuckled, and Nikki felt her compassion and gentle humor wrapped tight and warm around her. "Well, I can tell you the Board's decision now."

"They've decided?"

"Oh, yes, they were fairly sure halfway through your assignment. We had to be sure of you, though, before we could start to act."

"Even before all this trouble with Pastor Wally and Brock and those two slimes trying to blackmail him?"

"Such things are only... how does Sophie say it? Temporary blips on the screen. Nikki, some people are born to the traveling life. Get in, assess the situation clearly, act decisively, and move on without feeling their roots torn to pieces. They can care without needing to involve their hearts and souls, without needing to stay. You, however, are not made to migrate, so to speak. You are someone who must invest your whole being. For your own mental and emotional and spiritual health."

"And?" Nikki couldn't quite imagine what she would be told next. She felt empty, waiting, ready to move at the slightest breath of wind.

"We are definitely funding the Mission. It is too valuable an outreach to let it limp along as it has been doing. The people in Tabor have been doing marvelous things with their limited resources. It's a shining example of what God can do through His people when they are willing and committed. However, there are a few requirements." She paused, and Nikki heard a faint crackle in the phone lines. "We need to be more involved than simply quarterly reports and inspections. Between the Mission and the growth of Common Grounds, and other hints of budding ministry opportunities throughout that area, we've decided we need a regional director."

"Regional director?" Nikki knew what the position meant, but she couldn't seem to grasp it and apply it to herself. That was what Elizabeth was about to say, wasn't it?

"We want you to stay in Tabor and set up a regional office for the Arc Foundation. People can come directly to you for help, instead of calling here or driving the distance. You'll be part of the Mission, sharing responsibilities with the very capable staff. You will establish a stronger alliance with Tabor Christian and the other churches in Tabor, and stay more in touch with the pulse of the area. It's a vital position. Are you willing?"

"You wouldn't ask me unless you thought it was the best possible choice for Arc and for me." She blinked hard against sudden tears.

"Don't let that influence your decision, Nikki. You know the drill."

"Pray about it, think about it, talk with people who really understand, pray some more, and then decide. I know."

When she hung up a few moments later, Nikki wrapped her arms hard around herself and flopped back on the bed. She shivered, but that tense, tight, ready-to-burst feeling inside wasn't from fear or tears. A tiny giggle escaped her tight-clenched lips.

She knew she was going to say yes, even before praying and discussing this with her parents and Pastor Glenn and Rita, with Joan and her friends in town. This was right. She felt it deep down in her soul, in the place she had learned to ignore when she lived with Brock. It had taken blood and pain and grueling discipline to slowly make that part of her sensitive to God's leading again.

Nikki wanted this, more than she had wanted anything in a long time. Was it so wrong to accept the position just because it would let her stay near her family? Near Mercy Grace's grave?

Near Brock?

She thought about his reaction when she told him she would be staying in the area. What would that news do to the wistful light she saw burning in his eyes sometimes?

*Sunday, May 4*

Sunday afternoon when Brock showed up at the house and asked her to walk with him, Nikki didn't hesitate to accept. She hadn't told him yet about the news from the foundation and the Board's offer, and she felt guilty about it. Then on top of everything else that had happened, the ugly rumors were spreading through town with gale force speed. Nikki was glad to see that the people who really mattered at church weren't listening to the rumors. They treated Brock as they always had, willing to wait until proof came before letting judgment fall. There were others, though, who didn't hesitate to speak their feelings — to Brock and anyone who would listen — and urged others to act against him. They were the same people who told her she got what she deserved when she lost her baby, so Nikki remained calm by reminding herself to consider the source, and ignored them as inconsequential. It still hurt, though, to see Brock treated so badly by people who claimed to be Christians.

They walked through downtown Tabor, stopping at Rick's Bakery to get some cookies, Nikki's favorite blueberry scones, and cans of iced tea. It was nice to walk in silence and enjoy the warm weather and sunshine. Gray ran ahead of them as they turned down the road to the Metroparks entrance.

"Funny how things work out, huh?" Brock finally said, as they strolled along the side of the road, through the thick shadows cast by the tall trees. "I was all set to leave town to protect everybody and now... Some folks are ready to run me out of town."

"They don't count."

"Everybody counts. That's what I forgot for so long. Well, at least one good thing came out of this." He waited until Nikki turned her attention from the sloping, curving road to look at him. "I came here to town to win you back, and you're sticking with me stronger than anyone else."

"Brock—"

"How come you never told me about those two cops you were named after?"

"Huh?" She stopped short, more stunned by his lopsided smile than by the unexpected question itself. "I did."

"Yeah, the bare bones. Not the details. The scary details. They gave me a good lecture on how they're your adopted uncles and they're kind of careful of your feelings. Then they told me how you stood up for me. Especially when that phone call came in with that false witness."

"You know—" Nikki bit her lip to keep from blurting what could still be a department secret.

"It was a relief, let me tell you. I thought I was paranoid, thinking I had a shadow the last few weeks. Turns out the local cops and the DEA are taking turns watching me, figuring Angelo will try to contact me again. I'm kind of glad to have those kinds of bodyguards. I mean, I'm learning to trust God, but it's nice knowing there are some guns between me and Angelo."

"I'm so glad."

"What, you were worried?" He stopped them as they emerged from the trees. The road rose up ahead of them to the short raw stone bridge across the river, then dipped down again to meet the main road through this section of the Metroparks.

"Well—yeah." Nikki stopped with her intended joke withering on her lips. The hungry, aching look was back in his eyes. It made her want to cry. "I always worry about you. Even when I'm so mad I could just pound you."

"Thanks." He touched her cheek, his touch so gentle Nikki barely felt the tips of his fingers against her skin. She did feel the sparks that seemed to leap between them and settled in the pit of her stomach.

Brock leaned closer, holding her still with his gaze and the feather touch of his hand. Nikki knew he was going to try to kiss her.

A dark green Bonneville with tinted windows roared past them, spitting up gravel and dust. They stepped apart, choking a little, grinning as if they had been caught doing something embarrassing and foolish.

"Was that a message?" Brock pointed upward with his thumb.

"Maybe. To find a more appropriate place."

"Is there one?" He hooked his arm through hers. Nikki didn't pull away. A moment later, as they settled into stride together, she realized she wanted his arm around her waist, hips bumping gently as they walked.

Like old times, back when they were lost in their false happiness and security. When she didn't know about Ringo's shady business. When Brock made her feel like a fairytale princess.

"Maybe," she said, finally answering his question. She looked around for Gray. He had run down the slope, under the guardrails, and stood with his nose to the mud and rocks and reeds along the water's edge. Nikki felt a flash of guilt that she hadn't taken Gray on more walks while they were here.

She grinned, remembering the news from Elizabeth. She could take Gray to the Metroparks three times a week if she wanted.

"I've been thinking about us. A lot," Brock said, as they strolled up the incline of the bridge.

"Us." Nikki felt him tense—waiting for her to pull free? She adjusted her arm in his grip and leaned close to him. "I've been thinking about us, too."

"Yeah?" he breathed. Then he cleared his throat. "Well—you were right, you know. We were wrong. We did it all wrong. But part of me can't be sorry, because you were my lady. I loved you, and you loved me." He squeezed her hand as they went down the slope of the bridge to the other side. "As much as we were both able."

"We know the right way now."

"Yeah, we do." They had reached the intersection with Valley Parkway and Brock pointed right, then left. "Which way?"

"Right." She smiled a little when his eyes widened a little. Did he sense she was answering a few unspoken questions? Neither one said a word as they turned right. They walked a few dozen yards in silence before Brock cleared his throat again.

"So, what I'm trying to say is, I want to do it the right way now. I love you, Nikki. I loved you even when I was so furious with you. My life is a mess—was a mess, when you left."

"You can't depend on me to fix things."

"I know. And I'm right with God, and I know He's the foundation for everything. But there's this part of me that'll always ache if you're not part of my life. Or maybe, it's if I can't be part of *your* life. Know what I mean?"

"Yeah," she could barely whisper.

"I know you're moving on, but I'm staying here and I'll be here when you come back. And I hope that'll be enough for me."

"It wouldn't be enough for me."

"I hurt you. I almost got you killed. Our daughter's death is my fault, in a lot of ways. I'll try to be happy if you just let me be your friend. Maybe I can help you with your work. Who knows?"

"What if I fall in love and want to get married?" Nikki stopped them at a spot on the asphalt walking path where it curved into the leading edge of the forest, hidden from passing traffic until cars were almost on top of them.

"You mean, once I get over wanting to curl up and die?" Brock managed a grin, but his chuckle sounded sick and weak. "I'll try to be noble."

"I can't do that to you. You mean too much to me." She had to laugh when light blazed in his eyes and he stared at her. "You'd better convince me you're the one, or we're both going to be miserable."

"Do you mean it?" Brock grasped her shoulders, to draw her close to kiss. She was sure of his intention this time.

Another green Bonneville, perhaps even the same one, roared past, spitting up more gravel as it swerved off the road for a few seconds. It vanished around the bend in the road.

"That guy's timing—" Brock sighed as tires squealed. Nikki imagined the Bonneville swerving into oncoming traffic.

It reappeared a moment later, and jerked sharply to the right, crossing the other lane and flying across the grass straight at them.

"Nikki!" Brock grabbed her hand and ran.

The Bonneville swerved, narrowly avoiding a tree. The door flew open and Angelo leaped out as the car skidded to a stop. Brock flung Nikki away from him. Angelo lunged at Brock and brought him down with a bad, but still effective tackle.

Nikki stumbled but didn't fall. She kept going a few steps before she could turn back. Fists clenched, she braced herself to leap on Angelo. Marcus emerged from the car's driver side. The click of his gun cocking to fire echoed hard through the clearing. He said nothing, just grinned, begging her to move so he could shoot her.

A dark gray blur broke from the trees along the river, leaped, banged off the trunk of the Bonneville and landed on Marcus before he could even start to turn to face it. Gray made no sound as he took the man down, teeth clamped around the wrist of his gun hand. Nikki jumped, hitting the trunk with her hands and flinging herself across the trunk to follow up. She grinned, giddy with terror, refusing to let it master her. Vincent would applaud that move. It definitely had to be God moving her body, because she had messed up that move every time she tried it in practice.

Nikki kicked the gun from Marcus's hand at the same moment Gray released the bleeding wrist. Marcus broke his silence with shrieks and a filthy stream of curses.

"Hold!" she ordered, and went to retrieve the gun.

Gray dropped down on top of Marcus's stomach, silencing the man by driving the wind from his lungs. Nikki had the bag from their cookies in her pocket. She pulled it out and used it to wrap and pick up the gun. One of the first rules she had learned from Vincent was to never handle a weapon with bare hands, even to protect herself. It was too easy for something to go wrong, and too easy for innocent people to be framed by circumstantial evidence.

"Guard," she said, and put the bag down where Gray could watch it. Marcus held perfectly still, gripping his bleeding wrist and staring in uncharacteristic terror at Gray. Nikki ran around the car to help Brock with Angelo.

# Chapter Twenty-Three

The big Jamaican roared at her and turned, cocking his arm back to slam his clenched fist into her face. Brock was just getting up from his knees. Nikki leaped and spun in midair with a pair of high kicks, reacting without thinking, knocking herself to the ground, and slamming the toe of first one sneaker and then the other hard into Angelo's chin. His teeth clacked against each other and he let out a grunt as he tumbled to the ground. Nikki hit the ground, rolled and leaped to her feet again. By this time, Brock was on his feet. He gave her one incredulous glance, then stomped on Angelo's hand as the man reached for his dropped gun.

"Nobody move—you're under arrest!" a female voice called.

Nikki let out a yelp and turned, searching for the newcomers. A man and a woman in jeans and dark blue windbreakers came around either end of Angelo's car. They both carried guns. Tires crunched on gravel as a windowless blue van pulled up onto the berm. The sliding door banged open and three more people in jeans and windbreakers piled out. Every single one had DEA in white block letters on the backs of their jackets.

"Brock?" Nikki reached out a hand to him. He wrapped both arms around her and held her close. He shuddered. She didn't care that his nose was bleeding and his lip was split and he was getting blood in her hair.

"Where did you learn to fight like that?" he blurted.

"Brock Pierson?" the first agent asked, after his partner had yanked Angelo to his feet and confiscated the gun.

"That's me. Ah—how much did you guys see of this?"

"Way more than enough." He smiled, transforming from an icy blond machine soldier into a human being. Nikki sagged a little in Brock's arms as the adrenaline suddenly kicked off.

More tires crunched on gravel and Nikki looked over to see a Tabor black-and-white car and a Metroparks brown vehicle pull up behind the DEA van. Mike Nichols leaped from the cruiser and came running over. Nikki could finally smile.

~~~~~

"They say they weren't anywhere near the Mission that night," Mike said, following Dr. Holwood into the kitchen.

Brock, Nikki, and Doria were already there. Nikki put ice in a fresh washcloth to exchange for the one Brock held against his sore nose and swollen mouth, while Doria fed Gray strips of the sirloin roast she had
~~~~~

planned on making for dinner the next evening.

"Think they're lying?" Nikki asked.

"Wouldn't make any difference now." He sat down slowly, as if stiff, and shook his head as a wide grin spread across his face. "I saw the video of the take-down. Where'd you learn those moves, little girl?"

"Basic survival. You don't think Arc would really send us out on the road with just a cell phone and a big dog for protection?" She folded the washcloth once more over the lumpy bundle of ice and guided it up into position on Brock's face. For a long moment, they just looked into each other's eyes, smiling with relief and a thousand other feelings that couldn't be put into words. But she knew he understood exactly what she felt right that moment.

"Your teacher must have been with the Marines or the SEALs."

"Among others." Nikki hoped he wouldn't ask, because she honestly didn't know. Vincent had as dark a past as anyone who had come to join the family at Quarry Hall. He didn't talk about it, except in cryptic remarks that were meant to frighten his students into working harder and not asking about his past.

The doorbell rang and Dr. Holwood went to answer it. The sound of children's voices in the back yard filtered through the windows. Nikki closed her eyes, feeling close to tears with the glad relief that life was going on like normal everywhere else.

"There's the hero of the hour," Todd said, hurrying into the kitchen. He wore sweats that were dark under the arms and down the back, and she guessed he had been working out. He caught Nikki by her shoulders and turned her around in her chair, almost causing her to knock Brock's icepack free before she could let go of it. "You're really okay?"

"You should see what she did to the other guys," his partner said.

"Yeah, I heard. For crying out loud, Nikki, did you have to play ninja queen on my day off?" he grumbled, and dropped heavily into the nearest empty chair.

"Sorry, they didn't give us any time to ask for a rain check," Brock mumbled through his swollen mouth.

"Oh—hey—sorry. I really am glad you weren't too badly hurt. You've been a good sport, playing decoy for us. The DEA is really grateful. And speaking of which—" Todd looked around the room, making sure of their attention before he continued. "There's a reward posted for the capture, or assistance in the capture, of that pair of dirtballs."

"How big?" Mike asked when neither Nikki nor Brock could respond immediately.

"Before or after taxes?"

"Uncle Todd!" Nikki scolded.

"Well, you two will split it... Start thinking of what you could do with your share of $20,000." He grinned widely and sat back, waiting for their reaction.

"That's a lot of equipment for the Mission," Brock said slowly, enunciating his words with painful care. He watched Nikki as he spoke.

"Yeah." Her voice caught, and suddenly there were tears in her eyes. "It is."


*Monday, May 5*


"Are you crazy?" Rich staggered back from the playground doorway and his mouth dropped open. For a few moments, he couldn't speak.

Nikki wondered why it had taken him until almost noon before he heard about the capture of Angelo and Marcus and the reward money. Had he come into work late again, or was he just in one of his anti-social moods, so he avoided the Mission's staff? She suspected whoever had told him had done it deliberately, to irritate him. From the splash marks on his pants, he had been mopping something when he heard the news, and came running to find her and learn the truth.

She wasn't surprised that Rich thought first about the reward money and her plans for it, and didn't show any concern for whether she had been in danger or had been injured. The truth was that she feared she had jammed a couple toes when she kicked Angelo. Sneakers just weren't made for that kind of activity. She wasn't going to admit the problem to anyone unless the aches in her feet persisted.

She definitely wouldn't tell Rich. He was too busy having a hissy-fit about the money she was giving away. How long would it take before he complained that she should have offered it to him?

"Nikki," he finally moaned, "that's a lot of money, and you're just giving it away?"

"I don't need it. Arc pays all my bills."

"Yeah, but what about when you retire?"

"I'm taken care of." She thought of Kathryn, who had died at Ringo's hand while trying to rescue Nikki from him. She had known that retirement was something she might never have to worry about, if she worked for the Arc Foundation.

"Well, just think of the people who could really use that kind of money!"

"I am," she hurried to say, cutting him off before he could make a list, with himself at the top. "That's why I gave my share of the reward to the Mission."

"Bet good old Brock has big plans for his half. I still don't believe he's innocent. I think he turned on his pals just to look good for you." Rich slumped against the wall, almost in tears, glaring at her.

"Yes, he has big plans for it. A new copier for the office. Computers for the senior center. More phone lines installed. A freezer for the kitchen. To start out." Nikki acknowledged her nasty delight in Rich's shock and refused to be ashamed of it.

"He's just trying to buy you, Nikki. Can't you see that?" He stepped back to the doorway where she leaned against the frame, enjoying the fresh air coming through the door that glorious, warm, bright Monday morning.

"Buy me?"

"You gotta believe me. He's just putting on a good act to get you back. But he's not worth it, understand? He's no-good rotten slime and he's sure not good enough for you."

"That's not your judgment to make."

"Nikki!" For half a second, she thought Rich would burst out crying. "Come on, honey, give me a chance. I'm doing the best I can. I just gotta get a better paying job, and move on up in this world, and you and me, we'll be great together. Just like in high school."

"We're not in high school, Rich. I'm not the girl I was, and you certainly aren't the guy I knew in high school." At least he had pretended to listen to people back then. She couldn't believe he was using this same tactic, when she had already made it clear that they weren't getting together. What was wrong with him? Had he experimented on drugs and fried his brain, maybe destroyed his short-term memory?

Would she have to kick him in the jaw, like she had Angelo, before she finally got through to him?

"Why can't we be like we were before?" He rested his hands on her shoulders, just like Brock had the day before. Nikki shuddered. His hands were like cold globs of heavy clay, burying her.

"Because people have to grow up. You either become a better person or you become a worse person."

"Oh—and since I didn't graduate from college, that makes me dirt? I suppose your ex-con hero went to college?"

"Yes, Brock went to college." Nikki grabbed his wrists and shoved his hands off her shoulders. She stepped out of his reach. "But that isn't what makes him a better man than you."

"Now he's a better man than me! Next, you're going to say you love him and not me!"

"Brock is a better man than you because he admits his mistakes and he tries to fix them. He doesn't have to be beaten into a corner before he accepts responsibility for the stupid things he's done. And yes, I love him."

"What about me?" he wailed, and reached for her again.

Nikki twisted away, hands raised, ready to pound him if he so much as laid a finger on her. After yesterday, she knew she could take on any opponent and win.

"What about you?"

"I love you, Nikki! I want to spend the rest of my life with you."

"No, you want someone to clean up after you and be a live-in babysitter for Aurora."

"You're crazy! You're jealous, is that it? You're still jealous of Sue? Or you can't stand me having a kid when you killed yours?"

"I didn't kill my daughter." She kept her voice soft and low because the alternative was to shout it. She consciously unclenched her hands, to fight the temptation to use that windmill technique Vincent had been trying to teach her, one swinging blow after another.

"Yeah, I'll bet. Well, Aurora is all your fault. I wouldn't have got Sue pregnant if you hadn't dumped me. Told the whole stinking church what I did and everybody was feeling sorry for poor little Nikki. What was I supposed to do?"

"Besides take a little responsibility in your life? I didn't have anything to do with you being stupid, Rich! You did that all on your own."

Gray appeared in the doorway and growled, soft and low. He had been outside with the children during their morning play, which was why Nikki had been waiting in the propped-open doorway. The big Akita took two steps into the building.

Rich froze.

"Nikki!" Claire skidded around the corner. Her sandals slid on the dusty linoleum Rich hadn't cleaned yet, and she nearly slammed into the wall before she could change direction. "Nikki! Pastor Wally is awake!"

~~~~~

Chief Cooper himself came down to get Pastor Wally's statement about the night of the robbery and attack. He was just finishing up when Nikki and Claire arrived at the hospital. Brock was there, having hitched a ride with Curt Mehdlang from the *Tabor Picayune*, and they both waited by the nurse's station for the police chief to finish. The swelling in Brock's face had gone down about three-quarters from what it had been yesterday. He grinned when he saw Nikki, and nearly skipped the few steps he took to meet her. They hugged. He kissed her cheek and Nikki dared hope she saw promises of better things shining in his eyes.

The door opened before anyone could say anything and Chief Cooper stepped out into the hall. He glanced toward the nurse's station and nodded, giving them a tight smile. He snapped his notebook closed
~~~~~

with a small cracking sound and strode off down the hall.

"Can't let this one get away," Curt said, and dodged around the circular nurse's desk. "Hey, Brock —"

"I'll give him a ride back to work," Nikki said. The blond, lanky reporter barely waved his thanks before he dashed down the hall in the police chief's wake.

"Can we see him now?" Claire asked the tiny head nurse, who had to stand on a little stool to see over the counter. She sighed, black eyes sparkling, and nodded for them to go on in.

"The only smart thing to do when it's Grand Central Station is go with the flow," she said to no one in particular.

Pastor Wally was too pale, even against the blinding white hospital sheets. He had a thick turban of bandage around his head and wires taped to his chest and an IV tube in his arm. He managed a smile that wasn't even three-quarters his usual warmth and energy. The hospital bed seemed to dwarf him, shrinking his bulk. Nikki thought he looked like someone had taken a vacuum cleaner and sucked out some of his life and presence.

"Chief tells me I've been out of things for a while," Pastor Wally murmured, beckoning for them to come over to the bed.

"Yeah, you missed a little excitement," Nikki said. She leaned against the foot of his bed and let Claire have the single chair. Brock rested against the footboard with one hand and took hold of her hand with the other.

"Sorry about missing our meeting." He nodded to Brock.

"I'm just glad I wasn't late. I feel sort of guilty, though. I feel like it was my fault, because you were meeting me," Brock added.

"Not your fault at all. It's that big idiot, Rich Thomas."

"Rich?" Claire squeaked.

"Oh, yeah. Hard to miss those ugly barge-sized sneakers he wears." Pastor Wally swallowed hard, and for a moment, it seemed like he couldn't quite catch his breath. He shook his head, waving away the glass of water Claire picked up and held up to him. "He thought he could hide himself with one of those stupid black ski masks. I knew it was him by those shoes and his class ring. The only one in his class who got an opal. Everybody else got sapphires because of the school colors. Rich always had to be different." A long sigh escaped him and his eyes fluttered closed. "The chief was awfully happy to hear me say it was Rich. He couldn't be bothered telling me why."

"Well, mostly because I was the number one suspect," Brock said.

"Hey, if Rich was the one, what do you want to bet he lied about that anonymous tip?" Claire said. "When I get my hands on that lying —" A frustrated little shriek escaped her. "Excuse me. I have a few phone calls to make." She gave Pastor Wally a quick peck on the cheek and hurried out of the room.

Nikki was thinking of the open-mouthed shock on Rich's face when Claire had found them and blurted the good news about Pastor Wally waking up. Now that she thought about it, she clearly recalled that Rich never showed up for the prayer vigil in the senior center. And when the staff had talked about the attack, he had been so sure Pastor Wally wouldn't recover from his injuries, or if he did wake up, he wouldn't be able to remember anything about the attack. Looking back, she supposed it wasn't Rich's pessimism speaking, but his hopes.

"If he has any brains left, Rich is long gone," she murmured, and squeezed Brock's hand a little.

"So, does anyone want to tell me what I've been missing out on?" Pastor Wally demanded.


*Friday, May 9*


Rich Thomas left town, after stealing his mother's car and leaving Aurora at the Mission. A check by the police department showed he had emptied out his bank account ten minutes after Claire received the phone call about Pastor Wally regaining consciousness. The general consensus was that he had robbed the Mission the other time it was broken into, and in all likelihood had been helping himself to funds and supplies whenever he wanted. The "borrowing" that he had complained about to Nikki multiple times, leading to discrepancies in inventory, missing petty cash and vanishing equipment, could most likely be laid to his account. He had probably hoped to take himself off the list of suspects by complaining and pointing the finger of guilt at others.

"Maybe I should apply for his job," Brock told Nikki as they headed for their now-regular walk through the Metroparks. It was Friday night and all the details of the case had finally been wrapped up.

"Give up your accounting work? But I thought they liked you at the *Picayune*."

"They do, but I've got things so straightened out, I worked myself down to a part-time job. I could probably keep collecting full-time pay and goof off half the day but... it just wouldn't be right." He slid his arm around her waist, once they stepped into the shelter of the shadows on the winding, sloping park road. "What's that smile for? Don't tell me I made you proud again?"

"Again. Actually, I was thinking that you'd probably love spending your days with the kids, but it just isn't the job for you."

"I could do both, I bet. From what I saw of Rich's work, he turned a part-time job into a job for three people. I've never seen anyone work so slow or make such a mess and such a fuss out of such simple things."

"There's going to be a whole lot more work to do, once we start expanding facilities and bring in more staff."

"We?" Brock stopped them short. "Arc is coming on board?"

"Full support. The Board even thought of a few things Pastor Wally and the trustees didn't think to ask for, outreach opportunities, uses for the empty rooms once they're repaired."

"That's great!" He hugged her, lifting her off her feet and spinning her around twice.

Behind them, Gray whined, as if jealous to be left out. They laughed at him. He rubbed against their legs, nearly knocking them off balance until they relented and gave him some brisk petting.

"Anyway," Nikki continued, "I was thinking there was a bigger job you could do. How'd you like to be the financial administrator for the new regional office for the Arc Foundation?"

"That sounds pretty important. What would I do?"

"I haven't the foggiest idea. I just have a vague idea right now what the office itself is doing."

"Would I see you more often?"

"Oh," she said, her voice going so soft she almost couldn't hear it over her racing heart, "I guarantee it."

"Then I'll take it."

"Don't you think you should ask some questions, first? I mean, how do you know you'll like it? Or the people you'll be working with?"

"From what I've seen of the Arc Foundation, I know I'll get along with everybody." Brock cocked his head to one side and studied her a moment. "What's going on? What do you know about this job?"

"Oh-- " She squeaked when he grabbed hold of her arms and shook her a little.

"Nikki? How can you offer me this job? Were you told to?"

"Nope." She studied the top button of his shirt because suddenly she couldn't look into his face. "I can offer this job because my staff is my choice. But if you don't want to work for me, I can probably make sure you get the janitor's job."

"Work for you? Like you'll stop in every couple months and get reports?"

"No. Work for me, like I'm the new regional director and I'm staying here in town, but if you don't want to work for me — " She broke off, laughing, as he kissed her. They had never kissed while they laughed before, and she liked the sensation.

"You're going to drive me crazy!" Brock shouted as he ended the kiss and spun them around again.

"Does that mean you don't want the janitor's job?"

"I've got a buddy who would love the job. He's got a little girl to support and he's great with kids, and it'd be a big change from what he's doing now."

"What?" Nikki didn't mind that Brock didn't let go of her. She rested her head on his shoulder and prayed no one would drive by for a long time.

"He's a counselor at the prison where I was. He's the one who led me home. And I'd sure like him to be best man when we get married," he added on a whisper. "That is, if the regional director is allowed to marry one of her employees?"

"I don't know. You haven't asked me yet." Slowly, Nikki pushed free of his embrace. She leaned back, almost to arm's length, and looked into Brock's eyes.

The last of the bruises had faded to ugly green-yellow and brown stains on his face, and that last bit of pain had finally faded from the back of his eyes. He smiled at her, a threat of tears making his eyes glisten.

"It's too soon, I know. But one of these days, I'm going to ask you to marry me, to do it right this time." He took a long, deep breath. "Any chance you'll say yes, when I do?"

She couldn't make her voice work, so she gave him the next best answer, going up on her toes and clutching the front of his shirt as she kissed him softly, slowly, and with all her heart.

**THE END**

# THANK YOU!

Thank you for reading this book from Mt. Zion Ridge Press.

If you enjoyed the experience, learned something, gained a new perspective, or made new friends through story, could you do us a favor and write a review on Goodreads or wherever you bought the book?

Thanks! We and our authors appreciate it.

We invite you to visit our website, MtZionRidgePress.com, and explore other titles in fiction and non-fiction. We always have something coming up that's new and off the beaten path.

And please check out our podcast, **Books on the Ridge,** where we chat with our authors and give them a chance to share what was in their hearts while they wrote their book, as well as fun anecdotes and glimpses into their lives and experiences and the writing process. And we always discuss a very important topic: *Tea!*

You can listen to the podcast on our website or find it at most of the usual places where podcasts are available online. Please subscribe so you don't miss a single episode!

*Thanks for reading. We hope you come back soon!*

# About the Author

On the road to publication, Michelle fell into fandom in college and has 40+ stories in various SF and fantasy universes. She has a bunch of useless degrees in theater, English, film/communication, and writing. Even worse, she has over 100 books and novellas with multiple small presses, in science fiction and fantasy, YA, suspense, women's fiction, and sub-genres of romance.

Her official launch into publishing came with winning first place in the Writers of the Future contest in 1990. She was a finalist in the EPIC Awards competition multiple times, winning with *Lorien* in 2006 and *The Meruk Episodes, I-V,* in 2010, and was a finalist in the Realm Awards competition, in conjunction with the Realm Makers convention.

Her training includes the Institute for Children's Literature; proofreading at an advertising agency; and working at a community newspaper. She is a tea snob and freelance edits for a living (MichelleLevigne@gmail.com for info/rates), but only enough to give her time to write. Her newest crime against the literary world is to be co-managing editor at Mt. Zion Ridge Press and launching the publishing co-op, Ye Olde Dragon Books. Be afraid … be very afraid.

And please check out her newest venture: Ye Olde Dragon's Library, the storytelling podcast. Interspersed between the chapters will be interviews with authors of fantastical fiction. Listen to the podcast on your favorite podcast app or listen on the website: www.YeOldeDragonBooks.com, and click on the Ye Olde Dragon's Library link.

www.Mlevigne.com
www.MichelleLevigne.blogspot.com
www.YeOldeDragonBooks.com
www.MtZionRidgePress.com

NEWSLETTER:
Want to learn about upcoming books, book launch parties, inside information, and cover reveals?
Go to Michelle's website or blog to sign up.

**Thanks for reading!**
**If you enjoyed this book, would you help Michelle by posting a**
**review on Goodreads?**

**Are you a member of Book Bub? If so, please follow Michelle on Book**
**Bub, and you'll get alerts when new books are coming out.**

**As a way of saying thanks, Michelle invites you to the Goodies page**
**on her website. It will change regularly, offering you a free short story,**
**a sample audiobook chapter, sneak peeks at new cover art, inside**
**information on discounts and new release dates, etc.**
**Please go to: Mlevigne.com/good-stuff.html**

Also by Michelle L. Levigne

*Guardians of the Time Stream*: 4-book Steampunk series
*The Match Girls*: Humorous inspirational romance series starting with **A**
**Match (Not) Made in Heaven**
*Sarai's Journey:* A 2-book biblical fiction series
*Tabor Heights*: 18-book inspirational small town romance series.
*Quarry Hall*: 11-book women's fiction/suspense series
***For Sale: Wedding Dress. Never Used***: inspirational romance
***Crooked Creek: Fun Fables About Critters and Kids***: Children's short
stories.
***Do Yourself a Favor: Tips and Quips on the Writing Life.*** A book of
writing advice.
***To Eternity (and beyond):*** *Writing Spec Fic Good for Your Soul.* A book
defending speculative fiction.
***Killing His Alter-Ego***: contemporary romance/suspense, taking place in
fandom.
*The Commonwealth Universe*: SF series, 25 books and growing
*The Hunt*: 5-book YA fantasy series
*Faxinor*: Fantasy series, 4 books and growing
*Wildvine*: Fantasy series, 14 books when all released
*Neighborlee*: Humorous fantasy series
*Zygradon*: 5-book Arthurian fantasy series
*AFV Defender*: SF adventure series
*Young Defenders*: Middle Grade SF series, spin-off of *AFV Defender*
*Magic to Spare*: Fantasy series
*Book & Mug Mysteries*: cozy mystery series
*Quest for the Crescent Moon*: fantasy series

*Steward's World*: fantasy series reboot and expansion
*The Enchanted Castle Archives*: fantasy series